She had just a moment of panic, when she wanted to pull away, but it quickly faded. She could do this. She could be this close to a man, close enough so that she could feel a whisper of warmth through the fabric of her dress. Close enough to touch, and not be terrified.

She could if it was Jakob.

He sighed deeply, his even, slow breathing falling in rhythm with the night.

Oh, God, she thought. It felt so normal. A man and a woman on the front bench of a wagon, their shoulders touching. Two boys on the backseat, sleeping, on the ride home from town.

They looked like a family. The family she had never had, had never even hoped to have, and didn't realize until this moment how desperately she wanted.

*   *   *

"Susan Kay Law writes about love with joy and passion! The perfect read to warm up with beside a cozy fire."   —Tanya Anne Crosby, author of *Kissed*

"A heartfelt story of survival and love. Once again Susan Kay Law has written a moving, remarkable romance!"   —*The Literary Times*

Books by Susan Kay Law

Journey Home
Traitorous Hearts
Reckless Angel
Home Fires

Published by HarperPaperbacks

Harper Monogram

Home Fires

⇒ SUSAN KAY LAW ⇐

HarperPaperbacks
A Division of HarperCollinsPublishers

This is a work of fiction. The characters, incidents, and dialogues are products of the author's imagination and are not to be construed as real. Any resemblance to actual events or persons, living or dead, is entirely coincidental.

HarperPaperbacks *A Division of* HarperCollins*Publishers*
10 East 53rd Street, New York, N.Y. 10022

Cover illustration by Aleta Jenks

First printing: December 1995

Printed in the United States of America

HarperPaperbacks, HarperMonogram, and colophon are trademarks of HarperCollins*Publishers*

❖ 10 9 8 7 6 5 4 3 2 1

For the entire GEnie Romex family
And most especially
Suzanna Mitchell Donovan
9/17/61 – 1/8/95
Suz, you taught me more about gentle strength
than a hundred heroines.
I know that, somewhere, you're still laughing with us.
But I sure wish Heaven would get an Internet link.
We miss you.

Home Fires

Home Fires

Prologue

A Westbound Train, 1873

Zero out of three isn't good.

Helga von Leigh considered herself an excellent judge of people. She was quite certain that the woman who'd settled into the seat across from her just before the train pulled out of Pittsburgh was a grieving widow, traveling with her young son, and on the verge of destitution.

She was wrong on all counts.

The long, harsh blast of the whistle startled the boy, and he turned to the woman with uncertainty in his blue eyes. She whispered to him softly, reassuring him. He nodded, tipped his head against her shoulder, and stared out the open window. Hot, humid summer air gusted through as the train slowly gathered speed, bringing with it the smell of coal and smoke.

Such a beautiful boy, Helga thought. Perhaps nine, just beginning to grow into his teeth and ears. He had gorgeous, thick dark curls and obscenely long lashes to go with his eyes. He'd be quite a looker someday. He must favor his father, she decided.

Not that the mother wasn't pleasant enough looking, in a quiet way. How good to see an Eastern woman who hadn't succumbed to the current fashion for thinness; this one looked nicely healthy, like a good *deutsches* girl. Helga patted her own plump stomach.

It was going to be a long trip; no reason to spend it in silence. She leaned forward, speaking loudly to be heard over the steady clack of the wheels. "I hope you do not mind if I introduce myself. Old women like me do not have to stand on ceremony; one of the privileges of age. I am Helga von Leigh."

For a while Helga wondered if the young woman was going to answer, then she took a deep breath. "I'm Amy Smith," she said, so low that Helga could barely catch it.

Such a shy thing. It was an affliction Helga had never suffered from. "And this is?" she prompted, smiling at the boy.

The woman hesitated again. "Daniel." She slipped her arm around the boy's shoulders and pulled him close. "My son."

"I am very pleased to meet you, Daniel. You may call me *Tante*; all the children do—except for my own grandchildren, of course. And perhaps later, if your mother agrees, you can try some of the sweets I brought along. It is a new recipe, and I am not certain it is right. I could use an expert's opinion."

What a shame. No little boy should be that timid. He hardly dared meet her eyes until he checked with his mother for approval.

The bereavement must not have been too long ago, Helga decided. And very painful. It wasn't right that two such lovely people should be in such obvious distress.

Clearly, their fortunes had taken a downturn as well, for Amy's gray poplin traveling suit, while of good fabric, had a large stain on the underskirt and a neatly mended but still obvious tear across the left sleeve. She must not have been able to buy new clothes for a while, because it no longer fit her properly, too snug in the waist and the shoulders.

Helga's soft heart melted. "Is your loss recent?"

Amy went white and still, a striking study in grief. "Yes," she whispered.

It was not right, Helga thought again. Someone should do something for the poor dears. "It will not always be like this, you know," she said briskly. "I am a widow myself. I had thirty lovely years with my Augustus, and I thought I should never be able to bear life without him. But the time will come when you realize that the richness he added to your life does not disappear with his."

Amy didn't answer, her fingers nervously working the strap to her handbag. Perhaps she was not yet ready to accept it. Still, it seemed a terrible waste if such a sweet family allowed grief to overtake their lives.

"Hmm." Helga narrowed her gaze speculatively. "Where are you going to on this trip? To visit family?"

"No." Amy gave Daniel a light squeeze. "We're going home."

"Home? Where is that?"

Her smile was tentative, as if she were unused to smiling, and heartbreakingly beautiful.

"We don't know yet."

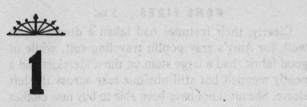

1

Dear God, please let me be doing the right thing.
The prayer had beaten, over and over again, in her
head and her heart since that mad dash from New
York. It thrummed in her now, as Amanda Sellington
clutched Daniel's hand and stepped from the 4:00 train
from Mankato.

New Ulm, Minnesota. She'd never heard of the
place before, until Helga had spoken of it on the train.
She'd decided to come here on no more solid reason
than that Daniel, who was usually so reserved around
adults, had taken a liking to Mrs. von Leigh. That, and
because Edward hated the Germans almost as he hated
the Irish, and it would give her a perverse satisfaction
to raise his son here.

"Mama," Daniel said, "you're squishing my fingers."

"Sorry." She forced herself to relax her grip and
smiled down at him as they took the last, large step to
the platform. Mama. Of all the lies, that one was the
one that came the easiest. To both of them.

She took a deep breath, trying to calm the panicked knocking of her heart. Every instinct she had told her to keep running, as far and fast as she could. But Daniel needed a home, a place to grow up in stability. She'd taken him away from his birthright; she couldn't force him to live constantly on the run, no matter how much she wanted to keep running.

She set her case down on the wooden platform. On either side of her, the town was tucked neatly into the river valley. Trim brick buildings, widely spaced, stepped up toward the rim of the lushly wooded valley, so different from the empty plains the train had passed through.

The air was thick with summer. Beneath the tinge of smoke from the train, there was earth and growing things, the scent of water from the river, herbs from carefully tended kitchen gardens, and wildly blooming summer flowers.

So different from New York, she thought. There, no matter how carefully she'd been shut away, no matter how many expensive blossoms perfumed her rooms, the odors of concrete and smoke and too many unwashed bodies still lurked.

She gulped another, steadying breath, and smelled freedom.

"You like it, *ja*?" Helga came up beside her, the warm August sun gilding the tight knot of her brilliant, improbably red hair that looked so strangely right against her plump, wrinkled face. "It is very different from Pittsburgh."

"Yes, it's very different." She couldn't afford to get into a discussion of Pittsburgh. Though when Helga asked, Amanda had named it as their hometown, they'd only been there a day on their way through.

Daniel's small hand was still tightly in hers, and he

was quiet by her side, but his eyes were bright with curiosity, an expression she'd seen there all too seldom.

"And yes, I do believe we like it." The town was large enough that a new person wouldn't stick out like a sore thumb, and it would give her plenty of business. It was also small enough that she could feel a part of the community, small enough to feel snug and safe, hidden away from the world. And from Edward, please God.

"Now then," Amanda said briskly, determined to get on with it, now that the decision was made. "If you could recommend a hotel—"

"Well, look who is here," Helga said, her voice too bright. "Jakob, you did not have to come and fetch me."

"You knew I would." As the strange man came up, Daniel huddled closer to Amanda's side, and she automatically slipped a protective arm around his shoulder.

"I had a shipment to get off on a barge, in any case," the man went on. He was of near average height, perhaps a bit taller, and too powerfully built for her peace of mind. Too stocky for his elegant gray suit, his shoulders pushing against the seams of the vest and his starched linen shirt.

"And where is this one bound?" Helga asked.

"To Indiana. South Bend." His voice was deep and smooth, his accent not nearly as pronounced as Helga's, just a slight German flavor to his words.

"So far!" Helga beamed approvingly. "Amy, Jakob's brewing is known all over the Midwest. He is sending his beer all the way to Indiana this time!"

Jakob gave Helga a puzzled frown. "Helga, why are you making such a fuss? We've been shipping there for six years, I think."

"I am always impressed, Jakob. You have managed so much." She clapped her hands together in front of her large chest. "Now, I shall introduce you to my new friends, and you will be kind to them, Jakob."

"Helga," he said warningly.

"Oh, hush."

It was the first time the man had really noticed her presence, Amanda realized when he turned to her, a frown drawing his eyebrows together, and she rather wished she'd remained invisible, for there was no welcome in his manner or eyes.

Oh, he was handsome enough. The short cropping of his dark hair couldn't disguise its rich curl, and the gold-framed spectacles he wore couldn't hide the strong, even bones of his features.

There was power, tangible and terrifying, in this man. And that was enough to make her breath shorten and her heart pound, enough to make her ready to grab Daniel and bolt back to the train, ready to run again.

It didn't matter where they went. As long as it was somewhere, anywhere, away from powerful men.

But if she gave in to the fear now, she knew she would never stop running. And damned if she would let Edward do that to her, even now. So she stiffened her spine and forced herself to keep her gaze from the ground.

"Jakob, this is Amy Smith and her son, Daniel," Helga said cheerfully. "Amy, this is Jakob Hall. I am his housekeeper, you know; I work for him out at the house."

"You do? I don't remember ever hiring you." He nodded at Amanda curtly, just enough for politeness' sake, and turned abruptly away. "Are you ready to go?"

"Jakob!" Helga scolded. "There is no need to be in such a hurry."

"Work to do."

"You always have work to do. It would be better for you to slow down. It is not so good for you to be in such a rush all the time."

Jakob sighed and gave in. There was no use arguing with Helga, and she seemed set on his standing here on the platform and being polite to her new acquaintance.

"Hello, Mrs. Smith. Daniel." From the corner of his eye, he watched the trunks being taken off the train, wishing they'd hurry up and unload Helga's so he could get back to the brewery. "Are you visiting someone in town?"

"No." The woman's voice was so soft he had to strain to catch her words. "We're staying."

"You're moving here?"

She hesitated and then gave a slight nod.

"Why?" He hadn't meant it to come out like that, so brusque and short. Hadn't meant to make her drop her gaze to her toes, either. But he'd never really learned the niceties of small talk and of putting people at their ease. He'd never had the time. "I mean . . . there are so many other places to choose." Not that he'd ever had the chance to see them. "Usually people who come here do so because they already have family here."

Damn it. She looked ready to bolt.

"We just—" She paused again, then lifted her head. The sunlight struck her, reflecting off her soft brown hair, sparking gold into her hazel eyes. She had skin like whipped cream, fine-textured, smooth, pale. "We needed a new home. Here seemed as good as any."

The softness of her voice snared a listener, Jakob thought. Made him pay even more attention than he would otherwise, drew him in like she was whispering to him alone. So quiet, as if she were afraid to disturb the air.

"It is that." She still looked unsure, one hand fluttering by her side, the other still latched onto the boy.

The boy. Jakob registered his presence for the first time. He couldn't be more than a year or two younger than Nicolaus. Daniel looked pale, his clothes too clean, and he was quieter than any boy in Jakob's experience. Too quiet, like his mother.

Jakob knelt down, so he could look into Daniel's downcast eyes. "Hello, Daniel," he said softly. "Welcome to New Ulm. And I bet you were lured here with some of *Tante* Helga's sweets, weren't you?"

"Yes, sir," he said politely without looking up. Jakob crouched there a moment, trying to think of something to draw the bashful boy out. He was the exact opposite of Jakob's impetuous nephew. Perhaps each of them would balance the other a bit.

"Nic, come on over here and meet—" Jakob glanced around and bit off a curse. Nicolaus had managed to make himself scarce again. Jakob stood up and bellowed, "Nicolaus!"

Nicolaus barreled around the corner of the train station, his limp brown hair dangling over one eye, his dirt-streaked shirt pulled out of his trousers and flopping around his hips, and wearing a grin as wide as the Minnesota River. His bare feet pounded across the wooden platform, and he threw his arms around Helga in a quick, exuberant hug before grabbing her arm and towing her off in the direction he came from.

"I found kittens, Helga! Four of them. Come and see."

"Nicolaus," Jakob said sharply. "You disappeared without telling me again."

"Oh, sorry. Come on, Jakob. You can come see them, too. Only don't frown. You'll scare them."

"No manners at all," Jakob grumbled before snagging Nicolaus and dragging him back.

The boy was spoiled rotten; there were no two ways around it. It was the whole town's fault. All of them, and Jakob worst of all, had done everything they could to make it up to the baby who'd lost both his parents and grandparents in one swoop, leaving him with no one to care for him but an inept 17-year-old uncle who'd also been saddled with the brewery that was the town's biggest employer.

Keeping his hands on Nic's shoulders to hold the fidgety boy still, Jakob introduced him to Amy and Daniel. He had to remind him to shake Amy's proffered hand—her shyness, it seemed, didn't extend to males under the age of twelve—and then Nic quickly invited Daniel to see the new kittens.

"Mama?" Daniel asked. "Do you think I should go?"

An odd way for the child to phrase it. Not "can I" or "may I," but "should I?" At least he'd asked, which was more than Nic was prone to do.

"Daniel, I . . . I don't think, I—" She stopped, clearly torn.

"It'll be safe enough," Jakob assured her. The whole town watched out for Nic; Daniel would be well looked after, by extension.

"But—" The rest of her body was utterly still, but her hands seemed in constant motion, brushing back a strand of her son's hair, smoothing his collar, as if she couldn't stop touching him. "We need to get our things and find a place to stay."

Helga spoke up. "You should get settled, and then come and collect him. The boy has been shut up in that train long enough." When she gave orders in that tone, Jakob followed them without stopping to think about it. It seemed to have the same effect on Amy.

"All right, then," she agreed.

Amanda had to force herself not to call Daniel back

as he, with one last uncertain look at her, trailed Nicolaus around the back of the building. She was simply going to have to get used to letting him out of her sight. She wanted him to have a normal life, and a normal life for a boy of his age was not having a mother who hovered over him constantly. It was good he'd found a friend already.

"Ah, they finally have everything unloaded." Jakob spun and strode over to the pile of crates and luggage stacked haphazardly at one end of the platform.

Helga patted Amanda's shoulder. "Jakob does not mean to be rude, dismissing you as he did. Though I try my best, I have never gotten the boy to slow down and be sociable."

"It's fine." The last thing she wanted was a man to be *sociable*. Especially one who managed to throw a crate over his shoulder and pick up two bulging valises in one large hand as though they weighed nothing. She was accustomed to being overlooked. Better that than the alternative.

She had better fetch her own things, too, and she moved to do just that, even though what she really wanted to do was slip around the corner and check on Daniel.

Jakob had already loaded the wagon with Helga's luggage by the time Amanda dragged her case over to the pile and located her other two trunks. She started to remove the heavy wooden crate that was stacked on top of one of her trunks when it was plucked right out of her hands.

"Let me do that." Jakob set it easily aside.

She hadn't flinched. Even though this powerful man had reached over her shoulder and taken the crate right out of her hands. She was proud of herself for that small victory. Perhaps she was stronger already.

"You needn't help me," she murmured. "I'm sure a porter will be along soon."

"There are no porters." The barest trace of amusement softened his deep voice. "This isn't the East, Mrs. Smith."

"Every woman for herself?" she said, astonishing herself. She'd even managed to dredge up a light remark.

"Not exactly. Usually families and neighbors help out each other. But you haven't been here long enough to collect those yet."

"Which is why you have us," Helga said, her wide smile creasing her round cheeks. "Jakob, load her things into the wagon, please."

"Yes, ma'am."

"No, really," Amanda protested, but it was too late. She winced as he tossed a trunk into the back of what was apparently his wagon, parked along the right side of the station. She hoped the straps she'd used to secure the trunks would hold. If they burst and the contents came spilling out, it would be difficult to explain why they were stuffed only with old rags, crumpled newspapers, and a few rocks for weight.

She'd bought them in a hurry, in Pittsburgh, just after they'd arrived, figuring that a widow and her son looking for a new home would look rather suspicious if they didn't have a few trunks of mementos with them.

They had nothing, of course. When the chance to leave had presented itself, she'd snatched it, having time to take nothing.

Or almost nothing. She pressed a palm against the lump in her corset, where it bit into her side, a painful reminder of what she had taken with her.

She needed no reminders. She was going to do her best to get rid of as many of the memories as possible, both for herself and Daniel.

The wagon was all loaded, and Jakob was looking at her expectantly. "Where to?"

Even that was new for her. To be asked where she wanted to go, instead of to be told. Choices. They were heady things, wonderful and more than a little frightening.

"I'm not certain. Perhaps you could recommend a hotel."

"There are three," he said, a trace of pride in his town showing through. "The Dakotah, perhaps. The food is quite good, and—"

"Don't be ridiculous," Helga broke in, a fiercely determined look on her gentle, homey features. "A hotel is no place for a young boy. You will be moving in with us, of course."

2

"Oh, no." The last thing in the world Jakob needed was to have them move in, to be faced every day with a too quiet young boy and an obviously fragile widow with whipped-cream skin. They clearly needed someone to watch over them, someone who could bring the joy back into their sad eyes. He wasn't the man.

Her "oh, no" echoed his, softer but only half a beat later.

Thank God, he thought. She wasn't going to take Helga up on it. And that wasn't a twinge of worry he felt mixed in with his relief. He couldn't worry about anyone else. It wasn't that he was afraid of responsibility; he simply *couldn't*. The last ten years had already used up all the worry he had to give.

"There, Helga, you see? She doesn't wish to," he said.

"Ridiculous." Helga dismissed his words with a wave, as if they were no more significant than a housefly. "She is polite, this one. That is all. We will change her mind, won't we?"

"No, we won't." He loved Helga dearly. Ignoring his protests, she'd simply moved in after his parents, his sister, and her husband had been killed. He knew there was no way he could have managed everything without her, and he was immensely grateful for her help in raising Nic. But there was no denying the woman liked to arrange other people's lives as she saw fit. She was always certain she knew best.

"Really, Mrs. von Leigh, we couldn't impose. The hotel will be fine."

Amy Smith's protests held a barely hidden edge of desperation, and Jakob wondered if he should be a bit insulted. Most of the unmarried women in town would have leaped at the chance to stay under his roof, giving them an inside edge at the town's most eligible bachelor—most eligible simply because he'd inherited the brewery along with his nephew.

"The hotel will not be fine. Oh, it is a perfectly nice hotel," Helga admitted, "but it is a hotel. There is no place for the boy to play. And we all know children must eat more often than the assigned dining times."

"But, Mrs. von Leigh—"

"*Nein!*" Helga barely paused for a breath. "You must call me *Tante*, too, I have told you this. Staying at the Dakotah would be too dear, for all it is a nice place. You should not waste your money on it. Also, it would be so much better for Daniel not to have to be so quiet as he would in a hotel."

"But you hardly know us, and it would be most improper." Mrs. Smith's voice still hadn't risen, merely picked up speed with her growing agitation, matching the rapid flutter of her hands.

"How can it be improper? I am there to chaperone. I do not mean you should stay in the main house, of course. There is that ridiculous guest house that

Jakob's father insisted on building—he always had to
be a bit better than the next, that one. It is hardly ever
used. The two of you would do well there, I know."

Jakob knew he should step in. Helga, when she had
her heart set on something, was unstoppable. There
was no way this quiet woman would be able to with-
stand Helga by herself.

So why wasn't he rushing to add his voice to her objec-
tions? Better yet, why didn't he simply ignore Helga and
go ahead and drop her and the boy off at the Dakotah?

Because he wasn't going to, that was why. He felt
one more chain, this one delicate and silvery and new,
adding to the many that bound him to this town and
this life.

For even though he couldn't take on one single addi-
tional worry, it seemed that, somehow, he'd already
accepted this one without even meaning to.

Well, that was just too bad. Chains could be broken.
The fact that, thus far, he hadn't managed to find a way
to escape even one of those chains didn't mean he
couldn't start now.

"There is one more thing." Helga played her trump
card. "A hotel will always only be a hotel. Daniel needs
a home."

Amanda was so tired. Weariness sapped all strength
from her bones. She didn't have the strength, nor the
heart, to fight Helga.

It didn't matter if she hadn't the strength. She simply must do it anyway.

The cost wasn't really an issue. Though she'd chosen
to pose as an impoverished family, assuming they'd be
less conspicuous that way, Daniel wasn't the only thing
she'd taken from Edward. She didn't really want to use
the money. She intended to save as much of it as possible; by rights, Daniel should have inherited a fortune

when he grew up, and this was all of it she'd been able to salvage for him.

But she simply couldn't do as Helga suggested and move in with her . . . and Mr. Hall. She went cold at even the thought of it; never, ever again would she put herself in a position where a man would have dominion over her. Particularly a man as strong and hard as this one.

"Helga, please," she said finally, resting a hand on Helga's sleeve to gain her attention. "Let me just call Daniel now, all right?"

"Then you'll come?" Helga's cheeks rounded like ripe apples as she grinned.

"I shall . . . think about it." At least long enough to come up with a good way to refuse Helga, once and for all. Perhaps she could enlist Jakob's aid; surely he did not want her there. It was a horrible imposition, for it hadn't even been his invitation, and he'd done nothing but stand there and frown throughout the entire conversation.

"Ah!" Helga bobbed her head. "We make progress!"

No, they didn't, Amanda thought. She just had to think of a better way to deflect Helga's insistence.

"Daniel!" She cupped her hands around her mouth and called his name.

The late afternoon sun was hot, slanting across the rim of the valley, beating down on them. Too warm in his suit, Jakob rolled his shoulders, wishing he'd worn something cooler. But when he was conducting business outside the brewery, he had always felt it necessary to dress as a businessman.

"Daniel!" she repeated.

Even when Mrs. Smith shouted, she was no louder than a sparrow chirping. He added his voice to hers. "Nicolaus!"

She jumped slightly at his bellow. "Sorry," he said quickly, then shouted again. "Nicolaus!"

There was no answer, just dense silence soon broken by the long whistle of the train preparing to pull out again. When the echo faded, she turned to him uncertainly. "They didn't come."

"I'll go and fetch them."

"I'm coming with you."

"There's no need."

The wind blew a strand of light brown hair across her cheek, and she brushed it away with a hand that trembled slightly. Fear? Just because the boys had gotten busy playing and hadn't come when they called? Hadn't her son ever misbehaved?

"Yes, there is." Her voice was firmer now, determined. So there was a bit of stubbornness there, after all. He'd wondered.

"Fine." He strode across the platform.

Expecting Daniel to pop out any minute, Amanda trailed Jakob around the back of the small brick train station. Daniel never went far from her if he could help it. Surely he was there and simply hadn't heard her call because he'd been occupied with the kittens. He'd always liked animals, especially small, warm, helpless ones. Just another way that he was completely different from his father.

Jakob stopped dead just around the corner to holler again: "Nicolaus!" Heavens, the man was loud. Certainly they could hear him back in Mankato.

"Damn it!" he swore, then flicked a brief glance at Amanda. "Sorry," he said, but without any apology in his voice.

"It's fine." She was long past the point where a swear word bruised her sensibilities. There were so many things much more dangerous than words. "Do you know where the kittens are?"

"No. I guess we'd better find them." He jumped

down from the high platform, then turned and grabbed her around the waist, setting her firmly on the ground. She inhaled sharply at the feel of strong hands against her ribs, but he let her go and started to hunt along the edge of a thick stand of grass growing beside the rough dirt road before she had time to recoil.

It took her only a moment to locate the animals, tucked safely under a sheltered corner of the platform, in a small basket stuffed with old rags that must have been placed there for the cat's use. Four small, round kittens mewled contentedly by their mother's side.

But still no Daniel.

She blinked against the dark shadows and peered farther under the platform, certain he must in be there somewhere. Thin beams of light leaked through cracks between the boards overhead, vaguely outlining stunted grass, lumps of dirt, and piles of discarded lumber.

It was otherwise empty. Daniel was gone.

The hot, stuffy air started to close around her, and she leaned weakly against a wooden beam. Dear Lord, had she made such a horrible mistake?

When she'd stolen him from New York, she'd only wanted to protect him. Had she lost him already?

Her throat closed, and she drew in a labored breath. Blackness blotted out the corners of her vision, creeping across her sight, tempting her with sweet oblivion.

It would be so easy; always so easy, to curl up inside herself and escape into that empty darkness, into a place that was far away and free from pain of any sort.

She couldn't afford to do it anymore. Daniel needed her.

She shook her head, and the darkness retreated. Cold dread still lumped in her stomach, lodging up under her heart, but she could think again.

"Mrs. Smith? Are you all right?"

"They're not here."

Jakob ducked, quickly checking underneath the overhang himself.

"You found the kittens?" he asked.

"Yes. But the boys aren't here." The breadth of his shoulders blocked the slanting rays of the afternoon sun, throwing her in shadow, and she shivered, suddenly cool. He didn't crowd her, staying a full, long step away, and she was grateful for that.

"Well, I guess we'll just have to go find them, won't we?"

His voice was confident and brisk. Either he wasn't worried at all, or he hid it extraordinarily well.

"Where do we start?"

"You don't know this town, and you still look a bit pale. You should wait here."

She glared at him then, angry that he assumed she would trust anyone else to do it. "He's *my* son."

"Come along, then." He turned on his heel and headed off down the street. Amanda hurried to catch up with him.

He didn't pause as they passed Mrs. von Leigh, just called "We'll be back in a bit" as he strode by.

"Got himself off again, did he?" Helga shaded her face from the sun and peered down from her roost on the wagon.

"Yes."

Amanda found herself a bit breathless as she trotted along beside him. He had long legs, and he made good use of them. Eschewing the boardwalks that marched in front of buildings hedging the town square, he took off down the middle of the hard-packed street.

"Apparently he does this often?" she asked.

"Nicolaus?" He frowned. "Yes."

"Well, why don't you keep a closer eye on him?" she snapped, then bit down on her tongue. She'd sounded accusatory, and she, of all people, knew how well men took to being blamed for anything.

The dusky flush of anger tinged his broad cheekbones. "I do the best I can," he said harshly.

"But what if they're in danger?"

"The only danger he's in is from me."

Stunned, Amanda stopped talking. The familiar, sick fear lanced through her.

She should have known better.

Her worry had made her angry, upset that this man's misbehaving nephew had dragged Daniel into his escapades. But the last thing she'd intended had been to spur Jakob's anger, too. If he took that wrath out on his nephew, she'd never forgive herself. She knew no way to stop him.

She never had.

Not all men are like Edward, she reminded herself. Intellectually, she believed that; her father had been all that was gentle, if ineffectual. But as she eyed the dark, determined man at her side, a large part of her remained unconvinced.

They crisscrossed the town from one end to the other; past the new, solid courthouse and jail at the end of the town square, down Center Street to the ferry that crossed the river, past the Eagle Roller Mill and the baseball fields.

They checked the livery stables, half-filled with horses; Jakob peeked in the back of Hummel's Billiard Hall and asked at two different sausage shops. He ignored Amanda, trotting along beside him, and only barely acknowledged the greetings of all the townspeople who grinned broadly at his appearance and seemed unsurprised by his barked question: "Have you seen Nicolaus?"

Amanda's worry and guilt grew with each stop they made, with each "no" they received. If Daniel had somehow been hurt, it was all her fault—for not guarding him closely enough, for bringing him here in the first place. But she couldn't quite believe that something had happened to him; surely fate couldn't be that cruel, not after all they'd gone through already.

The town was a blur of well-kept, mostly brick buildings and cheerful, ruddy-faced people with varying degrees of accented speech. Having spent nearly a decade being driven everywhere in a carefully guarded coach, she soon became breathless from all the walking, sweat beading her forehead and the back of her neck as her mind replayed all the possible disasters two young boys could stumble into.

"What if there are snakes?"

"There aren't any."

She hadn't realized she'd spoken aloud until he'd snapped an answer.

"At least, none that are poisonous," he amended.

"You don't suppose they got kicked by a horse?"

"Nic is eleven years old, for Christ's sake. He's got enough sense to stay away from the back end of a horse, even if that's all he's apparently got sense for."

"Abducted?"

"Why the hell would anyone want to kidnap them?"

She'd almost forgotten. No one here knew that Daniel's father was one of the wealthiest men in the United States. The danger of being kidnapped for ransom was something else she'd gladly left behind in New York, along with the guards she'd never been quite sure were for her and Daniel's protection or imprisonment.

"But—"

"Anybody dangerous in these parts hightailed it out eleven years ago, I promise you. Mass hangings tend to do that."

Mass hangings? What kind of place had she come to?

All she'd wanted was a home for the two of them. Someplace quiet and safe. Someplace like everyone else had. Was that so much to ask?

"Drowning?"

"Nicolaus can swim."

"Daniel can't."

"Damn." He wheeled around and headed down a small side street that soon ended, narrowing into a slender, overgrown path.

"Where are we going?"

"The river."

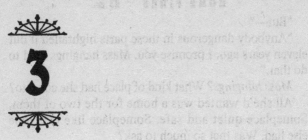

3

They found the boys in a tree, perched on the lowest branch of a spreading oak. The limb jutted out from the trunk, swinging wide a good eight feet over the river.

Amanda gasped. Oh, Lord. She wasn't sure if she should be relieved that Daniel was, for the moment, unharmed, or scared to death that he could so easily tumble into the water.

Daniel was the farthest one out on the branch that looked far too thin for Amanda's peace of mind. Next to him, Nicolaus sat, jabbering away about something, his legs swinging back and forth with just enough force to cause the limb to bob slightly.

Daniel was absolutely still, his white face set, and he was hanging on for dear life, clutching on to the gnarled, rough-barked bough. Below, shadows and sunlight chased across the brown surface of the wide, slow-moving Minnesota.

"You boys get over here right now!" Jakob bellowed.

A dark, curly-haired miniature of his uncle, Nicolaus sprang up and nimbly ran along the branch. Amanda pressed a hand to her heart, expecting him to slip and go crashing to the tree, the water, or the earth.

"Uncle Jake," he said breathlessly, gaining the bank and swinging down from the tree. "It's such a good thing you're here!"

"We're going to be talking about this later, Nic." Jakob's frown was dark and severe, but Nicolaus seemed undeterred. "Daniel, you need to get off there, too. I don't know how sturdy it is."

Daniel's eyes were huge, like large, purple bruises against his pale skin. He peered down at the water, then back up at Jakob and shook his head slowly.

"That's the problem, Uncle Jake. We got out there okay, but Daniel doesn't want to get back. He's scared or somethin'. He won't move."

"What? Why didn't you come get me right away?"

"You didn't think I'd leave him out there all by himself, did you?" Nicolaus said indignantly.

"No, I suppose not." Jakob stepped to the edge of the bank, resting one hand against the dark trunk of the oak. "Daniel?" he said softly, his voice gentle and patient, markedly different from the brusque tones Amanda had heard him use before. "It's going to be just fine. Have you ever climbed a tree before?"

Daniel swallowed visibly and shook his head, his black curls shining softly in the light that filtered through the broad, green leaves of the old oak.

"It's easier getting up than down, isn't it?"

Daniel bobbed his head in agreement.

"But it's not, really," Jakob went on. "It just *looks* scarier coming down."

Doubtfully, Daniel's gaze traced the length of the branch.

"All right, then." Jakob stretched his arm toward Daniel, his hand large, brown, and steady. "All you have to do is get over this far—just a few steps—and then I've got you."

Daniel finally found his voice, expelling a rush of air with the words: "I can't!"

"Of course you can." Jakob sounded entirely sure. "I won't let you fall."

Daniel simply shook his head again. Amanda moved to Jakob's side, trying to smile around the lump in her throat. What did she know of small boys climbing trees? She'd always kept Daniel so safe. "Come on, Daniel. You can do it," she said, trying to sound encouraging. "I know you can."

"Mama?" She could see his struggle, trying to be brave behind his white, still facade. Daniel had learned too young that to break into tears solved nothing. She'd ached as much for that as anything, at his loss of the freedom to cry and to give in to young, strong emotions.

"Come on," she urged again.

"Look," Jakob said patiently, "can you just scoot over a bit on your butt? If you can get over a little ways, I can probably grab you."

Daniel tried. He managed to inch one leg over a bit, but when he lifted his hand, he wobbled on his perch. With a smothered cry, he quickly grabbed hold again. Then he looked up fearfully, as if expecting someone to damn him for his weakness.

"Never mind, Daniel. It's okay," Jakob reassured him. "Just hang on a minute."

He stripped off his vest and handed it to Amanda. "Here. Hold this."

"What—?"

"I'm going out to get him."

She crushed the slightly scratchy wool, warm from his body, between her fists. Hopping on one foot, he tugged off his leather half-boots and socks, dropping them in a small pile. He reached up for a handhold and then, upon further reflection, pulled off his spectacles and handed them to her, too.

Broad, strong, and nimble, she thought. Fabric pulled over his shoulders as he hoisted himself easily up into the tree. Leaves shook and twigs quaked with his motion, but he was soon perched comfortably where a large limb segued into the trunk.

"Hey, Uncle Jakob, that's pretty good. You want a climbing race after you get Daniel down?"

"No." Jakob shot an exasperated glance at his nephew.

He slid one bare foot along the branch, testing. It bowed a bit under his weight and Daniel hunched down.

"Easy there."

"Would you be more careful!" Amanda shouted, worry adding force to her words.

"So," Jakob looked down at her, "you *can* talk above a whisper." He returned his attention to Daniel, who still clung to the same spot. "Okay now, kid, I'm going to stretch out as far as I can, and you see if you can reach over here to me."

With one hand touching the trunk behind him for balance, he spread his feet wide and leaned toward Daniel, his other hand outstretched. "Come on." His bare toes curled around the groaning branch. "Grab on."

Shooting a quick glance at his mother, Daniel took a deep breath. Do it, Amanda prayed silently. Come on, Daniel, do it. You've managed so much already. We got this far together.

Not moving any part of his body but his arm, Daniel reached for Jakob.

It wasn't even close. A good two or three feet separated their outstretched hands. "Come on," Jakob said again, tendons standing out on his neck as he tried to stretch farther.

"I can't," Daniel said, sounding very young. "I'm sorry."

"Don't be sorry." Jakob moved back into a more stable position. "I guess I'm just going to get to climb trees a bit more than we expected."

"What are you going to do?" Amanda asked.

"I'm just going to trot on out there and get him."

He blew a breath out through his cheeks and stuck his arms straight out for balance. He inched his feet along the limb, creeping forward, wavering only slightly. The branch that had seemed almost adequate beneath the boys now seemed very frail and thin below this large, solid man.

"Hang on, Daniel," he muttered as the branch bent down under his weight, the tips of the end nearly dipping into the water. "I'm coming."

A loud creak from the tree revealed the strain. Amanda had a sudden vision of the both of them plummeting down into the depths of the river. "Get down from there right now!" she shouted.

"What?" Jakob frowned, bewildered. "What's the matter?"

"I want you out of that tree right now." Before he snapped the thing in two, she thought; though, unwilling to frighten Daniel any further, she didn't say it out loud.

"But—"

"Now!" she repeated. "Get down before I drag you off."

"How are we going to get Daniel down, then?" he asked reasonably.

"I'll do it."

"You?" Clearly dubious, he looked her up and down. "I don't think that traveling getup is exactly the best thing for tree-climbing. Especially that bustle."

"I'll manage."

"Look, we're doing okay here. Just let me finish it."

"Now!"

"Okay, okay." He slid back to the trunk. "Just wait a minute, Danny. Seems your mother and I have something to get straight first."

He jumped down, landing with a soft thud, taking most of the impact with his knees. "What exactly is the problem?" He brushed bits of bark off his pants. "I'm not sure how safe that branch is."

"My point exactly." She was already unlacing her high-topped boots. "I don't weigh as much as you do. It's less likely to crack under me."

He had to concede that point. "But I suspect I'm a bit more experienced than you in hanging around in trees. Not to mention in rescuing little boys who get themselves into trouble."

"Apparently so." For a moment, she wondered about the propriety of stripping off her black lisle stockings as well as her boots. Propriety, however, was hardly her foremost concern right now, so she tugged them off. "But I simply don't think it will support you. Now—" She looked up at him expectantly. "Are you going to give me a boost?"

He shrugged. "Apparently so," he echoed. She reached for a lower limb, and he practically tossed her up into the tree.

"There," she said, finally gaining Daniel's level. "All safe and sound." She hoped. Her heart knocked heavily against her ribs, and the ground seemed very far away. She studied the length of branch out to Daniel. Six feet? Eight? Not so much. Yet the distance yawned before her, surrounded by far too much open air for her peace of mind.

"Mama? What are you doing up here? Are you sure it's safe?"

That was her Daniel, always worrying about her first, no matter how frightened he must be. "You didn't think I was going to let you sit up here all by yourself, did you?"

"I can't get down," he said dolefully.

"Well, then, I guess the two of us will just have to stay up here, won't we?"

"We can't do that, Mama," he said, in the voice children use when adults say something utterly stupid. "We'd get hungry."

"I'm sure we could talk Mr. Hall into bringing us some food."

"Then we'd have to . . . you know." He wrinkled his nose.

"Perhaps we would at that. Well, then, we'd better get down."

Though she was lighter than Jakob, the bough still seemed terribly thin to support her, too, and the rough bark bit into her bare soles. There was no way she was going to be able to dance right out there like a tightrope walker, the way Nicolaus had scurried back. No, there had to be another way.

Hitching up her skirts, she squatted down and straddled the branch, her legs sticking out ungracefully on either side. "Ouch!" She stuffed her petticoats more carefully beneath her for protection and heard a muffled snort of laughter beneath her.

"Now you stop that," she said.

"It wasn't me." Jakob's face was still serious—too serious, too innocent, as if he'd just wiped a grin off it. "I'm just standing right down here, waiting to catch you if you need help."

"Uh-huh." She couldn't lean back; the solid lump of her bustle prevented that, and she thanked her stars that this dress only required a small, practical one. If she'd still been wearing the grand dress she'd left New York in and quickly traded in Philadelphia for these plainer clothes, this would have been impossible.

"Here we go." She reached forward a few inches, firmly grabbed hold, and scootched the rest of her along behind. Reach, scoot. Reach, scoot. Not exactly graceful, or efficient, but functional.

She must have been way off in her estimation. Surely this wasn't six or eight feet. Twenty, maybe. Thirty-five, at least.

And then she was there at last, with Daniel wedged safely against her, his face against her shoulder. Carefully, she put one arm around him to hold him tight, and she could feel his slight trembling.

"I'm sorry, Mama," he whispered, voice muffled against her.

"Shh. It's all right, Daniel." It was a habit she wanted much to break him of, this tendency to apologize immediately, for anything and everything, whether he was at fault or not. A habit she intended to break herself of, too. "It's okay."

"I was scared."

"Me, too." It felt good to be able to say that she was afraid, right out like that, instead of merely hearing it over and over in her head. Fear was something she'd tried to deny for so long. Edward had gotten too much pleasure out of it. "But you're safe now."

Crack!

The branch sheared off, plunging them down into the water, their screams echoing long after the large splash.

Instinctively, Amanda tightened her grip. She threw her other arm around Daniel, holding him close. Unfortunately, she hadn't shut her mouth quickly enough.

After the warmth of the summer air, the river was a cold shock. They hit the water hard, almost as if it were solid rather than liquid, and she gulped in a mouthful of water as they sank beneath the surface.

Amanda knew how to swim a bit; it was one of the things her father had taught her and her siblings on infrequent childhood trips to the country. As soon as they slammed into the water, she started to kick, propelling them back to the surface.

They broke through, gasping for breath, Daniel's arms clenched so tightly around her neck she was nearly strangled.

They were going to go down.

It was almost impossible to tread water without her arms, which were still wrapped around Daniel, but no way was she ever going to loosen her hold and let him go. Her skirts tangled around her legs, hampering her frantic kicks.

It didn't matter how difficult it was. She *had* to do it.

If only she could look around and find out where the shoreline was. It couldn't be that far away.

You can do it, Amanda, she told herself. You've gotten this far.

Her head bobbed beneath the surface for an instant. But then there were strong arms there, pulling her back to the surface, supporting both her and Daniel, towing her back toward shore.

Relieved of the necessity of maintaining their position, she simply hung on to Daniel, feeling the warm wetness of her tears on her cheeks mixing with the cold chill of the water.

Jakob made it seem so easy, tugging them steadily through the water, that she gave in gratefully and let him do it. Daniel was shivering against her, whether from the cold or emotions, she wasn't sure. Perhaps both.

"It's okay, honey. We're safe now. Jakob has us."

They hit ground perhaps twenty yards downstream from where they'd gone in. For a current so seemingly slow and easy, it had done a remarkably good job of nearly sweeping them away.

The bottom of the river sloped off near the edge to a nice, shallow ledge. The sand beneath was firm, but Amanda's legs were too weak to hold her up. The bank pitched up sharply, three or four feet to a shelf that hung over the water.

Jakob deposited them safely on the sand. He plucked Daniel from her arms and lifted him, water streaming down from them both, and set him carefully up on the bank. "There you go." Placing his hands on the edge, he gave a heave and shoved himself out of the water, too.

"Mrs. Smith? Are you all right?"

"I'm fine," she answered, though she made no move to clamber out of the water but simply sat there, sopping wet, her skirts heavy, her hat gone, and her hair draining rivulets down her back.

"It would probably help if you got out of there."

"I suppose so." But that required effort, and darned if she hadn't used up just about all the effort she had to give.

"Here." He stuck out a hand. "If you can stand up and grab on, I'll get you up the rest of the way."

Squinting, she looked up at him. Perched up on the ledge, he looked overwhelmingly large, backlit by the bright August sun. The light rimmed him with gold, sparkling the droplets of water that clung to him. His thick, dark curls, plastered to his head, were already springing free. The water made his linen shirt almost transparent, delineating impressive ridges and swells of muscle.

He was the image of male power, strong and solid and tall. Power that should have terrified her. Perhaps it did, for, already short of breath, Amanda had all the more difficulty getting in enough air. But she was suddenly aware of the fact that male power had its uses.

It had saved her and Daniel. Quickly and easily, with barely a struggle. Trussed up in corsets and weighed down with petticoats, she would have had a hard time doing it herself.

He was waiting for her now, his hand stretched toward her. A large, strong hand, unwavering, the long fingers widespread, ready to enfold her own.

When was the last time she'd voluntarily moved to touch a man? She couldn't remember. It wasn't something that came easily to her.

Yet, this time, it seemed wholly natural.

She leaned forward, fighting the tug of the water on her weighted, drenched clothes, and placed her hand securely in his.

4

The woman wasn't all that light, especially soaking wet. Jakob gave an extra heave and she scrambled up the bank. He didn't mean to pull too hard, but he must have, because when she gained the rim of the bank she came flying forward, knocking into him.

It was only an instant. She jerked away quickly, mumbling an apology. But he felt her; their sodden clothing wasn't much of a barrier. All softness, she was lush and round and utterly feminine.

Jakob felt color burn his neck and cheeks, and he turned away. Darn it, why should he be embarrassed? He couldn't help his reaction.

With so little time to spare, he'd wasted little of it thinking about women. He wasted none in pursuing them. Apparently, he had a whole lot of pent-up awareness locked inside, just waiting for a woman to set it off. Well, it could darn well just go back into storage. There wasn't anything he could do about it now.

"So, then." He rounded on his nephew. "What the

hell did you think you were doing?" His volume escalated with each word. One of these days the boy was going to get in serious trouble, and Jakob seemed unable to find a way to teach him to be more careful. "You didn't even tell me where you were going, damn it!"

Amanda winced at Jakob's bellow. He was clearly angry, his eyes dark and severe. She found she felt almost as much compunction to protect this little boy as her own, and she moved a bit closer to him, ready to step in between them if Jakob raised a hand.

"I forgot," Nicolaus said simply.

"You *forgot!*"

Surprisingly, Nicolaus didn't seem at all cowed. He stepped forward, looking boldly up at his uncle. "I'm sorry, Uncle Jakob. I didn't mean no harm."

"And what if you'd gotten Daniel hurt in the process? Just how did you talk him into it, anyway? Dare him?"

"Oh, no, mister." Summoning his courage, Daniel barely managed to get the words out. He couldn't let his new friend take all the blame. "The tree was all my idea. I swear."

His jaw working, Jakob stood tall, glowering down at the boys. Then, to Amanda's complete astonishment, he dropped to one knee, spreading his arms wide, and Nicolaus threw himself into his embrace.

"Hey, Jake, you're getting me all wet."

"Sorry," Jakob said, but he didn't let go. His large, brown hand cupped the back of Nicolaus's head, pressing it into his neck. "But you've just got to be more careful, Nic." His voice was low and harsh. "I can't lose you, too."

"You won't. You always look out for me."

"Yeah." Jakob released Nicolaus and stood up. "Well, then, I guess *Tante* Helga will be wondering what happened to us, won't she? We'd better get back."

Amanda grabbed her skirt in both fists and twisted them, forcing out a small, dirty stream of water that puddled on the dusty ground. Deciding the trek back up to the town was too much to be undertaken on bare feet, she plunked down, knowing her dress was going to be coated with dirt, but deciding it was too far gone to really matter.

It was difficult pulling her socks over damp skin. She glanced over at Jakob, who was having the same problem. His white shirt and gray trousers were now splotched with black, and the wool of his pants had stretched, leaving it baggy and misshapen.

At least she had shoes to wear back. Daniel had lost one in the river, and the other one squished when he walked. Worse, she didn't think she *had* another pair of shoes for him. She hadn't wanted to risk taking any bags with them when they'd sneaked away, and she hadn't thought to buy an extra pair of shoes when she'd exchanged their clothing.

Jakob noticed, too. "Hey, Dan, you seem to be short a wheel there."

Daniel gave a small shrug, as if it didn't matter. "It's okay."

"Come on. I'll give you a ride." He tossed him up on his back. Daniel's eyes widened, and then he gingerly put his arms around Jakob's shoulders. "You can grab on better than that." He jiggled Daniel's legs to get a firm hold.

"Here we go," Jakob said, motioning her on ahead, then Nicolaus; he and his passenger brought up the rear. He could keep an eye on Nic that way, making sure the monkey didn't scamper off on another adventure.

Jakob had no idea what to do with his nephew. He

was disobedient and mischievous, but he didn't have a mean bone in his body. Aw, heck, what was Jakob supposed to do? He couldn't be a mother. He wasn't even a father. He did·the best he could, but it clearly wasn't enough.

His thighs and calves began to burn slightly as they trudged back up the narrow, rutted path. It had been much easier going down than up. The sun beat through the overhanging trees and was trapped in the still shelter of the woods, heating the air. It felt like his soggy clothes were starting to steam.

Plus, he had the boy on his back, who was now clinging firmly to his shoulders and was heavier than he appeared.

He was a lot more than he appeared, actually. Though he looked timid and sickly, there was an underlying core of toughness that Jakob admired. As scared as he must have been, Daniel hadn't given in to hysterics, either in the tree or in the water. And he'd certainly jumped in to defend Nicolaus quickly enough, making sure Nic didn't take all the blame for the tree escapade.

He obviously needed some feeding up. Some fresh air and exercise wouldn't hurt; maybe he'd take to baseball. But damned if Jakob didn't rather like the kid.

And damned if he didn't rather like the mother.

She was ten feet ahead of him, tromping up the path like a trooper, leaving a trail of droplets in the dirt. Her hair, darkened from the water, had come undone, and was hanging in a long, twisted rope down her back.

He'd thought she was so fragile and timid. She could barely get her voice above a whisper.

But when her son was threatened, she'd turned into a mother hawk, fierce and fiery. And loud! She'd climbed right up on that branch without a moment's hesitation, even though she clearly wasn't too happy about it.

Maybe Daniel had been sick; that would account for his pallor and thinness. At first Jakob had thought maybe it had been because Daniel's mother had coddled him too much. But if there was one thing he was sure of now, it was the fact that she was a good mother. The bond between them was evident, and she hadn't blamed the boys for going off and getting themselves into trouble.

And he'd seen the expression in her eyes when she looked at her son. A kind of love that was all too rare, and that every child should have the chance to grow up with.

The kind he wished Nicolaus had had a chance to have. Helga did her best, but she was getting older, after all, more like an indulgent grandmother than a mother.

He froze when he realized he'd nearly decided to ask them to move into the guest house, after all.

He wasn't going to do this, damn it, he reminded himself.

And it had nothing to do with the way he'd felt that brief instant when she'd pressed against him by the river. Not a chance. He'd forgotten that already.

"Mr. Hall?" Daniel bent down to his ear. "Are you okay? I can walk. Really."

"No, Daniel, I'm fine. I was just thinking about something."

"If I'm too heavy for you, I won't tell."

"I bet you wouldn't."

Yep, baseball, Jakob thought as he started down the trail again. Maybe third base.

*   *   *

When they made it back to town, Jakob had to take the lead again. Though they'd crisscrossed much of New Ulm in their search, and most of the buildings they passed seemed familiar, Amanda couldn't remember the way back to the train station. She'd been too worried before to pay much attention.

As he led them parallel to the river, back toward the center of town, Jakob kept turning around to check on Nicolaus, clearly concerned the boy was going to slip away again.

"Nicolaus? With all the excitement, I'm feeling just a little bit shaky. I don't suppose I could impose on you to lend me an arm?" Amanda suggested.

"What? Oh, yes ma'am." Nicolaus straightened proudly and offered her his elbow. She tucked her hand through the crook, then took a firm hold.

"You're such a gentleman." One young enough that she felt comfortable having him perform this common courtesy.

The next time Jakob turned around, she gave him a small nod to indicate that she'd keep Nicolas close. Jakob's smile was so brief, she almost wondered if she'd imagined it. But she noticed he no longer turned around to check on Nicolaus, either, and her water-logged steps grew a bit lighter.

They made quite a procession. A dripping Jakob, Daniel clinging to his shoulders, briskly acknowledged the greetings of the people they passed as if he did it every day. Amanda's sopping skirts trailed after her, leaving a wide track in the dust, and her bustle had settled down around her thighs. Nicolaus escorted her with all the proud airs of a grand gentleman.

Amanda knew that people were looking at her as

they passed. But it was nothing like the stares she was used to in New York: greedy, speculative, cold. These were curious, friendly, and amused. She supposed she could give them that; her little company really must look a fright.

Mrs. von Leigh seemed thoroughly delighted with their return. Perched comfortably in the wagon, her blazing hair bare to the sun, she smiled broadly at their appearance and slapped her palms together.

"Well, *there* you are." She looked them all over and nodded. "Had an adventure, did you?"

"You might say that." Jakob lifted Daniel down and proceeded to finish loading the remainder of the luggage.

"I have just the thing for that." She patted a box that rested on the seat beside her. "Brigitte Kiesling saw me here and stopped by to welcome me home. She brought us a *Schwarzwaldertorte*. After a slice, you will all be restored, good as new!"

Food. Amanda's mouth watered. She had no idea what *Schwarzwaldertorte* was, but it sounded like something with sugar in it. Maybe even butter. And, if heaven were kind—ah, just the thought of it—whipped cream!

"I don't want it," Jakob said.

"Now, now." Helga clucked at him. "Even if you and Brigitte have differing opinions on the eventual outcome of your . . ."

"Acquaintance."

"Acquaintance, you must admit the girl can cook."

Both boys had already clambered up into the wagon, claiming seats on each side of Helga and keeping a proprietary eye on the ribbon-tied box. Jakob handed Amanda up to the front seat and went around to the other side.

The front seat was fairly narrow, and when he sat

down, his thigh was only a few inches away from Amanda's. She was too tired to care. She sagged against the plank back of the seat and wished that it was high enough to support her head, too.

She was wet. She was tired. And oh, my, was she hungry.

The Dakotah could be the worst hotel in America and it would still look like paradise to her, as long as it had food and a bed. She couldn't decide which she wanted first. Maybe a bed. All she'd have to do was strip off her soggy clothes to go to sleep, whereas she'd have to put on something else to go down to the dining room.

Yes, sleep must be first. "How far is it to the Dakotah?"

"Not far. But we're not going there."

"Which hotel, then?"

"None of them. We're going back to our place."

"What?" She was too tired to fight this battle now. If she had a cake or two first, maybe then. Or a beef-steak, and ten or twelve hours of sleep. But now? No, not now.

She tried to summon up the energy to argue with him. She knew she should insist on being taken to a hotel. But the only image she could seem to dredge up was him, kneeling down, talking softly to Daniel.

Maybe, just for tonight, she'd go along with it.

Tomorrow was soon enough, she thought as she closed her eyes and let her head drop to her chest.

Yes, tomorrow she'd fight.

Jakob snapped the reins over the head of the two large, sturdy horses and they pulled away from the platform. A slight jerk, and then the wagon settled into a slow, easy, lulling motion.

The warm sun dried her hair into soft wisps around her face. Her head bobbed up and down, and she drifted easily into and out of a nice, warm place that was almost sleep. Behind her, she could hear the boys chatting cheerfully with Mrs. von Leigh, recounting Daniel's dip in the river. Above, there was the occasional whistle of a thrush, the swoop of a wren. She only vaguely noted that they'd climbed out of the town, that the dense growth of hickory, cottonwood, oak, and maple gave way to undulating, gold-washed prairie.

"Where do you live?"

"Only another mile or so." He shifted on the seat, the leather creaking below it. "Darn, I'm sticking to the seat."

"Is your place up here on the prairie?"

"No, down in the valley, where the Cottonwood meets the Minnesota."

"So far out of town? Don't most of your workers live in town?"

"Well, they don't have to smell the brewery in New Ulm this way." She blinked, trying to focus on him. His glasses were back on his nose, and his vest was folded over the back of the seat. A fat fly buzzed around his ear, and he waved it away with a quick flick of his hand. "Of course, *you* will, a bit."

Only if she stayed long enough, she thought, but didn't say it. Time enough to worry about that later. Now, she was simply happy that Daniel was being entertained and nothing more was required of her than slumping on this seat, soaking up the sun like a turtle on a log. It seemed like such a long time since she'd relaxed. Weeks, certainly. Since she'd first begun to believe that there might actually be a way to escape.

The rest of the trip passed in a haze. She couldn't have said if it had taken a few minutes or a few hours, and she didn't much care. The angle of the road tipped, and they were heading back down into a green-shaded valley.

"There it is." Jakob pointed down.

"Why . . . it's very lovely." And not at all what she'd expected, out here in what seemed to her to be the middle of nowhere.

The house, set back perhaps a hundred yards from the river, was large, solidly built of dark red brick. The gables were steeply pitched, the roof sheathed in gray slate, and large square stones decorated the corners of the house. Big diamond-paned windows faced the water, taking advantage of the view.

"As Helga said, always the best for *mein Vater*." He jerked his chin, pointing upstream. "The brewery's over there." She could catch only a glimpse of brick, screened by a thick stand of poplars. Lush lawns, green and dappled with sunlight, spread in all directions, studded with young pines. Nearer the house, a thick tangle of red and pink spilled over the edges of neat, square gardens.

"He planted the pines, too—had to import them, but he said they reminded him of home. The gardens are Helga's, though."

So peaceful. Was there another world out there, beyond the confines of the trees and the green and the water? Surely nothing bad could ever happen here; nothing dark could ever find her. She wondered how she'd ever find the will to leave it.

They pulled up in the drive in front of the house and he halted the team.

"Helga, why don't you take Mrs. Smith and Daniel on ahead and show them the cottage? I'll unload."

"Oh, *nein*." Helga flapped a hand in front of her face. "I am too warm and too tired to go running all the way down to the guest house. I will go in and start feeding the boys the cake. You can get Amy settled and come join us later."

"But—"

She clambered down from the wagon with a speed that belied her claim to exhaustion. "You will show her it good, Jakob, *ja?* Leave nothing out. Take your time." She turned and winked just before disappearing into the house with the boys.

Amanda flushed, knowing her cheeks must be almost glowing red. She hoped Jakob would attribute that high color to the heat.

"I'm sorry," he said flatly.

"For what?"

"Helga's been trying to marry me off for years. I guess you're the next candidate."

5

"What?" Amanda knew she was gaping; she couldn't help it. Marriage? What was she supposed to say? That she couldn't get married, because she already was?

"She's not exactly subtle, is she?" Jakob deftly grabbed all of her luggage and took off down a stone-paved path that wound through the pine trees, around the back of the house. "I'd say I'd talk to her, but it wouldn't do any good. All you can do is ignore her."

Dumbfounded, she trailed along behind him. The way was lined with flowers: pansies, petunias, phlox, and a host of others she couldn't identify, their scents melding with the clean spice of pine. Lovely. Someone must have taken care of the gardens while Mrs. von Leigh was in Pittsburgh.

The guest cottage was set in a thick, sheltering copse of maple beyond the main house. Also built of brick, it was small and snug. Amanda glimpsed the lacy edge of a curtain through the square front windows.

Jakob shouldered open the door, then stepped aside to allow her to enter. "There's a lock," he said. "We don't bother, but you may want to use it."

She stopped cold in the path. If she went into that house, he would follow. And she'd be alone, in that small space, with a man.

Her legs locked; she couldn't make herself go forward. She felt her breathing quicken, the tight constriction in her chest. There wouldn't be enough air in that little house. There wouldn't be enough space between them.

"Mrs. Smith?" he said politely, with just a touch of impatience. He was still waiting by the door, looking at her expectantly.

Stop it! she scolded herself. It was no safer out here alone with him than it would be in there. There was no one else around, and no place for her to run.

He wasn't going to hurt her. She knew it in her head; if only she could believe it with the rest of her. She couldn't go through the rest of her life being frightened of all men just because she hated one.

She intended to live in a small town and run a business. She was going to raise a son. Sooner or later, she was going to have to deal with men without breaking into a cold sweat. Somehow, she was going to have to learn to put it all behind her.

Somehow.

Taking a deep gulp of breath, she made a mad dash for the door, brushing by him quickly. If he thought it was odd, so be it. It was the best she could do.

Propping the door open with one of her trunks, he followed her in. "I'll just leave the door open. It's stuffy in here. Never been used much."

He deposited the rest of her bags on the braided rug just inside the door.

"It's not too big. Bedrooms are back there. Two of them." He indicated a pair of oak doors that opened off the single central room.

"It's fine." It was small. It would likely fit in one corner of the massive, ornate ballroom in the Sellington Mansion.

It was also, quite probably, the most charming thing she'd ever seen. To the right there was a small seating area, filled with another circular, braided rug; a small couch; and two chairs, one of them a rocker. Everything was blue, yellow, and white, the wood softly rubbed to a warm gold-brown.

To her left sat a big, sturdy oak table and the small open kitchen, dominated by a large, black cookstove. Speckled blue-and-white enameled pans hung along the walls.

There were scattered vases of dried flowers and bittersweet; fat yellow pillows piled in the living room chairs. And, as Jakob quickly moved through the cottage, throwing open the curtains and windows, the room was filled with sunlight, screened just enough by the trees to be mellowed of all harshness.

He left her alone and moved into the back rooms. Though Amanda could no longer see him, she could hear the scrape of opening windows.

She was no longer sure why she'd been so concerned about being in this house with him.

The man was all business. He wasted no more time in showing her around than he had to. She knew he'd only done that much for Helga's sake.

He left one bedroom and disappeared into the other without so much as a glance her way, and her tension relaxed another notch.

But he wasn't all business, she remembered. Not with the boys.

With Nicolaus—even with Daniel, whom he barely knew—his voice had softened and his pace had slowed. There'd been patience there; with Nicolaus, perhaps a bit too much patience, for the boy clearly needed someone to take him in hand.

Gentleness. That was it, what curbed his abrupt manner and mellowed the severe expression on his broad-boned face. The sharp, frowning man whom she'd first met on the train platform clearly had a soft spot for children.

Well, so did she. And a man who felt like that about children couldn't be that bad, could he?

But then, she hadn't thought that Edward could possibly be what he was, either.

No, better not to relax too soon. Safety had come at a horrible price; she was not going to take it lightly.

Jakob came out of the back room and headed for the door, frowning. "There aren't any sheets and pillows. I—"

"I'll ask Mrs. von Leigh. You needn't bother."

He stopped abruptly. "It's not a bother."

His brows were drawn together, his mouth compressed. Had she insulted him, by intimating she didn't want him performing even that small service for her? She hadn't meant to.

"I'll be back with them in a minute." He spun for the door. She trailed after him.

"You can wait here," he said.

"No," she said quietly.

He looked at her then, fully, the expression in his dark eyes shielded behind the thin, gold-rimmed lenses. His face softened, as it did when he looked at Nicolaus. "You must be tired. You should rest."

"I need to get Daniel."

"Helga will watch him." His smile was barely there,

so faint she almost wondered if it was a smile or simply a trick of the shifting light. "*I'll* watch over him."

"No." She shook her head, dulled with fatigue, but knowing there was no way she'd sleep without Daniel safely in the same house as she was.

"All right, then." He nodded curtly, that moment of softness gone as if it had never been there at all. He strode out the door and back toward the main house, leaving her to stumble along in his wake.

They found the boys and Helga in the large kitchen in the back of the house. A spacious, simple room with both a cookstove and a hearth, dried herbs hanging from the ceiling, the kitchen smelled as close to heaven as Amanda ever thought to come.

She smelled coffee. And chocolate. Her stomach rumbled and she followed the aromas right to the table that the three of them were clustered around.

"Hi, Mama." Apparently with few aftereffects from his dunking in the river, though she'd be willing to bet his clothes were still damp, Daniel smiled up at her with lips rimmed by whipped cream.

"You look like an old man with a white beard," she said, dipping her finger into the foam and dabbing his nose with it.

"I saved you some." He jabbed his fork in the direction of two plates. "A *big* one."

"My hero." She slid into one of the sturdy wooden chairs.

"You would like some coffee?" Helga asked, lifting herself in her chair to go fetch it.

"Stay there, *Tante*." Jakob headed for the cookstove. "You've had a long day. I'll get it."

"Actually—is that hot chocolate I smell?" Amanda asked.

"Helga, it's too hot for chocolate," Jakob said.

"And why is it any different to drink chocolate in the summer than hot coffee, I ask you?" Mrs. von Leigh's smile was apologetic. "The boys asked."

"You spoil them, Helga," he said reprovingly.

"Hah! As if I'm the only one."

He shrugged, splashed steaming, creamy-brown chocolate into a blue-and-white china cup, and set it down in front of Amanda. "Thank you," she murmured, uncomfortable that he would serve her.

She looked down at her plate, filled with billows of whipped cream, stripes of dark chocolate cake, and shining ruby-red cherries.

You're too fat, Amanda.

The words echoed in her head so strongly she nearly looked around to see if Edward was there.

It was one of the many, many ways she'd failed him as a wife. He'd wanted her slender, thin and willowy as the fashionable women who populated the society parties he kept dragging her to. As thin as Cynthia.

At first, wanting to please her new husband, she'd tried to obey his wishes. Later, as she began to realize exactly what her marriage was becoming, it had been her one small bit of rebellion and comfort. Though Edward had decreed her menus, his chef liked to see his creations enjoyed, and had often let her sneak into the kitchen and snitch a slice of cake or a fruit tart.

Food had been one of the few bright spots in her life. Food and Daniel.

She cut a small forkful and took a bite. Her mouth exploded with sweetness and flavor, rich chocolate and pure fruit. She closed her eyes in sheer enjoyment. Edward's overpaid French chef had nothing on this.

"You like it?"

She opened her eyes, expecting Jakob to be watching her with faint disapproval. Instead, he smiled at her. "Wait'll you taste *Tante*'s Christmas stollen. You'll think you've died and gone to heaven."

He assumed they'd still be here at Christmas. She wasn't at all certain they'd stay through next week. She'd been unable to plan ahead for so long that it now seemed almost impossible to think that far into the future.

So many ifs. If they were accepted in this town. If Daniel liked it here. If her business got off the ground. If Jakob was as kind as he seemed.

If Edward didn't find them.

She hid behind her cup, quickly gulping her chocolate. Strong and hot, it nearly burned her throat.

"And just where are you going, Jakob?" Helga demanded.

He'd gotten halfway to the door. "Back to work, of course."

"Don't be ridiculous. We have guests."

"We're boiling the wort today. I must be there."

"But there's something I need to talk to you about."

"Fine." He walked back to the table and spread his feet wide, folding his arms comfortably across his chest. "Talk."

"Can't you even sit down?"

"No."

Helga chuckled indulgently. "You are a good worker, I shall say that for you." She reached over and patted Amanda's hand. "Now then, forgive me for being forward, but how are you to support yourself and Daniel? I do not think you can afford to do nothing, *ja*?"

"Helga," Jakob interrupted, "this is none of your business."

"No, it's fine." Amanda said, rushing in, ready to explain her plans.

"Wait." Jakob nodded to the boys. "Nicolaus, if you

two are done with your *Schwarzwaldertorte*, perhaps
you want to show Daniel your room."

"Yeah. Come on, Daniel." He dashed from the
table, Daniel following him into the hallway at a
slightly more restrained pace.

"And don't try and climb up on the roof this time!"
Jakob bellowed after them.

"Sure thing, Uncle Jake." Amanda heard their feet
thudding down the hall and up the stairs.

"Thank you." She wrapped her stiff fingers around
the delicate cup. Even in the warm day, the heat from
the chocolate was welcome. "Now then, Mrs. von
Leigh, you are right, I will be needing some source of
income. I plan—"

"Not to worry! My Jakob will help you. And you
must not call me Mrs. von Leigh. I have told you this."

"Perhaps he *can* help me." She chanced a quick
glance at Jakob, wondering if he were annoyed at
Helga's volunteering his services. Certainly he would
be relieved to find out that the help she required from
him was so small. "Mr. Hall, would you happen to have
a newspaper around?"

"A newspaper?" Helga asked.

"Sure." He ducked into the next room.

"I am a seamstress. But I had to leave my machine
behind in—" She broke off, taking a quick breath.
She'd nearly said New York, without thinking. She had
schooled herself to be so careful, and had never come
close to slipping before. But something about being
here, in this warm, homey kitchen, had made her relax
a bit. Obviously, too much. "—back East."

Helga frowned at her. "A seamstress! That is not
what I had in mind at all."

"Nevertheless, a seamstress is what I am," she said
firmly.

It was the only marketable skill she had. She supposed she should be grateful that her father's fortunes had been erratic enough that she and her mother had been forced to learn to make the clothes for the entire family. They'd eventually become good enough that no one in their circle had suspected that her gowns had not come from the most fashionable modiste in New York. Of course, if her father's financial situation had been a bit more stable, she might never have married Edward.

Though she was certainly out of practice, she was sure she could still sew. And she had the advantage of coming fresh from the East Coast. She knew the latest fashions; she'd worn most of them.

"But you must spend time with—" Jakob's return stopped Helga's words. Amanda had a pretty good idea what Helga had intended to say.

Clearly, this was going to be a problem. If she were to stay in New Ulm, and remain friends with Helga, she was going to have to convince Mrs. von Leigh that she was most definitely not a suitable prospective bride for Jakob.

The easiest way to convince her would be to simply tell her that she was already married.

Absurdly, Amanda almost smiled at the thought. She would never do it, of course. But she would bet it would certainly put a stop to Helga's matchmaking quickly.

"Here you go." Jakob tossed a folded paper on the table in front of Amanda, stirring up a whoosh of air. "The *New Ulm Post*."

"Thank you." She unfolded the thin, crinkly paper, only to find that *New Ulm Post* were the only words on the page she could read. "It's all in German!" The old-world letters were thick and curvy. Sort of pretty, actually, but they did her no good at all.

"Of course it is." Was that a faint hint of amusement in his voice? He couldn't be teasing her. Yet, there was the slightest curl to his mouth, and when she unwillingly smiled back, it broke into a full-fledged grin which looked absolutely wonderful on him.

"What did you need the newspaper for?"

"I'm going to be a dressmaker. I need to order a sewing machine. There must be an advertisement for one in here."

"Probably." He came around the table to stand at her shoulder and reach over her, flipping through the rustling pages. Too close. She slid away, teetering on the edge of her chair, but he seemed oblivious to her discomfort. "Ah, there it is." He pointed to a black and white line drawing. "The millinery shop— it's on the first floor of the Dakotah. They'll order you a Singer."

"Does it mention how long it will take?"

"Let me see." He quickly scanned the paper. "No. A month or two at least, I'd expect. You're out here in the middle of the country now. You'll get used to waiting for things."

She sighed, deflated. "I suppose so." She really hadn't wanted to wait that long. She was deeply reluctant to use any more of the money she had brought than was necessary; it was all of his inheritance that Daniel would ever receive. And she thought she would become part of the community faster if she could contribute to it.

She wanted to belong here. She wanted this to be a home, both for her and Daniel, the kind they'd never had. Not to mention she needed something to occupy her hands in order to try to still her mind.

"Well, then." Oh, dear. The cheerfulness in Helga's voice told Amanda that Mrs. von Leigh had another plan. "Until your machine comes, you can help Daniel at the brewery. His office, it is always such a mess."

"What?" Amanda wondered if the word had sounded as strangled to everyone else as it did to her.

Jakob laughed low and shook his head. "Helga," he said, half scolding.

"What?" she said innocently. "It is a good idea. You know you never have the time to properly sort through all those papers and forms. You could use a woman's touch."

Amanda gaped at Helga. Surely she couldn't have been aware of what she just said. *You could use a woman's touch.*

Helga smiled beatifically and nodded. "It is all settled, then. You will like it there, Amy. Jakob is a good employer."

"Now wait just a minute," Jakob said. Amanda almost sagged in relief. She wasn't going to have to put a stop to this. Jakob was going to do it, thank God.

"Mrs. Smith." He looked down at her, directly, his gaze intent on her face. Irrelevantly, she tried to remember what his eyes had looked like without glasses when he'd taken them off by the river. She rather thought he had very nice eyes. "Do you *want* to work for me?"

He was asking her? She'd thought he was going to find a graceful way out of it. "But . . . but . . . what about Daniel? Who will watch him?"

"I will do it, of course," Helga suggested immediately. "I watch Nicolaus. And the school will be starting soon."

"But—" What excuse could she use to refuse? That she didn't really need the money? That Jakob made her uncomfortable, and she really didn't want to be around him every day? That she certainly didn't want to be indebted to him any more than she already was?

"I could really use the help," he said.

No one had asked for her help for such a long time. She'd forgotten how good it felt. But then, she'd forgotten how good a lot of things felt.

"Fine," she agreed.

6

He looked so much like his mother.

Gently, making no noise that might wake him, Amanda set her lamp on the small night table next to the bed Daniel slept in. She turned the wick down low, leaving just enough light so she could see him clearly.

He was washed in the low, gold light, a young, beautiful angel with midnight hair. He looked nothing like Edward, who was the image of classic golden handsomeness. Daniel whimpered in his sleep and turned over, his face pinched.

"Shh," she soothed him, gently smoothing a stray curl off his forehead. What nightmares haunted his sleep? She knew only too well what they probably were. He was too young, too perfect, to have such dreams. She could only hope that, with time, he would forget. As she would.

So much like Cynthia, she thought again. Cynthia had been her best friend at Mrs. Forster's School for Young Girls. Amanda's father's fortunes had been on the upswing then, and he'd scraped together enough money to send her to the school favored by the fashionable and wealthy.

She'd only been awkward and uncomfortable there, too plump, untraveled, and from a family clearly not as established as those of the other girls. Cynthia, who'd been the most wealthy and fashionable of them all, had, for some reason, taken her under her wing.

They'd kept in contact after she'd left school, when her father's business had nearly folded yet again, and she'd had to go home and help care for the rest of the family. When Cynthia had written that she was to marry Edward Sellington, the most eligible of New York's eligible bachelors, Amanda had been delighted for her.

Cynthia's letters had become less frequent, telling of a whirlwind of social events and glittering new acquaintances. And then she'd written to say she was expecting, and offering a position as her companion and helper after the child was born.

Amanda had known it was more than friendship that made Cynthia offer; Amanda's family's situation had reached a low point, and there was no money to send her younger brother to the school he so wanted to go to. Her salary would help, and Cynthia was merely kind enough to couch it in terms of desperately needing Amanda's assistance.

But when she'd arrived at the imposing manor right in the heart of New York City, she found Cynthia dead, Edward visibly grieving, and Daniel motherless. She'd fallen instantly, irrevocably in love with Cynthia's beautiful infant son.

If only she had known then what it all would lead to. And yet, perhaps she wouldn't change it, for it had brought her Daniel, and he was worth all she'd endured since then.

Bending over, she tucked the blanket more securely around his shoulders and pressed a kiss to his forehead. She stayed there a moment, eyes closed, her lips against his soft, fine skin, breathing in familiar, little-boy scents and wondering how long he'd still smell like that. The baby scent had gone so quickly.

Her throat burned. God, she loved him so much. She hadn't known it was possible to love so much.

"My son," she whispered, and knew it was true. He was not the child of her body, but he was the child of her heart.

Resisting the impulse to lie down beside him and pull him close, she finally scooped up the lantern and wandered back into the main room. The windows were open, letting in a cool breeze. She brushed back one of the lacy curtains and stared out into the night.

Peace. What a rarity. The moonlight was pale, silvery, starkly gilding the small pines. It was absolutely quiet, save for the small, soft rush of the river and an occasional hooting owl. Surprisingly, the quiet wasn't unsettling after New York, which, even in the dead of night, had never been completely silent. Instead, she found it utterly soothing.

Just after supper, she and Daniel had retreated to the guest house, quickly washed up, and pitched headlong into bed. She expected Daniel to sleep straight through until morning. He'd had an eventful day.

She, however, would not go back to bed until sunrise. When the night crept in, sleep left her. For too long, night had held the potential for pain. Too often, the reality of it. So now she slept during dusk and dawn, and nights were spent doing whatever would make her forget.

Perhaps someday she'd be able to sleep through the darkest hours again. But not yet, even here, where peace sighed through the trees with the wind and the moon smiled gently, where it seemed fear and pain could never creep in.

She sighed and set the lamp on the large kitchen table, turning up the wick as high as possible, the wavering light casting an oblong oval on the polished planks.

She fetched her sewing kit and an armful of clothes from her bedroom, piling them up on one end of the table. If she was to get any business as a seamstress, she'd need to be better dressed than she was now.

Her choices had been limited in Philadelphia, and she'd taken what she could get from the clothing resale shop. But most were outdated, often slightly damaged or stained. The fit, too, was not good, especially since without a maid to help, she couldn't lace herself tightly enough to slip easily into the snug-fitting waistlines.

She could fix all those things. But first, she had more important work to do.

The small, blue velvet pouch had ridden tight against her ribs, held in place with her corset, all the way from New York. Her fingers fumbled with the gold cords until the snug knots came free. Amanda dumped the contents onto the table, a soft clatter of metal and stone against wood.

The Sellington Diamonds. Amanda had always thought that was a ridiculous name for them, for they weren't heirlooms handed down from Edward's ancestors. He'd bought them just eight years ago, presenting them to her on their wedding day.

She poked at the necklace, arranging it against the gleaming wood. The diamonds captured the light, multiplying it, turning it into cold, blue-white glints. Dozens of round stones, so big she'd at first thought they couldn't possibly be real. But with Edward, everything was real—everything but his calm and smooth demeanor.

When he had first fastened them around her neck, they'd settled, cold and heavy, against her chest. The necklace was almost too small, the collar of it tight around her neck, nearly choking her. She should have suspected the trap she was entering into then.

She'd known that she didn't love him as she should, though she was slightly dazzled by his looks and money. But she'd also been marrying him for Daniel, and for the help Edward's fortune and influence could give to her family, even as she suspected he was marrying her for a mother to Daniel and, as she was Cynthia's closest friend, the last remnant of his first wife he had to hold on to.

But that day she'd felt hope. Surely he wouldn't be so extravagantly generous if he didn't care for her, too. It had taken her a long time to realize the diamonds were merely a showy display of his wealth. He was prone to displays.

As she picked up a sharp knife and bent to pry the stones from their settings, she wondered which loss Edward regretted the most: his wife, his son, or his diamonds.

The young, blond maid had finished the most important of her duties at the Sellington Mansion. Carefully, she wiped her mouth on the edge of her spotless white apron, then sat back on her heels and gave Edward a practiced smile.

"Nicely done, Corinna. As always."

"Thank you, sir." She bobbed her head in agreement.

"You may fasten me up now," he said, just a hint of impatience creeping into his voice. They were so hard to train properly. Why couldn't they remember to refasten his clothing when they were done?

"I'm sorry, Mr. Sellington." Her voice wavered a bit, and he smiled at her discomfiture. Good. She respected him properly already.

"Sir," he corrected.

"Sir," she said, her deft, clever fingers quickly working the buttons of his trousers.

"Good girl." He reached over to his desk, slid open one of the heavy, carved drawers, retrieved a single gold coin, and tossed it to her.

"Thank you, sir." She bobbed a quick curtsy, displaying the ample charms her uniform was cut to highlight. He waved negligently at the door and she skittered out of sight.

He tipped back the big, brown leather chair and studied his library. The two-story walls were lined with rare books. Underfoot, priceless antique Oriental rugs set off precious, mahogany furniture, all softly illuminated by gently hissing gas wall sconces.

The room was barely adequate. The entire mansion was barely adequate, he thought in disgust. In the last year, two men of his acquaintance had built ones slightly larger and grander. That would never do. Perhaps it was time to start interviewing architects.

He sighed and lifted a snifter of cognac, warming it in his hands. So much to do. No one ever seemed to understand the responsibilities and requirements of being Edward Sellington.

The soft whisper of silk against the plush rugs alerted him to her presence. "Hello, Mother."

She glided into the room. Even this late, long after midnight, she was perfectly coifed and gilded in jewels. The elaborate dress she wore had quite likely taken the seamstress a full month of non-stop work to finish properly. Her cool, silver-blond hair piled high on her head, her face perfectly painted—it was difficult to discern her age. Easy to discern money and power.

"I saw that maid leave." She selected a deep, silk-covered chair and lowered herself into it with all the airs of the queen he knew she would have loved to be. No one who saw her would ever suspect her modest start as the daughter of a Boston schoolteacher. "Are you feeling better?"

"I never felt badly." The cognac slid over his tongue, warming, easing down the back of his throat.

"Of course not." She inclined her head, deep red rubies ringing her throat like a trail of blood. "They aren't worth it."

"No."

"They were never worth it, neither of those wives of yours. This one, though, I never thought would have the spirit to defy you."

Neither had he. His fingers tightened around the heavy crystal. After one beautiful wife, a plainer one had seemed the obvious choice. He was tired of men hovering around Cynthia; Amanda, he'd thought, would be properly grateful for his attentions.

"Of course, I don't know why she would want to," his mother was continuing, her voice crystal-sharp in the warm, glowing room. "She never appreciated you properly, Edward."

No, he silently agreed, swirling the liquid in his glass, watching it flow and ebb. She never had, even though he'd taken such pains to instruct her.

"I never did understand why you married her."

"Didn't you, Mother?" He smiled and breathed in the warm scent of fine cognac; there was nothing to compare to it. "I married her because I could."

She looked puzzled, and faint lines furrowed her high brow. She wouldn't like that; he wouldn't mention it. Or perhaps he would. "I don't understand."

"Who else could marry a nobody like Amanda and not have it affect his standing at all?"

"Ah," she said, her voice sliding on the word. "I *do* understand." She nodded, setting her jewel-studded ear clips asparkle. "Have you found them yet?"

"No." He reached over to the cut-crystal decanter and refilled his glass. Truly excellent cognac was perhaps one of the few things that had never failed him.

That, and power, and wealth. Humans were decidedly more fallible, and disappointingly less reliable.

Her heavy skirts rustling, his mother sat back in her chair, diamond-decorated wrists resting elegantly on the smooth curve of the carved armrests. "Do you want to?"

"Not particularly. But I will, in any case."

"Good. He is your son, after all, even if he is a poor reflection on you."

He barely checked himself. His son! If only she knew.

The desire to explode with the injustice done him was so strong. But not with her. Never with her.

"Must you bring her back?"

"Yes," he said harshly.

He could see her disapproval; her lips thinned, her chin lifted imperiously. "Why?"

"She is mine."

"Even if she is unworthy?"

"Especially then."

"But—"

"Quiet!" The word exploded from him, ripping through the quiet, sheltered room, as out of place as a gunshot in a cathedral.

Her hand shook as she lifted it and pressed it to her chest, just over her heart. She swallowed and drew herself together, unwilling as always ever to show a weakness. One of the things he'd inherited from her. "What shall you do then? Hire more men to look?"

"No." He took two quick swallows, willing the aged brandy to cool the fire in his belly. Instead, it only made it burn the brighter. "The last thing I want is for news of this to spread around."

"Surely there are men who are trustworthy, if you pay them enough."

"Who doesn't like to revel in the troubles of their betters? No, it would be too tempting for them to tell someone. We'll have to make do with what I have on it already."

"And then?"

"And then?" The thought of what he would do then made him smile. He would teach them both their proper places. He would forcibly mold them into the wife and son they should already be, if he must. He would *make* them. "Why, then, Mother, I shall go and fetch them home."

"Don't, Edward," she said.

"Enough!" he roared. "I will do what I wish, Mother!"

Bright spots of color burst on her cheeks, deepening the rose already painted there. "I am sorry, Edward. I only want you to have a wife worthy of you."

"It is of no matter," he said, his voice firmly back in control, as smooth and polished as if he had never exploded. "All women are whores, anyway." His gaze flicked up to his mother. "Present company excepted, of course."

"There is no need." Her back ramrod stiff, she rose majestically from her chair. "You are quite correct, of course. The difference is, my darling, that I did it for you."

Just before she slipped through the door, he called to her. "Oh, and Mother?"

"Yes?" She turned back, eyes bright and bearing tall, ageless, queenlike, framed by the heavy velvet that draped the door.

"Send Corinna back in to me."

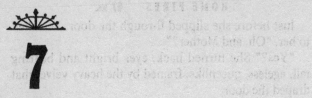

7

Almost done.

Amanda took the last few stitches that securely
closed the small cut she'd made in the heavy fabric of
her bustle. Daniel's future was now safely tucked away
in a mass of horsehair.

She stowed away her supplies, pulled on a light
wrapper, and stuck her feet into her boots. After
checking on Daniel one last time, finding him still
sleeping peacefully, she headed out the door and down
the path that led to the necessary behind the big house.

The small, square building was perched on a slight
knoll, where the wind could blow away any stray
odors. The door creaked as she pulled it wide. A yellow
shaft of moonlight streamed through, landing right on
the built-in shelf.

And she tossed the empty settings for her diamonds
right down the round, black hole.

A fit of laughter took her as she left the outhouse.
She wondered if someone coming across her right then

would have thought her mad. But it seemed as if so much had gone right down that smelly hole with those useless bits of gold. Things she wanted so much to be rid of: fears, burdens, the past.

She was no longer Mrs. Edward Sellington. She was Amy Smith, a widow with a young son, a seamstress, a resident of New Ulm, Minnesota. She rather thought she was going to like Amy Smith.

Throwing her arms wide, she spun, the light cotton of her wrapper floating out around her, giddy with the night and the freedom. Amy Smith wasn't a married woman! No one had power over her but herself.

Her feet skimmed lightly over the path back. The grass was wet with dew, dampening the bottom of her nightdress. The air was rich with the scent of pine and the river, and suddenly she didn't want to go back inside and start ripping apart and putting back together a dress.

There was plenty of time for work later. Now, the sound of the river drew her, and she wound between the trees, heading for its bank.

She remembered seeing a bench there in the afternoon, a simple, low-backed wooden seat beside a droopy willow. She'd sit there for a while and watch the water, giving herself a bit more time to savor this.

Edward was a thousand miles away. Surely even he, with all his power and money and seeming invincibility, would never find them here, in this little spot of a town hidden away in a valley she knew he'd never heard of. They were safe, she repeated to herself. Safe.

The breeze rustled the trailing leaves of the willow and the sound melted into the low murmur of the river. She paused, watching moonlight dance over the tiny ripples in the water.

"Good evening."

She shrieked and jumped, all her peace shattered. Energy pumped through her body, ready to take flight.

"Wait!" Jakob said. "I'm sorry. I didn't mean to startle you."

"I didn't see you there," she said, a bit breathlessly.

"I thought you must have seen me."

"No." And she hadn't realized it was he when he first spoke. For one second, just one brief, terrifying instant, she had thought perhaps Edward had found her after all. Would he always haunt her? Even now, when she knew she was safe, her heart didn't seem to realize it. It was racing along, pounding so hard she thought it might beat right out of her chest.

"I'm sorry," he said again. "I didn't mean to frighten you."

"I'm not frightened!" she said, too sharply. "I'm not frightened," she repeated more calmly. Surely she was beyond fright. One who'd already experienced the worst that could happen should no longer know fear, she thought. Now, only for Daniel would she feel it, she resolved. Never again for herself. It was useless, anyway; fear had never done her any good. It had never saved her.

"Would you like to join me?" He slid over on the bench, indicating the empty spot.

"Oh, no." She clutched at the neckline of her wrapper, tugging it more tightly around her. "I'm not dressed."

"That's okay. I am."

Was he teasing her again? It was not what she would have expected from him. But then, she certainly wouldn't have expected him to be sitting outside on a warm summer night and enjoying the moonlight on the river. She would have thought that, if he were up, he'd be in the brewery, hunched over some work left from the day.

Now he was comfortably sprawled on an old wooden bench, his long legs stretched out in front of him, crossed at the ankles. He slouched in the seat, arms spread along the long back.

"Oh, come on, sit down. I'm really quite safe."

"Are you?"

"Oh, yes. Helga would never allow me another breath if I weren't," he said. Withdrawing his arms from the bench, he leaned forward conspiratorially. "I live in fear of her, you know."

"And well you should."

"Ah, learned that already, have you?"

Taking the chance, she gathered her robes around her and perched on the end of the bench, as far from him as she could get, hugging the arm. "I'm here, aren't I? I'm still not quite sure how it ended up that way. I thought I was going to California. But she suggested Minnesota, and I was here before I realized what happened."

"That sounds like her."

She ducked her chin and looked at him out of the corner of her eye. The clothes he had on now suited him much better than the suit he'd worn that afternoon. These were simple, heavy canvas trousers and a loose cotton shirt that fit his shoulders well.

"Why, you're not wearing your glasses," she said before she thought.

"I don't really need them much. Just for reading."

She was surprised enough to look at him fully. "Why would you wear them, then?"

He shifted a bit, embarrassed. "I . . . well, I was very young when I took over the brewery. Too young to be taken seriously as a businessman, I figured, and I thought they made me look older. Now they're sort of a habit, I guess."

He had beautiful eyes. Dark, heavily lashed. And

solemn. Far too solemn, the eyes of a much older man, a man who'd seen too much and enjoyed too little. Solemn even when he was smiling, as he was now. She wondered what it would take to put an expression of another sort there.

"So," he said, "why are you wandering around in the middle of the night? Couldn't sleep?"

"No."

"It's sometimes hard to sleep in a new place. You'll get used to it."

"No, I . . ." She paused, surprised that she found herself willing to talk to him about this. And yet she was. "I don't sleep well at night."

"Me, either," he said sympathetically. "Nightmares, too?"

"No." A cloud shifted, obscuring the moon and cloaking them in darkness. It was easier somehow, when she couldn't see him, could only hear his voice twining through the darkness. "Memories."

The wind picked up, shivering the willow strands, blowing her hair across her cheek. She brushed it back.

What could haunt his dreams? He appeared to have a perfect life. Youth, strength, a thriving business, and a family that he clearly loved.

"What do you see in your nightmares?" She shocked herself by asking. But she had already shocked herself by sitting beside a man and a river in the middle of the night; what was a bit more?

She really didn't think he would answer; she was prying into something that was none of her business. For a long time, she heard only the whoosh of the water and the rustle of the leaves.

"Smoke," he said finally. "I see smoke."

*　　*　　*

Somehow, it didn't seem odd to him that she'd appeared to him out of the dark and the moonlight, wrapped in billowy white.

After all, he'd been thinking about her.

Which was odd enough in itself. Women were at the bottom of a very long list of things he usually thought about.

At night, unable to sleep, he tried to think of nothing at all. It was better than thinking of the things that kept him awake.

Often he tried to work. Almost always he failed, for the tight quarters of his offices closed in, reminding him of the days he'd spent crowded into a few small buildings with most of the residents of New Ulm.

So he wandered the grounds instead, wearing paths up and down the hill and along the edge of the water, until he was so exhausted that he was certain he could fall into at least a few hours of deep, dreamless sleep.

But tonight, as he'd paced through the gardens and along the banks of the river, he'd thought of her.

A very strange woman, alternately timid and fierce. He sensed there was much more there than she showed, and he was curious. Curiosity? He'd nearly laughed aloud. When had he ever indulged in curiosity?

Not that it could ever be more than that, despite the temporary job he'd offered her. It had been as simple as he'd told her: his office was a shambles, he had no taste for organizing it himself, and he had no time to hire help. It was convenient—she was right here—and perhaps the money would help her and her son out.

But now, as she sat beside him, bright moonlight glossing her light brown hair with silver, he wondered if it was that simple after all.

It was incongruous, her sitting here, wrapped in layers of white nightclothes and wearing her clunky boots.

She was skittish, leaning away from him, half climbing up the other arm of the bench.

He supposed she had a right to be concerned. She scarcely knew him, it was night, and they were alone on his land, miles from town.

Her voice was soft, barely audible above the rush of the river and the whispering of the wind, braiding with them both into a soothing sound, and he leaned closer to hear her. She smoothed away a stray lock of hair, and he wondered if she was pretty.

He wasn't certain. *Pretty* was not a quality that had ever had much value in his life. But she was soft, all billowing fabric and wisps of windblown hair. And her skin was white, pure, glowing faintly as if she'd captured a bit of the moonlight and made it her own.

"Smoke," he repeated. "Smoke, from the uprising."

"The uprising?" Her voice went high, thin and reedy.

"Didn't Helga tell you?"

"No."

"I would have thought she would have told you."

He'd never talked about it, he realized. How strange. But everyone he knew had been there; they'd lived through it, too, and had no more desire than he to rehash those few, torturous, endless days.

"It was the Sioux," he said finally.

Her silence was somehow encouraging, a gentle patience that drew out his words.

"They were . . ." he paused, searched. How could he give reasons when there were none? "Hungry. This used to be their land, everything in this part of Minnesota. I remember, my mother used to give them food." He gestured upstream, in the general direction of the brewery. "I guess that's why they spared this, when everything else was burned." Pain welled, deep and powerful, no less fresh for having been born a decade ago. "It didn't save her, though."

Clouds, dense gray, shifted in the sky; the river rolled slowly, unceasingly past. Quiet, peaceful, calm. Like it had been for a hundred years, and would be for a hundred more. Had it been quiet like this, just before the attack?

"You don't have to tell me this, Mr. Hall."

"I think we could probably dispense with the Mister now, couldn't we?" He knew his smile was a bit weak. "After all, I've seen you in your nightclothes."

"Jakob, then."

"Aren't you going to give me permission to call you by your first name?"

"Do you need it?"

"No, Amy, I guess I don't."

She nodded, accepting. "As I said, you don't have to go on. Not if it's difficult."

"Difficult." A narrow word. Difficulties were something one overcame, not something one fought with, lived with, every single night. "It was almost eleven years ago right now, do you know that?

"I was seventeen, and angry that they wouldn't let me go off and fight the Rebs like every other man in town." He grimaced, remembering what a fool he'd been, fool enough to think war would be a grand adventure. He'd learned otherwise quickly enough. "So angry, I stayed behind when they went out to visit my sister, Charlotte. She'd just had Nicolaus, you see. They lived northwest of town."

He flexed his hands, wishing he had something to hold on to. Wishing, irrationally, that he could hold on to her, could pull her close and fill his arms with softness while he remembered what he'd never been able to forget.

"That's where the raiding party hit first. I was in town when the first survivors came in. I didn't know . . . for days, I didn't know if they were safe or not."

He remembered the madness, the chaos. Fleeing settlers pouring into town, looking for shelter. Two thousand people packed into as little space as possible, four square blocks of brick buildings, as the town burned to the ground around them.

"We . . . there was nothing we could do! All the men had gone off to fight for the Union. We only had fifty guns between us. Hell, only twelve of them were rifles!"

He'd gotten his taste of war, all right. More than he'd ever wanted. Screaming children, crying women, old men trying to hold their places with small pistols that were grossly inadequate. Rapidly depleting food and ammunition. An overwhelming impotence; knowing there was nothing—nothing!—he could do to help them.

"It was only five days. We weren't even fighting most of the time, just hanging on, waiting for reinforcements from Mankato or Fort Ridgely."

He didn't dare look anywhere but her face. As long as he looked at her, he didn't see it. Didn't see any blood, didn't see any wounded, didn't see the black smoke curling up from the hundreds of fires.

"We only lost eight people in town. But then they started bringing wagons in from the countryside . . . wagons with bodies."

Don't see it! See her eyes, the soft shimmer of reflected moonlight. See the full curve of her cheek, the roundness of her chin.

"They found Nicolaus under Charlotte's body. He was little, and hungry, and they put him in my arms." He'd understood more about war then, about a murderous rage that made one care about nothing but seeing the enemy's blood run free and red. How a man could forget that the person on the other side was anything but a target to focus that blinding fury on.

"I wanted to kill them all."

She didn't flinch, just gave a small nod as if she understood. But what could she know of that black, horrible drive to kill? "What happened to them then?"

"They hung 'em." He shook his head. "Not all of them, of course. Just thirty-eight. Just the ones Lincoln decided had committed murder and rape, rather than had killed in an act of war." As if that made any difference to those who died—or those who lived, left behind and alone.

He shivered, suddenly chilled. "The day after Christmas, in Mankato. I went to watch. It was cold; I remember it was cold."

There'd been white snow on the ground, white as Amy's skin. And shadows; distorted, swinging shadows of all those bodies.

"I don't know what they did with the rest of them . . . the ones who weren't 'murderers.'" He laughed, a hollow, harsh sound. "Stuck them out on a reservation, I expect."

"Did it help?" she asked softly. "Seeing them punished?"

"No. No, it didn't help." It only gave him more nightmares to keep him awake at night.

He breathed in, filling his lungs with summer night air, warm and thick with growing things.

"That's how I got Helga, you know. Her husband was lost, too. The next day, she just up and moved in, announcing I'd need help with Nicolaus. I doubt I'd get her out now with a blasting iron."

Not that he'd ever tried. He'd put up with her bossiness, her matchmaking, and her endless opinions, because she'd needed him and Nicolaus as much as they'd needed her help.

There was a shimmer of sympathy in Amy's eyes, an echo of sadness. All at once he was sorry that he'd told her all this now. He hadn't meant to make her sad. He'd only wanted her to understand, though he wondered about that. Why should it matter if she understood?

He forced a grin, consciously trying to lighten the mood. "Well, now that I've kept you out so long—" He pointed at the moon, lower in the sky, edging towards the rim of the valley. "—I think we have a few hours left. Care to spend the rest of the night with me?"

Her laughter was so soft it was barely there at all. "No, I don't think so." But she made no move to leave.

"You could tell me all *your* secrets now. It would only be fair."

There wasn't a flicker of change in her expression. "I don't have any secrets."

"Everyone has secrets."

He wanted to hear hers, almost as much as he wanted to use them—or any other excuse he could come up with—to keep her out here with him.

The long, empty nights were easier when they weren't entirely empty, he found. Went faster when there was something to look at besides the trees and the river.

He hadn't intended it. He was quite certain he hadn't planned it. Perhaps his body and hand had moved on its own. All he'd thought of was that he simply had to know if her skin could possibly feel as fine as it looked.

He slid over on the rough bench and lifted his hand to her cheek. A slow stroke, a single glide down the softly rounded curve, and he knew. It felt even better than it looked. Plush, warm, alive, and incredibly soft. He cupped her cheek in his palm, his thumb lightly gliding, now utterly certain that there was nothing on this earth that could compare with Amy's skin.

She froze, her hands clutching the neckline of her wrapper, and her eyes went wide. Then, with a strangled gasp, she threw herself from the bench and hurtled down the path. Her nightclothes streamed behind her, yards of white floating above the earth, making her look like a fleeing ghost.

She never looked back.

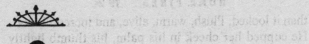

8

Helga arrived on the doorstep first thing the next morning with a basket full of hard rolls and a soft, white cheese for their breakfast. When Amanda carefully broached the subject of her and Daniel finding other accommodations, Daniel's face fell so dolefully that she quickly abandoned the topic.

All right, then, she decided. They'd stay for a while and see how it went. Her unease at taking so much from Jakob and Helga persisted, however, and she resolved that she must do something about it at the first opportunity.

It was one thing to accept kindness. Quite another to take advantage of it.

So, as soon as Daniel gobbled down his food—more than she'd ever seen him eat in New York—and he'd headed off to play with Nicolaus, she imposed on Mrs. von Leigh to keep an eye on him again. If she were to repay some of their generosity, she was going to have to get to work.

Now, she trudged down the road toward town. It was a lovely, clear morning, the sun sparkling off the broad river and sliding over the green-brushed land.

The way up out of the valley was steep and she wondered how the horses managed it with fully loaded wagons. On top of the bluffs, wind blew freely across the plains, tugging at her hair, which she'd drawn into a high chignon. With no trees to block the sun, wildflowers grew in abandoned profusion, white daisies, deep yellow black-eyed Susans, purple-topped thistles and clover tangling and tumbling together like fragrant, scattered confetti.

By the time she'd achieved the flats, she was puffing. Tramping a mile and a half into town was nothing like the decorous strolls through Central Park she was accustomed to. She had no idea how she was going to carry back home all the supplies she needed. Oh, well, she'd manage somehow. It wasn't as if she had too many other options.

She breathed in deeply, wondering how air could smell so beautifully different than it ever had before. Surely it was the same air she breathed in New York. Somehow it seemed to have more life in it, making her feel stronger and younger with each breath.

She laughed aloud at her absurd thoughts, knowing full well the only difference between this air and the air in New York was the fact that Edward didn't breathe in this air, too.

What more could a woman want? she wondered. The sky was blue, the air was warm, and she was free.

"Ouch!" She stopped and tugged off her low boots, shaking out a pebble.

Maybe a ride wouldn't come amiss.

Almost as if her wish had conjured it up, Jakob's wagon rounded over the edge of the bluff, pulling up

behind her. The huge hooves of his draft horses stirred
up tiny whirlwinds of dust with each clop.

The front seat was high, well over her head, and she
shaded her eyes to look up at him.

"Would you like a ride?"

"Did Helga send you?"

He grinned broadly. "Yup."

"I don't think so, then." She turned away and
marched toward town.

"Hey, wait a minute."

He hopped down from the wagon and hurried to
place himself in her path.

She stopped dead, unwilling to get any closer to
him. He was all dressed up again, in a dark brown suit
this time, his glasses firmly in place on the bridge of his
strong nose.

"I—" He gestured awkwardly. "About last night. I
didn't mean anything by it, you know."

Amanda swallowed and looked down, embarrassed
by her overreaction in rudely rejecting his offer of a
ride into town, which had certainly been no more than
common courtesy. What must he think of her? That
she was a skittish female who jumped to conclusions at
the slightest provocation?

"It was dark, and, well, I'm sorry if you took it the
wrong way."

She fiddled with the strings of her handbag. "It's all
right."

"It was just—" He seemed bemused, his dark gaze
drifting over her face. "Well, you have the most beautiful skin."

She went hot, incredibly, improbably flattered. It
had been forever since someone had simply paid her a
compliment. She wasn't certain anyone ever had.
Suddenly, she remembered the soft whisper of his

palm against her cheek, and she wished that, last night, she hadn't run away so quickly after all.

"Will you allow me to give you a ride?"

"Yes, of course."

He climbed down, handed her up to the seat, and then took his own. A quick command to the horses and the wagon rolled on down the road.

"This really was quite unnecessary, you know," she said quietly.

"I had to go into town, anyway. Supplies coming in on the steamboat."

So that's why he was all dressed up. After the things he'd told her last night, she thought she understood his attire a bit better now. When he'd so prematurely been thrust into running the brewery, he'd been too young to be taken seriously as a businessman, and probably used such formal clothes to appear older. It had apparently become a habit.

She just wished he'd find a tailor who knew how to cut for those shoulders.

"But you said that Helga sent you."

"Well, she had a bit to do with the timing, I'll admit." He looked at her sidewise, serious now. "You could have asked, you know. I'd have given you a ride."

"I didn't want to bother you."

"If it's a bother, I'll let you know, believe me. Just ask anyone."

"I'm sorry."

He frowned at her slightly. "Don't apologize. I just don't believe in wasting time because people are too polite to ask for what they need."

Her hands fisted, curling around the strings of her bag. Darn it! There *hadn't* been any reason to apologize. But so much had been her fault for so long that it had become second nature; "I'm sorry" was her habitual response to almost anything.

"All right, then," she said firmly, determined to follow his advice. "There *was* something I'd like to talk to you about."

"Shoot."

"I want to pay rent for the cottage." She held her breath, hoping she hadn't offended him by questioning his generosity. She doubted he needed the money, but she needed the independence, needed to feel that she wasn't depending on his charity.

"Okay."

He'd agreed. Just like that. She knew she must have looked surprised, for he slanted her a quick grin. "Did you want me to argue?"

"No, but I . . . ."

"I don't have the patience for those kinds of games. You tell me something, and I'm going to take you at your word."

As if she were an equal. How completely unusual.

"What do you think is fair?" she asked.

"I'd say a quarter of your salary is standard."

"Agreed." Her hands fluttered a bit in her indecision, then she stiffly stuck out her right one. He took it, his grip firm, his hand warm, but nothing about those strong fingers closing over hers seemed threatening.

"It's a deal, then." His shake was brief and businesslike, then he turned back to driving the horses.

She allowed herself a nod of pride and settled back on the seat, feeling a good deal more confident than she had a half an hour ago.

Perhaps she could get used to being treated like an equal.

He didn't bother with any conversation the rest of the way into town. Amanda wondered for a moment if she was supposed to chatter, to keep up her end. But she'd never learned the art of small talk. Edward had preferred her silence to what he called "her foolish jabbering."

And Jakob certainly didn't seem as if he expected it of her. He just leaned back in his seat, getting comfortable, the reins held firmly in his competent hands, and studied the fields they passed.

For Amanda, silence had always held a note of fear, of dreading the possibility of impending pain. She hadn't thought silence could be so easy, but this was.

She spent the rest of the ride happily running through her plans, thinking of all the things she needed to buy in town. No reason to keep the list short now, for she had the wagon to carry things back. She could get everything she needed.

They reached town in what seemed like no time at all. As the wagon clattered through the wide, neat streets, what she'd missed the first time in town was perfectly obvious now: Nearly all of the buildings were of the same vintage.

It seemed as if there should have been some remnant of the tragedy; some dark shadows or charred remains of burned houses. All she found were straight, clean streets and well-kept buildings. Perhaps, however, the fires explained why so many of the buildings were built of expensive, fire-resistant brick.

The Dakotah Hotel was not. A white, two-story building with blue shutters and a small overhang above the front door, it squatted along a street lined with several other prosperous-looking buildings.

"Here you go," Jakob said, halting the team. "The millinery's right inside. Do you need any help?"

"Of course not." She hopped down.

"What time shall I pick you up?"

"Whenever's convenient."

He scowled at her.

She squared her shoulders. "I shall need at least two hours."

"Good," he said, nodding in approval. "Will you be here?"

"Is there a dry goods store nearby?"

"Kaufenburg's is right across the street."

"Then that's where I shall be."

"I'll pick you up there, then. In two hours."

He headed off down Minnesota Street without a second glance, leaving her there, alone in a strange town.

And she was flattered by it. How strange.

Two hours later, Amanda stood in the middle of Hans Kaufenburg's mercantile juggling her packages, trying to figure out a way to hold on to the one she'd just bought.

"Ma'am? Do you think you'll be able to manage?" Mr. Kaufenburg asked.

"Certainly . . . somehow!" She dove for the bag that toppled off the pile, and missed. It hit the floor, spilling out two rounds of cheese and a half-dozen hard rolls.

She'd been disappointed to find that it would take nearly two months for her to receive the Singer sewing machine she'd ordered. Despite that, she considered the rest of the morning a rousing success.

Mrs. Mueller, who owned the millinery, had a wonderful selection of trimmings, buttons, and laces; Amanda had already begun planning the dresses those notions could decorate. And once Mrs. Franzen had learned of her plans, she'd given a quick once-over to Amanda's newly altered dress and promised she'd steer potential customers in her direction.

The town appeared highly prosperous; there were more stores than she'd ever expected to find, which boded well for her own prospects. She'd bought cheese, sausage, and bread, which she figured she couldn't ruin and would keep herself and Daniel fed for at least a few days.

"Here you go." Mr. Kaufenburg grinned and scooped up her purchases, piling them back in her arms.

"I'll take that." Jakob deftly captured the majority of her packages.

"Oh, Jakob, there you are! Thank you."

"I see you must have been horribly disappointed in the selection in our small town. You hardly bought a thing."

She grinned at him, flushed with success. She'd wandered up and down the town, all by herself. She'd bought things, introduced herself, made new acquaintances. All without someone looking over her shoulder, guarding, spying, ready to report back to her husband.

"Well, Jakob, I did leave *most* of it back with that nice clerk at the hotel. You'll simply have to go back and fetch it. I wonder if we can fit it into the wagon?"

When his jaw dropped in surprise, she couldn't help it. She laughed, and was rewarded when his eyes sparkled behind his glasses and his laughter joined hers. So his eyes weren't always solemn, after all.

"Did you meet Mr. Kaufenburg?"

"She did indeed," Hans said, beaming at them. "I hear she is staying out to your place for a while?"

"Well, you know how Helga is. The more of us she has to watch over, the better."

"Yes, indeed."

"How is it you all know where I'm staying?" Amanda asked. "That's been happening to me all morning long."

"Ah, well," Hans said, looking from one to the other. "We all know what our Jakob is up to."

"Is that package yours, too?" Jakob said, reaching for a brown-wrapped bundle resting on the long counter.

"No," she said quickly, snatching it up. "I mean, yes, it's mine, but I can take it."

"Okay. Ready to go?"

"Oh, Jakob, are you in here? I thought I saw your wagon outside, and I just—" A woman breezed in the door in a flutter of blue cotton. "Oh, there you are!"

"Yes, but not for long." He juggled Amanda's purchases more securely and took a step toward the door.

"No need to rush off," she said, her voice as bright as the sheen on her hair.

She sashayed over, all lithe curves in her ice-blue dress. She was very pretty, Amanda thought. Though she'd be even prettier if she could be talked into a dress without all those lacy frills drowning her. Definitely a potential customer.

The woman gained Jakob's side and smiled up at him. "Hello, Jakob. Did you enjoy the cake?"

"I didn't have any."

She made a lush pout. "But I made it for you."

"I thought you made it for Helga." Jakob adroitly stepped aside, closer to Amanda. "Brigitte, I'd like to introduce you to Amy Smith. She's just moved here."

"So I've heard." The blue of her eyes was every bit as cold as that of her dress. "So you are the *Ausländer*."

"I'm very pleased to meet you," Amanda said. "And I, on the other hand, quite enjoyed your cake."

"I'd imagine you did." She cocked one hand against her tightly laced waist. "Have you been to Turner Hall yet?"

"No, I haven't—"

"Well, perhaps you would join us for a gymnastics class sometime. The exercise is quite good for you. I never miss it." Dismissively, she turned back to Jakob. "Did you hear that Armando the Amazing will be there next Friday night?"

"Yes, I had heard that." He tried to slide a little nearer to the door. Amanda wondered if the woman didn't notice or simply didn't care; Jakob's anxiousness to leave was perfectly clear to Amanda.

"Are you going?"

"Well, I don't know yet," he said desperately, clutching the overflowing piles of packages. "I thought maybe Nicolaus would like—"

"Oh, you should go," Hans broke in. He rocked back on his heels, broad hands resting on his apron-covered belly, and beamed at them. "Mrs. Smith certainly must see the Hall and meet everyone, do not you think?"

"Well, I—"

"You should take her, Jakob." Hans winked directly at Amanda.

"Yes, of course I'm taking her," Jakob said quickly. "The boys wouldn't miss it. Amy, do you have everything now?"

"I believe so."

He steered her out the front door with a determination that was more than a bit obvious.

Hans chuckled. "It was very nice to meet you, Mrs. Smith!" he called after them.

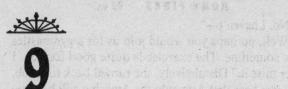

9

"Just what exactly was all that?"

Jakob grinned and slapped the reins over the backs of the two horses. He'd wondered how long it was going to take for her to get around to asking. Any other woman of his acquaintance would have burst with questions the minute they had gotten out the door. Amy had waited until they got out of town, and only then asked in that quiet, calm voice.

"Brigitte?"

"She's in love with you, of course."

That made him laugh. "No, she's in love with the brewery. I just come along with it."

She looked at him in disbelief, and he was oddly flattered. So she thought Brigitte must be in love with him, did she? Well, she could think it all she liked. He'd known Brigitte all his life, and he knew very well what put all that lust in her eyes.

"And what about Mr. Kaufenburg? Why did he insist you take me to the magic show?"

"I guess he thought I wasn't offering quick enough myself."

"Why would he care?"

"Oh, he's just matchmaking, too. Don't worry about it."

"Don't worry about it? Does everyone in town plan to marry you off?"

He glanced over at her. She was sitting straight-backed on the bench, the sun shining off the upsweep of her light, fine hair, and she was studying the passing landscape with rapt absorption. Simply dressed, the brown-wrapped bundle she'd gotten at Kaufenburg's resting in her lap, she seemed absolutely content to follow the river.

"Pretty much." She fit here surprisingly well, he realized. Not at all like any Easterner he'd ever met, who usually turned up their noses at the wares and the people in a town they saw as hopelessly provincial.

"Why are they all so interested in getting you married?" She looked up at him then, her hazel eyes soft and curious, and he felt an awkward, unwanted jolt of warmth. "And why would he want you to marry an outsider like me?"

"Well, they've tried every girl in town already. Could be you're their last hope."

She scowled slightly, light brown brows drawing together, and he grinned at her discomfiture. "But why do they insist you marry?" she asked.

"I think they believe I'll be more content here if I marry. That way I'll never sell the brewery."

"I didn't realize you had any plans to sell it."

"Not immediately, but—" He broke off and pointed to the river. "You know where that river goes?"

"No, not really," she said, faint puzzlement wisping through her voice.

"The Cottonwood joins with the Minnesota. You know that." He nodded at the river. It swept constantly on, rolling undisturbed, slow and powerful. Once, just once, he wanted to jump right into it and let it take him along for the ride. "That joins up with the Mississippi, and goes on down to the ocean, and then on out to the world." A world that he had never seen. Maybe he never would.

"I've never been past St. Paul," he said.

"So why don't you go?"

"How can I? I can't leave Nicolaus."

"Take him with you."

He stared at her incredulously. "Are you serious? You see the trouble I have with him here. I can just imagine what he'd do with things like trains and oceans and mountains."

She laughed then, throwing back her head, and he saw the even flash of her teeth. A soft, beguiling laugh, as understated and subtly compelling as she was. "I guess not."

"And then there's the brewery. I can't just up and take off. Nobody in town's willing to run it—it's always been Hall's brewery, and I'm the only Hall around. Tradition runs too strong. And, too, nobody seems to have the right feel for the beer. Father always said you had to be born with brewer's taste buds."

"Can't you find someone from the outside?"

"That's exactly what no one wants." He searched for a way to explain it to her, so she would understand what Hall's meant to this town. "After the attack, when everything burned, there *wasn't* anything else left. The brewery was about the only way most people had of making a living. If it had gone, so would the town."

He'd known it even then. Known it in the fearful,

worried, expectant looks people had turned on him, in their anxious questions. He'd been scared to death he was going to let them down.

"But what about now? Surely no one would begrudge you a bit of freedom."

"Things are better, but the last few years the grasshoppers have gotten most of the crops. The brewery has always been there to fall back on if they needed a little extra money to make ends meet."

"There must be some way," she said, her voice rich with sympathy he hadn't realized he needed. He had dozens of friends and acquaintances, but they all had as much tied up in the town and the brewery as they did in him. They did not want to hear about how much he wanted to leave it all behind.

In the few days he'd known her, he'd talked to her about things he'd never talked about to anyone else. It felt surprisingly good.

"It doesn't matter right now, anyway. Not until Nicolaus is older. Then, perhaps, he'll want to take over. If not, I'll find someone else."

He would, he vowed silently. Not that he regretted one moment of the last eleven years. But someday, surely it wasn't too much to ask for a bit of time for himself. To see mountains and oceans and cities, to find out if the sky in California or New York looked the same as it did in Minnesota. To find out if there were places that didn't have memories lurking in every damn corner, where he could sleep the whole night through without dreaming of the wagons that had rolled into a destroyed town, carrying the bodies of his family.

"Tell me about where you're from," he said.

"What do you mean?"

"The East. Pittsburgh. Whatever."

She shook her head, and her fingers pleated a bit of the loosely gathered blue fabric of her skirt. "It's crowded. Busy and loud. There's a lot of smoke." She tipped her head back, lifting her face to the sky, revealing a bit of her smooth, white throat. The skin on her cheek had been so soft, like featherdown beneath his fingers. Surely, the skin of her throat would be even finer, and he wondered how that was possible. "Often, at night, you can't even see the stars."

"It doesn't sound like you like it all that much."

She smiled gently, then her gaze swept the shallow valley of the Cottonwood and the flat, green-gold fields of grain on the other side. "I like it here just fine."

"Yes, I think you do," he murmured. The city still sounded exciting to him. Perhaps he wouldn't like it, but he wanted to find out for himself. But, right this moment, as he watched her delight in the rapid wheel and dart of a hawk overhead, he thought perhaps nowhere else would be quite as good as right here with her.

She glanced over at him and must have caught his expression, for she took a deep breath and squared her round, sturdy shoulders. "I can't go to the magician with you, Jakob."

Ah, damn. He hadn't intended to scare her off again. Had his inappropriate thoughts been that clear on his face? He'd thought she was over her skittishness with him. "What do you mean, you can't go with me? You can't possibly abandon me to Brigitte's attentions."

"You'll have to manage."

"Ah." He clapped a hand to his heart. "You are too cruel."

She barely smiled, so he pulled the horses to a stop and turned to give her his full attention.

"The boys would like it."

"I'm certain they would. The answer is still no."

"Why can't you go to the Hall with me, Amy?"

Her lashes swept down to cover eyes that were nearly the shade of the ripening fields—mostly green, with a warming hint of rich golden brown.

"It's not because of last night, is it? When I touched you?" he asked. "Because I already apologized for that."

"I wouldn't want you to—" She fidgeted, clearly nonplussed, sliding her fingers back and forth along the string that secured the package she'd bought in Kaufenburg's. "I realize that it's quite ridiculous, of course, but just in case you thought that there . . . that there might be something between us—" she gulped and continued "—I wouldn't want you to get the wrong idea."

"I'm beginning to think there *is* something between us."

Her eyes flew open then, wide with panic. "No, there can't be!"

"Why not?" he asked, genuinely curious.

"My husband—he—" She snapped her mouth shut, and nearly crushed the package between her hands, crumpling the brown paper.

"I understand," he said sympathetically. "Your loss is too new."

"No, it's not just that! I couldn't ever . . ." She trailed off helplessly, and he was immediately sorry he'd ever brought the subject up. The pain in her eyes was too fresh, too deep, and there was nothing he could do to make it go away.

"You must have loved him very much." The lucky bastard.

She stilled, her eyes glistening wetly.

"Look," he said, "you really don't have anything to worry about. It's not that I don't find you attractive, because I do."

The flush heated her cheeks at once, a becoming rose that bloomed underneath her pale skin.

"But that really doesn't matter, Amy. My plans have no place for that sort of thing, either."

He watched relief flood her, and felt just a twinge of bruised pride. "But since neither of us has any . . . intentions . . . what I thought might be between us is, well—" What a stupid thing to propose to a woman he barely knew. Yet it was precisely how he thought of her. "Friendship."

"Friendship?" she said wonderingly, as if the thought were alien to her.

"Yeah," he said, embarrassed. What need would she have of his friendship? He wasn't sure he even knew how to be friends with a woman like her. "Friendship."

He was shocked to find out how strongly he wanted her to agree. He shouldn't want this so much. Wanting was a very dangerous thing.

A pleased smile lit her face, and he knew that "pretty" really had nothing at all to do with it. When a woman smiled like that, just for him, she was beautiful.

"I would like that very much, Jakob."

He stuck out his hand. "Agreed, then?"

"Agreed."

Her palm was in his for only the briefest instant, a tiny little squeeze of a shake. Her hand was small, soft, and white, nearly swallowed up in his big brown one.

He had a very strong notion that a *friend* wouldn't remember quite so well the feel of another friend's hand in his.

*   *   *

After Jakob and Amy returned from town he gulped down his dinner and then spent the entire afternoon and a good part of the evening at the brewery, making up the work he'd missed by going into town to meet the steamboat loaded with his supplies.

When he finally came home that evening, the sun hadn't set yet, but the light had softened, casting deep shadows across the path that led to the back of the house. His stomach rumbled, reminding him that he'd probably missed supper. Well, Helga would have saved a plate for him. She always did, and he was used to eating alone. It didn't bother him.

The kitchen was brightly lit and filled with activity. Helga and Amy sat at the big oak table, their knives flashing silver as they worked. In front of Helga was a large, neat pile of apple slices; Amy had a smaller and much less uniform heap in front of her. Both Nicolaus and Daniel hovered around them, snitching bites of apple and chattering away.

"Good evening," he said. "You've all been busy in here tonight."

All four of them looked up and smiled greetings, and Jakob felt a peculiar little catch of warmth in his chest. After a long day of work, he was lucky to have this to come home to.

Helga began on another apple, slicing off a steady spiral of bright red skin. "Daniel was hungry."

"Oh, he was, was he?"

"Mama burned dinner," he mumbled around a mouthful of apple.

"Really?"

Amy looked abashed and industriously attacked another apple with her knife. "Well, I don't cook nearly as well as I sew. That was one of my sisters' jobs."

"Mama's learning to make an apple cake. I mean, an—" Daniel darted a quick glance at Helga and searched for the right word "—an *Apfelkuchen*."

At her nod of approval, he beamed.

"Well, I'm trying," Amy muttered, staring down at the apple she'd just butchered. "It *looks* so easy."

"Sit, Jakob." Helga jumped to her feet, a cloud of flour showering from her white apron. "I saved you some supper."

He sat down across from Amy, who was frowning in concentration, her mouth puckered up like a young girl's kiss. "Nicolaus, you get away from that hot stove," she said without glancing his way.

Jakob smiled in amusement as Nicolaus shot a guilty look at her and jumped away from where he'd been preparing to poke at the smoldering fire.

"Do you suppose you could go get me another bowl of apples, Nicolaus? I've nearly used up this one."

"Yes, ma'am." He scrambled to do as she asked. Strange. He never moved that quickly when Jakob or Helga asked him to do something.

Helga set before him a steaming bowl of potato soup, a large chunk of dark bread, and several thick slices of sausage. He murmured his thanks and picked up his spoon to dig in, but his gaze never wavered from Amy. The knot of her hair was nearly undone, leaving tendrils clinging to her neck, along the edge of her lacy high collar. Her pale skin was flushed pink from the heat of the kitchen, and a streak of sparkling sugar decorated one cheek. He had the most absurd notion to lick that sweetness right off her skin.

"Ouch!" He jumped. A bit of the hot soup had sloshed over the spoon and into his lap, soaking through his pants, and was just hot enough to be uncomfortable.

Helga smothered a chuckle and he glared at her knowing grin.

Darn it. Apparently he'd neglected this *woman* thing long enough.

Well, that was just too bad. There simply weren't that kind of women in New Ulm.

He lowered his gaze to his bowl of soup, deciding it would be a good idea to pay more attention to what he was eating. But he couldn't seem to help it; he kept peeking up at her. She popped a chunk of apple in her mouth, and when she breathed deeply, closing her eyes and smiling with delight, he took a good sniff, too.

The air was rich and warm, full of the scents of caramelizing sugar, vanilla, cinnamon, and tart apple. It smelled homey and good, and it was nothing he'd ever bothered to notice before.

Helga piled the slices of apple into a deep blue crockery bowl. "If we slice much more, we will have apple cake for the next month. Now we will mix the dough."

"But I was just getting good at this part," Amy said.

Helga chuckled. "*Ja*, well, you will be good at the next part, too. I am a good teacher. I taught my daughter, though I—" A quick rap on the door stopped her. "Who could that be at this time of the evening?"

"Probably someone from the brewery." Jakob pushed back his chair, sighing, and wished he'd gotten through more of the soup before he got summoned back to work. He was still hungry. "Come in!" he called. "It's open."

A man he'd never seen before came through the door. He had a wide, barreled chest and belly; a red, beaming face; and a shiny head rimmed with wisps of snow-white hair.

"I'm sorry to intrude," he said. "I am looking for *Herr* Hall."

The loud crash and crack of splintering crockery echoed Helga's small shriek.

She stood frozen in the kitchen, the shattered bowl and sliced apples strewn around her feet. Her hands pressed to her plump chest, her mouth wide, she stared in disbelieving shock at the visitor.

"Karl!"

10

How very interesting. Helga was as flushed as a young girl, her hands fluttering up to check her hair. And as soon as this Karl fellow's gaze had landed on her, he'd lit up like an eager bridegroom.

"I take it you two know each other."

"Well, *ja*, I . . ." Helga gasped, clearly flustered. Jakob was quite certain he'd never seen her in this state before. If asked, he would have said it was impossible. "Oh, I had better clean up this mess." She bent to pick up the broken bowl.

"Oh, no you don't." Amy hopped up from her chair. "You must introduce Jakob to your friend. I'll take care of this." She brushed Helga aside and attended to it herself. As she knelt, she gave Jakob a quick, conspiratorial glance, her eyes sparkling with amusement.

She looked quite nice with that animation lighting her features, a hint of a smile playing at the corners of her rose-blushed mouth. Clearly she, too, realized that there was something interesting afoot.

"Yes, Helga, why don't you introduce us?" Jakob suggested.

"Oh, well, this is Karl Mueller. I met him when I went to visit my daughter, in Pittsburgh. He worked with my Anja's husband, and—oh, dear!" She reached for the back of a chair and gripped it. "What are you doing here?" she burst out.

"Helga," Karl said chidingly, "you did not really think I would leave it at that, did you?"

"You should not have come here!"

"Why not?" His voice softened and he stepped forward into the room, his big, rough hands clutching the soft brown hat he carried. "You said you could not stay with me. And so I come to you."

Helga's mouth worked, as if she wanted to speak but couldn't find any words. Then she threw up her hands, burst into tears, and ran from the room.

"Oh, my." Amy straightened, lifting the enameled pan now filled with shards of crockery and smashed apple pieces. She looked at Jakob in dismay, and he merely shrugged. He was at a complete loss.

Karl crushed his hat, his rounded face the picture of dejection. "I should not have come."

"Oh, no, of course you should have." Jakob rushed to pull out a chair for him. "Please, sit down."

"Are you *Tante* Helga's *Verehrer*? Her boyfriend?" Nicolaus piped up, his face bright with interest.

"I do not know," Karl said miserably, slumping into a chair.

Jakob could see that Nicolaus was just warming up for a barrage of questions. He doubted poor Karl was up to it and rushed to head off his nephew's curiosity, but Amy beat him to it.

"Nicolaus, didn't you say you wanted to show Daniel the minnow you caught this morning?"

Nicolaus leaned over to Daniel. "They're just trying to get rid of us, you know."

"Yeah," Daniel agreed. "But they're not going to say anything good when we're here, anyway."

"Oh, shush, you two," Amy said, setting the basin down by the sink and herding the children toward the door. "Perhaps I'll go check on Mrs. von Leigh."

"Maybe you should," Jakob said as she left. "Oh, and Nicolaus?"

"Yeah, Uncle Jake?"

"Why did you bring a dead minnow into the house? You'd better get it out before it starts to smell."

"Oh, it's not dead. I put it in water."

"What did you find to hold it?"

Nicolaus grinned over his shoulder before Amy guided him through the doorway. "It's okay, he's a little minnow. I put him in your shaving cup."

So that was why he hadn't been able to find it this morning. However, at the moment it appeared Jakob had more pressing concerns than his shaving cup. He tipped back his chair and contemplated the stranger in his kitchen, who, he was willing to bet, didn't usually look so dispirited. There were wrinkles fanning from the corners of Karl's eyes that indicated a man who spent a great deal of time smiling.

Karl studied his hands and shook his head. "I really thought she would be happy to see me."

The truly strange part of it was that, despite Helga's tears and abrupt departure, Jakob was almost certain that she was.

He debated a minute. Did he really want to interfere here? Did he have any right?

He thought of Helga's endless matchmaking, her well-intentioned poking into every corner of his life. And he thought of the way she'd looked when her husband had been killed, all shocked and still, as if someone had torn away a piece of her soul and she had no idea how to get it back and so had simply shut down to stop the bleeding.

Aw, hell. Of course he wanted to interfere.

"Would you like a beer, *Herr* Mueller?"

"A beer?" He shrugged his massive shoulders. "*Ja*, I guess so."

Jakob went outside and down to the root cellar under the house, where it was slightly cooler. He selected two bottles of a recent batch of pilsner that he thought had turned out exceptionally well.

When he returned to the kitchen, full darkness had fallen. The room still carried the rich, yeasty scents of cooking. It was almost too hot inside, a fire snapping in the big black cookstove, and the light from the two lamps filling the room with a mellow glow warmed the white walls to butter yellow.

It looked like a home, like the kind of place where no one would ever be alone. And in the center of it sat a man who looked terribly lonely.

Just for a moment, Jakob wondered if he'd be that alone when he reached Karl's age. Then he dismissed the thought; after all, being alone and unencumbered—at least for a while—was exactly what he'd always wanted.

He handed one bottle to Karl, who took it without appearing to notice what he held. Jakob regained his seat and uncorked the bottle.

Stalling, trying to figure out what to say, Jakob took a long swallow. The beer was cooler than the air, and the bite of it eased down his throat. Yes, he'd been right. The addition of just a bit more malt had added an extra depth of flavor. An excellent batch. He was very good at making beer.

But what did he know about affairs of the heart? There was no recipe to follow, no long tradition passed down from his father that told him what to do. And yet, somehow, he must figure out a way to help Helga.

Perhaps if he knew a bit more about the situation something would occur to him. "How did you meet Helga?"

"Ah." Karl eased back in his chair and smiled, lost in remembrance. "Her daughter invited me to supper. She is quite the matchmaker, you know, that Anja."

"She comes by it honestly."

"Well, I did not want to go, but she insisted. And I never could resist Anja's *sauerbraten*. When I walked in the door, there Helga was, her hair all lit up like fire, and I thought to myself 'Karl, now *there* is a woman.'"

Uneasily, Jakob gulped half the bottle of beer. He was suddenly not entirely sure if he wanted to hear this. It was disconcerting, to say the least, to hear Helga talked about in those terms.

"And she . . . she felt the same way about you?"

"I thought so." Karl's smile faded. "A man can tell these things, you know."

"You asked her to stay?"

"Of course." Karl rolled the unopened bottle between huge palms. "She said she could not."

"She tell you why?"

"No."

Because of me, Jakob thought. Nicolaus and me. Because she thinks we need her, and she would never do something for herself if she thought it wouldn't be good for us, no matter how much she wanted it.

And they did need her. But she'd given unselfishly to them for all these years. Jakob could not let her give this up if it was what she really wanted. He owed her that much.

"Why don't you try your beer?" Jakob suggested. He wanted to keep Karl here while he figured out what to do, but he couldn't think of another excuse.

Karl looked down at his bottle in surprise, as if he'd forgotten about it. He expertly flicked it open and took a deep swallow.

"Ah, that is good. You use the Hersbruck hops, *ja*?"

"Yes, we do," Jakob said in surprise. "How could you tell?"

"Oh, it is all in the taste buds." Karl took another taste. "Have you ever thought of trying the Hellertau?"

"They don't grow well here." Jakob looked more closely at Karl, who, his despondency momentarily forgotten, was inspecting the bottle of beer, holding it up to the lamplight to test the clarity. "What exactly is it you do in Pittsburgh?"

"I was the master brewer, of course." He nodded proudly. "Twenty years at the Hauenstein Brewery. Best in all of Pennsylvania."

"I bet they'll be glad to get you back when you return."

"Oh, *nein*." Karl's shoulders sagged. "I quit. I thought if Helga could not stay with me, I would prove to her that I was willing to stay with her."

"Really?" Jakob grinned and sat back in his chair. "*Herr* Mueller, there's something I'd like to talk to you about."

Amanda awoke the next morning with one thought in her mind: today she was going to work. She was going to earn a real paycheck, for the first time in her life.

Among the women of her acquaintance in the East, it was a scandalous notion, working for money. In an office, no less; worst of all, a brewery. How ill bred.

Her own mother would have been horrified; it had taken weeks of discussion to get her to agree to let Amanda take the post as Cynthia's companion.

Yet, though it ran contrary to the lady she'd been brought up to be, Amanda could not deny she was anticipating working, and she would have been out-and-out excited if she weren't so worried about leaving Daniel for the time she was at work. But she consoled herself with the fact that she would only be a few steps away, easily reachable if he needed her.

That, and the fact that Daniel himself seemed completely unconcerned. As they walked along the path to the main house, he inspected all the plants along the way and captured two ladybugs to show Nicolaus.

"Look, Mama. One has two spots, the other four."

"Very nice," she said, admiring them properly. "Now, remember, I will be coming back to have lunch with you."

"I know, Mama. You told me already."

"And Mrs. von Leigh knows where to find me if you should need me."

"Yes, Mama." He turned over a rock, hunting for slugs.

She sighed. It seemed that this brief separation would be harder for her than him.

His entire life, they'd rarely been apart, except for the few occasions when Edward had insisted she accompany him to some society function or another. Those instances had been rare; her lack of beauty and polish did not reflect well on him, so why would he want her there? Only when he knew it made her miserable and awkward to attend did he force her to come.

She was going to miss Daniel today, though she tried hard not to allow him to see it. She marveled at these small changes in her son, who had always been so timid and had shown such reluctance to ever stray from her side, at his new willingness and comfort to stay with Mrs. von Leigh. Had simply no longer having the threat of Edward's presence freed him so much? If so, she would no longer wonder if she'd done the right thing in fleeing New York.

She had.

When they reached the house she realized they were interrupting breakfast. Helga, pale-complected and unusually quiet, her red hair drawn into a severe knot, was dishing up a mixture of leftover meat and potatoes mixed with eggs that Nicolaus called *hoppel poppel*.

Amanda hadn't expected to see Jakob, assuming that he'd have left for the brewery long ago, but he was still there.

He pushed back his chair, scraping the legs on the polished, wide-planked floor and leaving a half-finished plate of food. "Ah, there you are. I was waiting to walk over with you."

"You shouldn't have waited. I would have found it." She was not accustomed to a man interrupting his routine for her. She wasn't sure she liked it; there was a vague feeling of being in his debt.

"It's fine," he said briskly. "Are you ready now?"

"But your breakfast? I certainly didn't mean to disturb you."

He grinned. "That was the third helping."

"Oh."

"Would you like some, Daniel?" Helga asked, reaching for another plate.

"He's already eaten," Amanda protested. She couldn't let them keep feeding him, she thought. They were giving far more than she could ever find a way to repay as it was, even if they didn't seem to realize it.

"It sure smells good," Daniel said.

"Oh, let him." Jakob stood up and headed for the door. "Are you ready to go, Amy?"

"Good-bye, Daniel." She edged hesitantly toward the door, needing to go, wanting to stay.

"Wait, Mama." Daniel spun and gave her a brief, abashed hug. "You're going to be back at lunchtime, right?"

"Absolutely," she promised, running her hand quickly through his soft black curls. "Lunchtime."

"Dinner," Helga corrected.

"Dinner?"

"What we call lunch is the snack in the mid-morning and mid-afternoon in these parts. Supper is at night. You will come back for the dinner at noon."

"How many times a day do you eat here?"

The laughter rolled out of Helga, full and booming, the first time that morning that the worry lines between her brows had eased. "As often as possible."

"All right, then. I'll be back for dinner."

"I expect you to make certain that Jakob comes home, too."

"*Tante*," Jakob said on a sigh, reaching around to open the door for Amanda.

"Do not you *Tante* me, Jakob," she scolded. "You work through dinner much too often. You will wither away to nothing, and people will say I do not take proper care of you."

Unable to stop herself, Amanda snuck a quick peek at the man who stood framed in the doorway. He certainly didn't look like he was withering away to her. In fact, he seemed overwhelmingly . . . healthy.

"I am depending on you, Amy," Helga added.

"All right, then," she agreed. "I will make sure he returns for dinner, even if I must drag him home."

11

"And just how do you plan on dragging me back to dinner?" Jakob asked once they'd left the house.

"I guess I'll just have to think of something." The morning was new and fresh, clean sunlight pouring over the ridge of the valley. A very good morning for fresh starts.

"You must be stronger than you look."

"No. But I don't always play fair." Actually, she didn't play at all, but she figured it was long past time she learned.

"You can't do that. I'm your boss."

She looked over at him, walking beside her but a half-step ahead, as if he were having difficulty slowing his pace to her own. She suspected he usually dashed along this path, impatient to get to work.

He was dressed for brewery work this morning, not business work. No glasses, no suit; just a loose white shirt that showed the edge of a knit undershirt at the collar, plain tan pants, and boots. Despite that, he looked every inch the boss. It had nothing to do with clothing and everything to do with the command and confidence that was as much a part of him as having dark hair.

"I'll find a way," she insisted again. "After all, I'm more frightened of Helga than I am of you."

What an utterly ridiculous thing to say. Of course she must be frightened of him; she'd long ago learned to be wary of powerful men.

And yet, strangely enough, she wasn't. She had the path; he walked through the grass along the edge, giving her plenty of space, not crowding her a bit. For all his occasional abruptness, he'd never given her a hint of hidden violence.

But then, she'd never suspected it in Edward, either. Not until she'd married him, and he'd had the right to do with her anything he wished. And he had.

Don't make assumptions, she reminded herself. Not even about Jakob. So much better to be careful than to regret it later.

"You really didn't have to wait for me this morning."

"I needed to ask you about something." He hesitated, jamming his hands in his pockets. "Did you talk to Helga last night?"

"A bit." Though Amanda had tried to gently probe for information, Helga, between sniffles, only told her a little about Karl. However, her misery had told Amanda every bit as much as her few words.

He kicked at a leaf, sending it scooting across the deep green grass. "Does she love him, Amy?"

"Yes." Amanda brushed at a wrinkle in her skirts. "Yes, I believe she does."

"Did she say that?" He looked hopeful.

"No. Which is exactly why I think she does." She laughed as his face fell into a puzzled frown.

"Aw, hell, what am I doing? I don't know anything about this stuff."

"'This stuff?'"

"Love."

"Who does?"

"Helga has spent a lot of time telling me that she does, if only I would listen to her."

"Only about other people," she said. "I don't think it applies nearly so well where she herself is concerned."

"Do you really think she loves him? I need to know."

"Yes, I really do."

He scrubbed his huge palm through the jumbled waves of his dark hair. "I sure hope so."

"Why?"

He winced. "I offered Karl a job and he accepted. He's staying here. She's going to have to deal with him whether she wants to or not."

Amanda tipped back the creaky leather chair and surveyed Jakob's office. She'd put in a solid three hours of work and the place still looked as if a giant hand had simply reached in, thrown thousands of papers up in the air, and let them fall where they would.

It seemed impossible that Jakob could run a successful business with his office and files in this condition. It was clearly a low priority for him; this morning, he'd merely showed her to the office, waved a hand at the mess, told her to "do something," and disappeared somewhere into the brewery.

She'd decided that before she put anything away, she must make some attempt at sorting through the mayhem. From a quick perusal of the papers, it was clear that Jakob *was* running a successful business. It was also equally clear that it had been months since he'd made even a cursory attempt to straighten either the files or the books.

So she'd devoted herself to separating the papers into years and then into months. Though she'd yet to even peek into the oak file cabinets that lined one wall—she shuddered to even contemplate what could be carelessly shoved in there—at least now neat piles covered the large desk and marched along beneath the bank of windows that faced the river.

The other half of the office still hadn't been touched, and the square, tidy piles she'd completed looked odd next to the scattered fans of white that she had yet to touch.

She figured there was enough work to keep her busy at least until her sewing machine got here.

She stretched, easing out the tension in her lower back caused by so much bending and lifting. The windows were wide open, letting in the bright sunshine and the clatter and shouts of the men coming and going in the yard below. The office door was shut to the rest of the brewery, but she could hear an occasional loud hiss and metallic clank.

It should have been a boring morning, stuck away up here all by herself with only the sunshine and the papers to keep her company. Instead, she'd loved it.

Had she ever done productive work? she wondered. Work that clearly needed doing, and that she was trusted to do right? Certainly she'd never been left alone to do it as she saw fit, without anyone checking over her shoulder or telling her she wasn't doing it properly. That she wasn't quite bright enough or pretty enough or clever enough to even be by herself for a few hours.

She hadn't realized the incredible freedom of simply being alone for a little while.

She stuck her booted heels up on the desk and laughed. In that horrible, dark, formal house she'd lived in for so long, it would never even have occurred to her to put her feet on the furniture. She'd never even felt quite comfortable *sitting* on it, even in her own bedroom. Mostly because it had never felt like hers; it was all Edward's.

And she was going to get to come back and do this again tomorrow. She'd thought the world was a scary place; she'd been half-certain she'd never be able to survive away from Edward, though she wasn't sure what she'd been doing *with* him could be called living, either. Why hadn't she known what it could be like? She would have summoned up the courage and the will to leave years ago.

Well, there was one more part of her job to perform—this one, the duty that Helga had given her.

She popped up from the desk and headed out the door, into the main section of the brewery.

The brewery was mostly brick and white-painted wood, a haphazard collection of additions that sprouted from the central brewhouse. The office was on the second floor, so that when she left it she was on the wide balcony that rimmed the edges of the two-story room.

Steam and heat rose to greet her, the yeasty, earthy smells rolling up like lifting fog. The roasting grain added a smoky, sweet layering to the scent. She slipped between the mash tubs and reached the white-painted iron fretwork that bordered the upper floor. She leaned over, searching the space below for Jakob.

The huge brew kettles were beneath her, rounded copper tubs that squatted on the scuffed, sanded floors like oversized elves waiting for their huge bellies to be filled with brew. Men milled between them, rushing around doing things that Amanda could only guess at.

Jakob was easy to find; he had the broadest shoulders in the place. Steam swirled around him as he barked out orders to the other men without pausing in his own labors. He bent next to a tub and his dark, wavy hair reflected, distorted, in the burnished copper of the massive kettles.

He'd discarded his outer shirt, and the thin knit undershirt that remained was damp, clinging to the bulge and swell of his muscles. He lifted a bushel basket of hops to his shoulder, and the diffuse light gleamed off the bronze skin of his arms, lightly misted with sweat.

Her hands curled around the warm iron of the balcony railing.

He was so different from any man she'd ever known. Between her husband and his acquaintances, the men she knew must have owned dozens—hundreds—of factories in New York. She doubted any of them had ever set foot inside a single one of them, unless it was to find a way to eke out a bit more profit by forcing more demands on the poor souls who labored there.

Certainly none of them would ever have thought to work beside his employees. It was so far beneath them that the idea would never have occurred to them.

No one had yet noticed her up on the balcony, and she was caught by the unique opportunity to simply watch a man work. Tendons stood out, taut and prominent, along the sides of his neck; his bared, powerful forearms were traced with veins.

This was what strength was for, she thought. Not for intimidating weaker humans. It was for working, for building a business and a life that others could depend on. There was nothing frightening about it.

Instead, it was terribly, awfully exciting. Her heart sped up and her breathing deepened. A low, warm humming seeped through her limbs, her chest, and deep in her belly. Heat flushed her skin; her breasts, her cheeks, her thighs.

All women are whores.

Cold lanced through her and, shaking, she stepped away from the railing, shamed to her bones. Had she learned nothing? It was her worst failing, her deepest flaw; she had desires, forbidden, immoral, sordid desires she had never been able to properly rid herself of. In this, at least, Edward had been all too horribly right.

She had to get away. Away from this building, away from Jakob, away from her sinfully weak self. Jakob would simply have to miss lunch today. Where was the quickest way out?

She whirled; too late. One of the workers on the floor had seen her. The man was middle-aged and burly, and he winked at her and poked Jakob, pointing up to the balcony.

Jakob glanced up at her, then looked around and frowned. He must have too much work to do. Maybe he wouldn't come with her. Good. She skittered along the edge of the balcony, inching toward the stairs.

The man laughed and gave Jakob a good-natured shove, urging him to go. *No,* Amanda thought. *Let him stay!* She didn't want to walk beside him on that green-shaded path, as that stray lock of hair fell over his forehead and his powerful shoulders stretched the confines of his shirt. It was asking too much of herself; it would have been far better if she still feared him. Instead, it seemed as if she must fear herself and her body's demands. She caught herself just before she shook her head "no."

Jakob shrugged and spread one hand over his belly, long brown fingers wide on the cream-colored knit of his undershirt.

He was hungry, she realized, clearly torn between the demands of his stomach and his job. And the only way he would get out of here to eat was if she insisted he come to dinner.

She thought about leaving, right then and there, and letting him go hungry. But he shouldn't have to suffer for her weakness and unholy urges. It wasn't his fault; he'd done absolutely nothing to entice her.

And she didn't have to give in to them, either. Surely a woman who was strong enough to leave Edward was strong enough to subdue the shameful demands of her body.

She squared her shoulders, leaned over the balcony, and gestured toward the door.

His eyebrows curved upward and he folded his arms across his chest. She could read his expression as easily as if he had spoken. *Oh, really? Are you going to make me?*

Scowling in what she hoped was a determined manner, she jammed one hand on her hip and flung the other toward the door again, insisting he leave.

He scowled back. She glowered. And then a huge, delighted grin broke over his features, and she could see his shoulders start to shake with laughter. He shrugged in submission. The worker who'd been watching the entire episode with great interest clapped him on the back, and Jakob waved for her to come down the stairs.

She smiled and decided she'd just earned her own lunch.

The week passed as quickly as any she'd ever known. Each morning, Jakob waited to walk her to work, though she insisted that it was ridiculous. He simply told her that Helga had instilled better manners than that in him and would speak no more about it.

Once at the brewery, she rarely saw him. He was never in the office, which she was slowly transforming into a rough semblance of organization. She made sure he came home for lunch—dinner—each day. He didn't even bother to argue the point anymore, and she felt a bit of satisfaction that she was able to make sure that he was eating properly, for in just the short time she'd spent at the brewery, she knew he was prone to work to the exclusion of all else, even food and rest.

To her immense relief, there was no repeat of that sinful surge of desire. She could see him at work without imagining him stripping off his shirt; she could sit across a table from him without noticing the shadows in the hollows of his throat. That one time on the balcony was apparently a horrible aberration.

She was still uncomfortable with many of the men at the brewery. They were too big, too loud; there was apparently no concept of a respectful distance from a lady here. They considered her a coworker. It was also completely, awkwardly clear that they considered her *Jakob's,* and could never seem to resist a slight nudge in that direction, for when she had to speak to Jakob about something, the men grinned and melted away, pointedly leaving the two of them alone.

Despite that minor problem, she settled into her new life with an ease that surprised her. Working all morning, she had the afternoons free to spend with Daniel, who gained more healthy color in his cheeks every day, though he complained mightily about her cooking and couldn't understand why she wouldn't allow them to eat every meal over at the main house. After all, Helga had invited them, and his new *Tante* Helga knew how to cook.

She liked the work, and the easy, simple days. She didn't mind not having servants a bit; no one to damn her with wordless disapproval, no one to dress her or change her hair. No one to change *her*.

The nights were still long and empty. That was when she felt Edward the nearest. And though she no longer spent the dark hours in rigid expectation, sleep was more than she could ask for. So she sewed by hand, wishing her machine would hurry up and get there, and she watched over Daniel.

It was enough to get her through the nights.

Until Friday, when she found out that Jakob had not forgotten the promise he'd made in the store, and he had every intention of taking her to see the magician at Turner Hall.

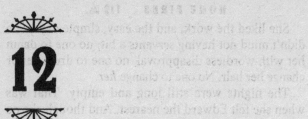

12

When Jakob ushered Helga, both boys, and
Amy through the double front doors of Turner Hall on
Friday night, it seemed as if most of New Ulm and a
good portion of the surrounding countryside had come
out.

Not that it was unusual; whether a dance, a lecture,
or a play was scheduled, the turnout was always good.
If there was one thing the residents knew how to do, it
was enjoy themselves. But anticipation was clearly high
tonight; the flags that topped the white posts decorating each corner of the hall flew with cheerful abandon.
The early evening light was sharp and golden, and the
talk, an exuberant blend of German and English, bubbled out of the open windows. They'd never had a
magician perform in town before, and Armando the
Amazing was the subject of much speculation.

"Uncle Jake?" Nicolaus tugged on his sleeve, and
Jakob bent down to hear him over the hubbub. "Can
we sit right down front?"

"I suppose so."

"Oh, good." Nic grinned broadly. "I heard he uses these real big knives, and—" He laughed at Jakob's aghast expression. "I'm just teasing you."

"You'd better be." He chucked his nephew under the chin. Beside them, Daniel was tight against his mother's side, searching the room with wide eyes. He looked a bit overwhelmed.

"Daniel, have you ever seen a magician before?"

"No, Father would never—" He stopped, gulped, and looked up to his mother. He appeared to be on the verge of tears. Poor kid. Probably missed his father.

"I'm sorry," Jakob said quickly. "I didn't mean to remind you of sad memories."

"It's fine." Amy brushed a hand soothingly over Daniel's head and smiled. "It's fine."

And it was fine, Jakob thought. No one could smile like that if it wasn't. It was the smile he waited for each day, as he rushed around the brewery attending to the million things that had to be done. The whole time, somewhere in the back of his mind, he knew that soon she would come to fetch him, and she would smile at him just like that.

The really odd thing about it was, it *was* just a smile. That was what appealed to him the most. There was no expectation in it; there was no obligation or calculation or wordless responsibility. People seldom looked at him without any of those things.

She asked nothing of him, and, because of that, he found the lure of giving. Easily, freely, and with enjoyment. He waited for her each morning because she didn't need him to, didn't want him to, but seemed to enjoy his company just the same. She did her job without fuss or any uncomfortable gratitude; just a calm acceptance of a bargain made and fair work given. And she did it well; today, he'd even been able to find a bill of sale the first time he'd looked for it.

Someone's elbow connected with his back, and he was uncomfortably aware that he'd been standing there unmoving in the middle of the crowded entryway grinning at her, blocking the paths of all the people who jostled around him, trying to make their way to the seats. And Helga was observing him with an entirely too smug expression on her face.

"Well, I guess we'd better go ahead if we want to get good seats," he suggested, tugging at his tight collar.

"Certainly." Gently, Amy placed a hand on each boy's back and steered them down the open center aisle, which ran the length of the main hall between the two rows of seats. Relieved, he plunged into the crowd after them, hoping to gain his seat before he did something else as stupid and obvious as stopping and gawking at her when he was supposed to be moving.

He should have known it would never be quite that simple.

Matthias Voehringer hailed him from the other side of the room and came rushing over, his wife Margarite in tow. The tall, bony Matthias was one of the local farmers who supplemented his income by growing hops for Hall's and occasionally doing a few days of labor there. He was also one of the least subtle men Jakob knew.

"Jakob, it is good to see you out. You rarely find the time to come to one of the entertainments."

"Yes, well." Jakob cleared his throat. Had it been so long since he'd attended a social event? It must be. He couldn't remember the last one. They'd often proved more awkward than relaxing, what with half the town talking up eligible females and the other half staring at him with barely disguised concern, so he'd bowed out of most of them with some excuse or another about work. "Nicolaus wanted to see it."

"Of course he did. I am sure that he did not want to see any of the shows at the Hall in the last six months, did he?" Matthias grinned. "It certainly has nothing to do with Mrs. Smith, does it?" He turned to Amy, whom he'd met earlier in the week at the brewery. "We *Deutsche*, we work hard, but we know how to play hard, too. Our Jakob, I have often wondered if he was somehow missing the 'play hard' part. I am glad you are here to help with that."

"Thank you, but I'm sure I truly had nothing to do with it," Amy replied. She was embarrassed, her eyes downcast, a becoming flush staining the gentle curve of her cheek. Jakob did not understand why everyone assumed he was her beau. Though, from his perspective, that state of affairs had a certain advantage. He hadn't yet been accosted by hopeful mamas with their sweet young daughters in tow, and he'd been in the Hall all of five or ten minutes.

"Of course not," Matthias said, clearly unconvinced. "I wanted to introduce you to my wife. Jakob told me about your dressmaking."

"He did?" She gave him a quick look, surprise and pleasure glinting in her eyes. He'd done nothing but mention it to a few of the married men who worked at the brewery that, if their wives were in the market for a new dress, they might consider Amy; yet damned if her reaction didn't make him want to rush right out and find her a dozen new customers.

"Yes," Matthias went on, drawing forward his wife, a lean, narrow woman in a dress that nearly drowned her in ruffles. "She had a few questions about the newest fashions, or some such woman thing, and wondered if perhaps Mrs. Smith could help."

Folding his arms across his chest, Jakob watched her chat with Margarite. Her reserved, quiet manner seemed to evaporate as she discussed her work, her arms gesturing quickly as she described some new sleeve treatment. She listened attentively to Margarite's questions. When Nicolaus tried to slip away into the crowd heading for the stage, her arm shot out, hooked in the collar of his shirt, and drew him back without her concentration wavering from her conversation.

Now what, exactly, was this warmth swelling inside him, puffing out his chest? It took a moment to identify the emotion, it was so strange for him.

Damn it, he was proud of her. He wondered for a moment if that was a really dumb thing to be; it wasn't as if he had any right to be proud of her.

Except that they'd formed a friendship, of a sort, though it wasn't quite like anything he'd ever experienced before. Just a quiet understanding between them, her allowance and acceptance of his flaws, that seemed to somehow lift the steady pressure that always hovered over him.

It didn't really matter if he had any right to be proud of her. He simply was, and that was all there was to it.

At first he was too busy watching Amy to notice the soft pressure against his arm. A petulant "Jakob" squealed low in his ear, and he realized the joggling against his side wasn't just the crowd milling around, trying to find their neighbors and friends.

He glanced down into Brigitte's avid, larkspur-blue eyes and knew he needed help. Experience taught him that, inside of a minute, Brigitte was going to start babbling about how beautifully she could decorate his house, if only she were to be given the chance and enough money. Shamelessly, he reached for Amy's hand and tugged her over to his side. She tried to pull away, and he curled his fingers firmly around hers.

Startled, she looked up at him. He inclined his head slightly toward Brigitte. Understanding dawned, and she plastered on a bright smile and took a step closer to him, close enough that he could catch a hint of her warmth through his sleeve.

"Brigitte," she said brightly. "How nice to see you." She placed her free hand against his upper arm, as if claiming possession, and he gave the hand he held a quick squeeze of gratitude. "Jakob, don't you think we should find our seats? The boys are getting restless, and you know they will complain if we do not get seats right down front."

"You're absolutely right. Thank you for reminding me." He shrugged apologetically and disengaged himself from Brigitte.

Nicolaus dashed ahead and found five seats right in the middle of the front row. After promising he would behave if they sat right there—no sneaking behind the stage to try and figure out Armando's tricks—they all filed in after him.

It was only after he'd taken his seat that Jakob realized he still held Amy's hand. It was small and soft, snuggled comfortably in his palm, and he realized he was reluctant to let it go. Which was probably why he should do it right away.

He uncurled his fingers, and she snatched her hand back to her lap, just barely brushing his thigh as she did so. That did it. He couldn't quit imagining what it would have been like if that touch had not been quite so brief and slight.

As she sat beside him, saying nothing, her head bent, rubbing a bit of her skirt between her fingers, he had the oddest urge to apologize. Small, pale brown wisps of hair had worked free of her topknot and drifted down to curl at the nape of her neck.

A cool wash of air brushed his palm, a startling contrast to the warmth there had been when she'd touched him. His hand fisted, as if trying to save the remnants of that warmth, and he dropped it to his thigh.

"*Mein Damen und Herren!* Ladies and gentleman! If you would all find your seats, Armando is about to begin!" *Herr* Kaufenburg, who also served as the town mayor, stood on the stage and shouted to be heard over the clamor. "Please, take your seats!"

Nicolaus started trying to shush every person within earshot. Daniel studied the stage, his body absolutely still, all his attention squarely focused. Helga, humming with an air of expectancy, scanned the room eagerly, then slumped back in her chair as if disappointed.

And Jakob, stunned into confused silence, still watched Amy, wondering why this, why now, why her? Not the right place, not the right time. Perhaps not even the right woman. She obviously had a very long way to go to get over the loss of her husband. She seemed to want nothing from him.

He did not want this. He didn't want the complications, didn't want one more restriction on his freedom. Certainly not now, when he could finally see the tantalizing possibility of it just a few years away.

Yet, as one by one, the lamps around the perimeter of the room were snuffed out, the light slowly fading and casting dusky shadows against her fine-textured skin, he knew that he was going to be very hard-pressed to make this stay at friendship.

Huge lanterns flared to life on the stage, throwing wavering golden light back through the darkness of the Hall. Dark smoke rolled from the front of the room, hanging low, seeping down and across the floor. In the center of the stage, the smoke boiled, bubbled. An eerie, black-cloaked figure appeared there, rising majestically, magically from the solid floor, and the crowd drew a collective gasp.

Jakob had to admit that Armando knew his craft. Fire appeared from his fingertips and birds from his hat. Sleek black canes hovered inches below his hands. Rabbits disappeared into nothingness; shiny silver rings waltzed in thin air.

Despite Armando's skill, Jakob was having much more fun watching his family. Nicolaus was fairly dancing in his seat, a bouncing, wiggling blur of energy. His hands mimicked Armando's gestures, and Jakob made a mental note to check his room for "disappearing" animals for the next few weeks.

Helga had one hand pressed to her formidable chest, and her mouth formed a round *O*. For the moment, she appeared to have forgotten Karl and whatever worries that had made her unusually subdued this week. That, Jakob supposed, was the real magic.

Jakob doubted that Daniel had moved since the lights had dimmed. Hard to believe a child that young could be so intently focused.

Amy was just to Jakob's left, her arm slipped around her son, absently rubbing his shoulder. The flames of the stage lights were reflected in her eyes. The soft light tossed shadows in the hollows of her throat, and her lips were slightly parted in what could only be wonder.

He never would have expected it. She was a city woman, an Easterner. Surely she'd seen many fabulous things, grand and glorious events. And yet she found joy in a traveling magician in Turner Hall in New Ulm.

The sudden, loud clap of hands drew his attention

back to the stage. Armando leapt off, a swirl of rippling black cape, and landed right in front of Jakob.

Why the hell was the man staring at him? No way was he getting up on that stage to "assist" with some trick or another.

It was such a simple illusion, and should have seemed poor after the grander ones that preceded it. A slight snap of Armando's hand and twist of his wrist, and a daisy appeared there, summoned from a lush, hidden garden. The petals were pale and creamy, trembling slightly, and kissed with dew.

"Take it," Armando said, his voice hypnotic. "I trust that you know what to do with it."

What's gotten into me? Jakob wondered. Thinking about magical gardens. Kissed by dew, for God's sake. Sentimental crap. He scarcely ever even noticed his own gardens.

Yet he reached out and took the flower. Armando nodded, satisfied, and, with a swirl of black satin, returned to the stage and his act.

Amy was watching Jakob now, the magician apparently forgotten. Her skin was as pale and flawless as the flower, and he fingered the petals lightly, remembering her softness when he'd touched her by the river.

The daisy was so much like her. Deceptively simple on the surface, sometimes overlooked for showier, more colorful flowers. The kind of bloom that slipped into one's life and brightened it without interrupting the rhythm.

Unthinkingly, he thrust the flower at her. She stared up at him, her eyes mirroring dozens of tiny gold flames, the fires smaller and smaller into the depths of her eyes, and he thought that, no matter how deeply he looked, he would never see the end of those lights.

Her mouth formed the words "thank you," her voice

lost in the thunderous applause that erupted around them. The sound sealed them off, distant from the crowd, as if the people who surrounded them were as illusory as the tricks the magician had created. Surely they were the only two who were real.

Her fingers brushed his as she took the flower, a soft whisper of a touch that was gone before he could capture the feel. She brought the bloom up to her face, the petals stroking lightly down her cheek, as he had done once and wanted—too much—to do again.

Ah, damn, he thought again.

It was going to be very, very hard to leave this at friendship.

13

After two encores, Armando took a final bow. With Daniel and Nicolaus firmly in hand—Nic had expressed an extreme interest in the huge, glittering daggers Armando used in his finale—Amy followed Jakob, who was making his way through the crowds to the front door.

He stopped every few feet to introduce her to someone. From their comments and shocked expressions, she gathered that, the occasional times Helga badgered him into attending some community event or another, he'd ducked out afterward as quickly as possible.

He was obviously making a special effort to introduce her to the women—her future customers. How incredibly thoughtful of him, a man who she'd first assumed had not a thoughtful bone in his body. How wrong she'd been.

They finally reached the front door, stepping into the brisk night air. Complete darkness had fallen while Armando spun his magic; the surrounding buildings disappeared into a blackness as rich as the magician's cape, broken only by the lemon-colored rectangles of light that marked the windows. A fresh breeze sprang up, sweeping away the August heat and humidity.

"Helga." Karl stepped out of the shadows, into the yellow light that spilled out of the open front doors. "Wait a moment, *bitte*."

"Karl." His name came out on a gasp, and her hands flew to check the twisted pile of her hair. "I . . . I didn't see you inside, at the show," she stammered.

"Did you look?" He held a cap, turning it round and round in his huge hands.

"Well, I . . ." She sniffed and lifted her chin in the air. "I might have noticed, just for a moment."

A faint, hopeful smile crinkled his face. "Helga, would you allow me to drive you home?"

She hesitated a moment, clearly torn, then spoke sadly. "I don't think—"

"You know, *Tante*, that would be ever so helpful," Amanda broke in, her voice bright. "It's been a very late night for the boys, and they are so tired. With a bit more room on the seat, they could lie down and sleep on the way home."

"I'm not ti—" Nicolaus's words were lost in a muffled *oof* when Daniel's elbow connected with his ribs.

"Yes," Jakob said quickly. "It would be doing us such a favor if you would escort Helga, Karl."

"Of course."

"But—" Karl took Helga's arm and guided her away before she had another chance to protest, steering her down State Street where most of the buggies and wagons were parked.

Jakob and Amanda looked at each other and burst out laughing.

"That was very quick thinking." Jakob made an approving bow.

"Thank you." Amanda bobbed a quick curtsy in acknowledgment. "I try."

"We make a good team." How easy it had been; how quickly they had understood and played off each other. And how strange that they should have that quick communication between them when they scarcely knew each other.

"I think maybe I should go with them." Nicolaus spun in the direction of the dark street that Karl and Helga had strolled down.

"Oh, no you don't." Jakob placed a firm hand on Nicolaus's shoulder, holding him in place.

"Who's going to protect *Tante* Helga?"

"With any luck, no one," Jakob murmured. Then, more loudly to Nicolaus, he added: "I'm sure Karl has things well in hand."

"She's acting like a *Backfisch*." Nicolaus's voice was heavy with disgust.

"A what?" Amanda asked.

"A baked fish," he explained.

"Excuse me?"

Jakob chuckled. "A *Backfisch* is what we call a young woman who's just old enough to be acting crazy with the boys."

"Ah. So, for instance, you could call Brigitte a baked fish?"

"Nah." Nicolaus's opinion was firm. "She's too old. Fish goes rotten fast."

"Nicolaus!" Jakob scolded, but Amanda could see he was just barely suppressing his amusement. The corners of his mouth quirked upward, and his dark eyes sparkled with laughter. He looked so wonderful like that, alive and alight, that her stomach did a slow spin. Maybe it was good that he looked so serious all the time. Like this, she was prone to think far too much about him, and she had no business thinking of him at all.

"I really think I should go with Helga and Karl. Just in case," Nicolaus insisted.

"You know what I think, Nicolaus?" Amanda bent down until her nose nearly touched his. "I think you just want to snoop."

"Oh, no," he said, his face the picture of innocence. Someday, she mused, this one, all big bright eyes and mischievous grin, would be real trouble for the ladies. "I wouldn't do that."

"Besides, if you go with them, who'll protect me?"

"Jakob will," he said with certainty.

Amanda snapped up, unable to keep her gaze from flying to Jakob.

Jakob will.

He was silhouetted in the light from the Hall, a dark figure limned in gold, as broad and powerful a man as she had ever seen. He was still and focused, not a single twitch or unneeded gesture wasting his energy, energy he had in abundance.

A man to protect. Not a man to be protected *from*, but a man who would protect. Out of the mouths of babes. Nicolaus, who knew him best, seemed so sure.

And suddenly, she, too, was absolutely certain. This was not a man she would ever have to be protected from. Not a man that she would ever need to shield a child from. Not a man whose anger she would ever have to fear.

Perhaps he had failings. Too impatient, too narrowly focused on work, too serious. But violence—no, not that. Not ever that.

And then she *was* frightened—not for her welfare, not for the children, but because she was all too vulnerable to him. He would be too easy to confide in, too terribly easy to believe in—and her life did not allow such luxuries. She must not forget it. She'd made the only decision she could; now she must learn to live with it, and all it meant.

"We'd better get going." Jakob shooed the boys in the direction of their wagon, then waited for Amanda to join him as they walked.

Jakob's heels clomped along the boardwalk. Her full skirts swished softly, sometimes brushing his lower leg.

Sometime during the last week, in their brief walks back and forth to the brewery, either his pace had slowed or hers had picked up. Jakob no longer strode half a step in front of her, as if impatient to get to his destination. Now they walked in perfect synchronization, side by side. How odd, Amanda thought. When had that happened?

Soon they were all settled in the wagon and on the road back out to Hall's. Her claim to Helga that the boys were exhausted quickly proved to be true. Though at first they excitedly chattered about all of Armando's tricks, deciding that they were impossible and he must be a true magician after all, by the time the wagon climbed out of the valley and rounded the top of the ridge, the two children had slumped together on the backseat and faded into silence.

"Are they out?" Jakob asked quietly.

She twisted on the seat, smiling at the picture of the two of them, curled together like tired puppies. "Soon, if not already, I think."

"Good."

"Thank you for taking us, Jakob. Daniel really enjoyed it."

"And you? Did you enjoy it?"

She still held the daisy. The white petals captured a bit of the moonlight, appearing to glow softly in the darkness. She spun the flower and the petals blurred together.

She'd had bouquets given to her, huge, lush arrangements of exotic blooms. This was just a single, simple daisy. Yet none of those lavish flowers had ever touched her as much as this solitary one, though she knew she had no right to be touched by it.

"Oh, yes," she said softly. "I enjoyed it."

"Good."

She tipped her head back. Above, the stars had arrived, thousands of pinpoints of light strewn luxuriously across a blue-black sky. So many of them, so bright. Not dimmed and smudged by smoke. Surely those couldn't be the same wan, lusterless stars she had seen in New York. Here, they were so much more vivid and distinct.

"It's a beautiful evening."

Jakob took his gaze from the horses and looked around. "Yeah," he said, sounding faintly surprised. "I guess it is."

"You didn't notice?"

"I did now." He gave her a quick smile, then leaned back on the bench, relaxing. The reins were looped loosely through his fingers; the team plodded along on the road they knew so well, the clopping of their huge hooves echoing through the silence.

All the focused energy drained out of him as he sat back. His legs fell wide, his knee brushing hers. When the wagon jounced through a rut in the road, his shoulder bumped against her, too.

She had just a moment of panic, when she wanted to jump away, but it quickly faded. She could do this. She could be this close to a man, close enough so that she could feel a whisper of warmth through the fabric of her dress. Close enough to touch, and not be terrified.

She could if it was Jakob.

He sighed deeply, his even, slow breathing falling in rhythm with the night.

Oh, God, she thought. They looked so normal. A man and a woman on the front bench of a wagon, their shoulders touching. Two boys on the backseat, sleeping, all going home from town.

They looked like a family. An ordinary, everyday family like a million others. A family like she had never had, had never even hoped to have, and didn't realize until this moment how desperately she wanted.

She took a shuddering breath, a warm, sad ache seeping around her heart.

She could never have it. Never, ever, and she'd do well to remember it; there was no use in even thinking anything else.

The stars blurred in front of her eyes, tiny, watery spears of light shooting out from each one.

Oh, Jakob. What would it have been like if she'd met him first?

As if to make up for his Friday evening off, Jakob went back to work with a vengeance. Except for a couple of hours to take them all to church on Sunday morning, he spent nearly every waking hour at the brewery. On two days, Amanda was unable to pry him away for dinner despite her best efforts.

So when Saturday rolled around again, she decided it was time to take off the gloves and pull out the big guns.

She used the children.

Primed with information that Helga had casually mentioned one day over afternoon "lunch"—though Amanda was skeptical about just how casual those comments really had been—she carefully made her preparations.

She rehearsed the boys on their lines. She packed. And she got herself invited to breakfast.

Jakob had given her the place of safety and peace Daniel and she had needed. In return, the least she could do was make sure the man had a little fun.

The kitchen was lazy and warm with Saturday morning sun, filled with the smells of coffee and baking bread. Jakob grabbed one last slice of cheese, bade them all a perfunctory good-bye, and headed for the door.

Daniel leaned toward his mother. "Now?" he whispered.

"Now."

"Jakob?" he called after him.

Nearly to the door, Jakob wheeled around. He rested his hands on his hips and looked straight at Daniel. "What is it, Dan?" No matter how rushed Jakob was, he always seemed to really listen to the boys if one of them spoke to him.

"Ah, well . . ." He paused, uncertain, and Amanda slid her hand over to cover his. You can do it, Daniel, she silently urged. Just like we practiced.

He gulped and went on. "Well, um, school's going to be starting pretty soon."

"Are you worried about that? You know Nic will be there. And the Franzen boys—you met them in church."

"No, it's not that. Nic says that everyone plays baseball at lunchtime."

Jakob nodded. "Yes, I think so."

"I don't know how," Daniel said. "Do—do you think you could teach me how?"

A shadow darkened Jakob's eyes, a soft echo of longing. "You want me to teach you?"

"You know how, don't you?"

"Yeah." He ran his fingers through his hair, leaving the dark waves mussed. "Yeah, I know how."

"Would you?" Amanda felt Daniel's fingers tense under hers, and she realized there was more than her plan and a free morning at stake here. Daniel really wanted this.

He had never been able to ask his father things like this. He'd learned all too well, early, not to ask. This was a huge leap on his part, to be able to ask a grown man for something he wanted, to risk being turned down or worse.

"Please?"

"Sure," Jakob agreed softly. "I'd be happy to teach you. And Daniel?"

"Yes?"

He smiled gently. "Thank you for doing me the honor of asking me."

Daniel's eager grin was something she hadn't been sure she'd ever see, and she blinked away the sting in her eyes. One more thing she must find a way to thank Jakob for. No matter how hard she tried, it seemed she owed him more gratitude all the time. Gratitude, she knew, was the last thing he wanted, but she felt it deeply all the same.

"Can we start now?" both boys asked together.

"Now?" Jakob looked startled at their enthusiasm. "Well, I don't know. You mean right now?"

"It just so happens Daniel and I had planned to take Nicolaus on a picnic today. You're welcome to join us," Amanda suggested.

"Oh, that would be so good!" Helga chimed in as if she'd had her lines scripted, too. "If I did not have to worry about feeding you dinner, I could get the washing done."

"Yeah! Let's go, Uncle Jake!" Nicolaus grabbed Jakob's wrist and began towing him to the door. A bewildered Jakob went along, wondering just how his day of work had turned into a picnic and a baseball game.

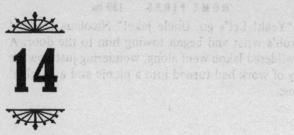

14

Amanda let Nicolaus suggest the spot, and she couldn't have picked a better place herself. On a bluff overlooking where the two rivers joined, the area was clear and sunny, studded with just enough maples to make a shady spot for her to sit in while the three of them had a broad, grassy spot for their ball game.

She spread out a blanket and spent the morning there, simply soaking in the sun and the breezes, watching Jakob teach her son to play, and watching the boys remind Jakob how to enjoy himself.

Daniel picked up the game with surprising speed, making up for his small size with absolute focus on the ball. At first, he looked fearfully at Jakob with each mistake he made, as if he expected Jakob to punish him for his errors. And Amanda knew that was exactly what Daniel did expect.

Jakob's response was always the same: after a quick smile and a word of encouragement, he patiently waited for Daniel to correct his own mistake.

Amanda had planned this morning to give Jakob a

break from the work, and because Helga had mentioned how much he used to enjoy baseball. Amanda thought it was a shame that he'd given up something he'd apparently once loved. Instead, again, he'd gifted her with something—his care and encouragement of her son, whose confidence seemed to grow with each ball he caught.

Jakob pitched to Nicolaus while Daniel hovered between first and second base. The tan leather ball arced slowly through the air. Nicolaus wound the bat back and whacked at the ball. It shot out, a pale streak against the deep blue sky.

"I got it, Jakob," Nicolaus shouted, his small legs pumping furiously as he backpedaled, his head tipped back to watch the ball. He stretched his arms high, reaching.

It sailed over his head and landed behind him, a few yards beyond his reach. He scrambled over to it, snatched it up, and whirled back to the playing field.

"Over here!" Jakob clapped his hands together, then held them up to give Daniel a throwing target. Nicolaus rounded first base and headed toward second, where Jakob stood ready.

Daniel aimed and hurled the ball, which soared up farther than he intended, above Jakob's reach. Jakob leapt, stretched full-length, capturing the ball with one hand, and came down on the base just before Nicolaus barreled into him.

The two went down in a tangle of arms, legs, and laughter. Daniel came running in from right field, then stopped, staring at Nicolaus and Jakob wrestling on the ground.

His expression was so wistful, so uncertain, that Amanda's heart nearly broke. *Go on,* she urged silently. *You can do it.*

She saw him take a deep breath, and then he jumped right into the pile. Jakob's arms went wide, gathering him in. Daniel's laughter joined theirs, and her heart did break.

Oh, Daniel. Never in her wildest dreams had she thought it could be this easy. That he'd be able to trust a man again, so simply, so sure. Perhaps she'd been quick enough. Perhaps she'd gotten him away from Edward before the damage ran too deep.

All she'd really thought about was survival. And now, to her astonishment, there was more than survival. There was the incredible, tenuous promise of happiness.

Jakob disentangled himself from the boys. He gave each one a hand, pulling them up and setting them easily on their feet. He slapped at his pants, beating up a cloud of dust.

"You two play catch for a while," he said. "This is hard on an old man."

"Aw, Uncle Jake—"

"Hey, you need the practice." He tweaked his nephew's nose. "I'll be back soon, and we'll see just how good you do when I'm the one batting."

He loped over the golden-brown grass to her and threw himself down on the blanket next to her. His pants were grass-stained, his shirt pulled out of the waistband, and his hair was all mussed. He wore a big, boyish grin and she was convinced she'd never seen anything so appealing in her entire life. She had no business being drawn by it.

He studied her briefly, and his smile faded. "Are you all right?"

She drew a shuddering breath and managed a shaky smile. "Oh, yes," she said softly. "I think I'm even better than all right."

* * *

It had been the kind of morning he'd forgotten existed.

A morning when he noticed the sunshine, not because it would be good for the new crop of barley, but because it felt so darn nice on his shoulders. When he stretched his muscles it was to reach for a fly ball, not another barrel of supplies. When he laughed, it was for the sheer joy of being alive. Had he *ever* done this, he wondered? If he had, it was so long ago he couldn't remember.

The entire time, as he'd played with the boys and tried to remember just how he'd bent his knuckles around the ball for his secret pitch, he'd been conscious that she was there. He was sure it was perfectly obvious, how he kept sneaking glances in her direction.

She was curled up on the blanket, her knees tucked beneath her, mottled sunlight and shadow falling over her glossy hair. She wore a light, pale green dress, looking as cool and ladylike as he'd expect from an Eastern woman. Except she warmly applauded her son's plays, and Jakob thought that maybe, just maybe, she'd sneaked a glance or two at him, too.

Finally, he convinced the boys to manage awhile without him and ran over to her, hoping that he didn't seem too eager. He plopped down next to her, knowing he was messy and sweaty but somehow knowing she, for all her neat appearance, wouldn't mind.

There was a shadow of sadness in her eyes, so he asked if she was all right. Maybe he'd offended her after all, thinking she might welcome his presence, even all mussed and dirty from the game. But then she smiled at him, a brilliant, beautiful smile that went straight to his head, and for the first time ever, he wondered if all adventures were to be found at the end of a far, distant trail.

"Are you hungry?" she asked. "It's almost time to eat."

"Already?"

She laughed, a bright sound that seemed to match the day. "You've been occupied."

"Yeah."

"You're not all that good at keeping track of mealtimes, anyway."

"I guess it's a good thing you're around to watch out for me then, isn't it?"

"Would you like some lemonade?" She uncorked a jug and poured two glasses. Beads of moisture dripped down the side of the glass she handed him, and he gratefully gulped down the tart-sweet liquid.

"Thank you for agreeing to teach Daniel."

"Thank you for asking me," he said, meaning it. How could he accept thanks for doing something he enjoyed so much? "I do believe he's going to be quite good at it. He's got good hustle."

"Oh?" There was a bead of lemonade clinging to her upper lip, and she licked it away. "Are you an expert?"

"I sure am. The last game I pitched for the town team, Sleepy Eye didn't get a single hit off me."

"Is that good?"

"Damn right, it's good."

"Why did you quit, then?"

"I don't know." Why had he quit, given up something that he'd enjoyed so much? At the time, joy had seemed inconceivable. How could he play a game, a stupid, useless *game*, when his family was dead? When there was so much work to do, and he was so inadequate to it? He wondered now if it had been necessary; surely it wouldn't have been so awful to keep something so small as baseball for himself. His family would probably have wanted that, he realized, though at the time he'd been too numb and scared to think of it.

"Why don't you start again?" Amanda asked. She wondered if she had the right to meddle here, but she could see it all so clearly: a youth, trying to do a man's job, who'd given up all things that seemed youthful. Perhaps she could give him more than a free morning; perhaps she could give him back something that he'd once loved.

"Maybe I will," he said thoughtfully. He flexed his arm. "Think the old arm still has it?"

Muscle bulged under his shirt, straining the fabric. She had no idea what he'd been like as an adolescent; now, he was clearly a man, with the kind of strength that made difficult tasks look effortless. "Maybe," she said airily. "Perhaps you'd better not try it. You might hurt yourself."

"Hey!" He looked affronted. "I'll have you know that I'm even stronger than I was ten years ago!"

She burst into laughter, and he looked abashed. "Why, you—"

"Hey, look out!" Amanda heard Nicolaus's shout and saw the flash of dirty tan heading for her face. Old habits kicked in, and she froze.

The ball smashed into her temple. Splinters of pain shot around her eye. Lights danced in front of her.

"Amy! Amy, are you okay?" In an instant, Jakob was kneeling in front of her, and his fingers gently probed her face. "Ah, jeez, why didn't you duck?"

She closed her eyes against the dark red haze that seemed to creep in from the corners of her vision. How was she supposed to answer a question like that? Tell him that she'd learned not to flinch when a blow was coming, because it only meant she'd get two to make up for the one she'd evaded?

"I didn't see it," she murmured.

The children must have reached them, for their

voices were close and frantic. "I'm sorry, Jake," Nicolaus said. "I didn't mean to throw it so hard!"

"Mama!" The word cracked on a sob. "Mama, are you okay? It was my fault, I should have caught it, I just missed it and—"

"No." She forced her eyes open. "It wasn't your fault." She could not allow Daniel to think he was to blame for this accident.

Jakob's fingers whispered over a tender spot, and she winced. "I don't think there's anything broken, but you're going to have a heck of a bruise." He dug into his pocket, unearthing a white handkerchief, and tossed it to Nicolaus. "Nic, could you run down to the river and wet this?"

Nicolaus grabbed the rag and took off.

"Mama?" Daniel said again. She tried to pull away from Jakob to reassure her son.

"Don't move yet," Jakob commanded. "You might be dizzy. I think you should lie down for a while."

"Oh, would you all stop making such a fuss!" she snapped. "You act like I've never been hit before!"

The sudden silence was heavy, almost surreal. Amanda's stomach sank as she realized what she'd just said.

Jakob's palms cupped her chin, and he tipped her head up to face him. His eyes were dark and startlingly intent. "What is that supposed to mean?" he asked, his voice soft but fierce. "Who hit you?"

He was going to know, she thought. His eyes were going to look straight through hers and see all her secrets, read all her lies.

It couldn't happen. Though his touch was still gentle, his body was taut, vibrating with tension, and she knew that all his protective instincts were rushing to the fore. It touched her, even as it frightened her. She couldn't let him be dragged into her past. He didn't deserve that nightmare.

"It's nothing," she said firmly. "I come from a big family. You know what it's like, Jakob. Sometimes when I was playing with my brothers and sisters, it got out of hand and one of us got hurt. That's all I meant."

Her family was her one regret, the thing that had kept her in New York long past the time she should have gone. Suddenly, she missed them, with a sharp, pure wave of loneliness that stabbed at her heart. She would never see them again, would never know if they were all right.

She'd been worried, for a time, that Edward would take her defection out on them. But she knew that, if she weren't there to witness it, they were probably beneath his notice or his effort, and so would be left alone.

"That's all, Jakob," she repeated, trying to make him believe. More lies, somehow getting harder and harder to tell him, harder to live with. She hated lies; Edward had used them too effectively for her to ever see them as good, no matter how necessary. She hated lying to Jakob even more.

"Okay," he said softly. "Okay."

"Here you go!" Nicolaus was panting from his rush to and from the river. He handed Jakob the dripping rag.

"Okay. Easy now, Amy." He lightly dabbed at the corner of her eye.

"Ouch!"

"Sorry." The cloth was cool from the water, moist and soothing. His fingers were very warm, and somehow not soothing at all.

He was very close to her. His broad chest blocked her vision, and she tilted her head back, so she could look up at his face.

Deep green leaves danced above him, shuddering in the slight wind. She could read the concern on his face, the worried frown that pulled at the corners of his mouth. His features were rough, blunt; nothing fine or elegant, but completely male.

"You're going to have a hell of a shiner," he said.

She shrugged. Bruises were nothing.

His scent drifted to her, soap and warmth mixed with sunshine. One hand still held the damp rag pressed against her face. His free hand came up, sliding down the other side of her neck, under her ear, a stroke that had nothing to with checking her injury. It was simply a caress, a gentle glide of skin on skin.

A simple touch that was anything but simple. Heat bloomed under the abrasive pads of his fingertips, and she wondered how a stroke so small could cause such a deep response. She shivered.

"Cold?"

"No."

She couldn't seem to look away from him, from the dark eyes that stared directly into hers. She didn't think Edward had ever looked deeply into her eyes, had ever wondered what went on inside her, beyond the surface. He'd never cared.

She started to lift her hand, to echo Jakob's caress. She wanted to sweep her fingers down his cheek and smooth away the frown creases that deepened around his lips.

"Mama? Does it hurt?"

Daniel's worried question recalled her to her senses. She couldn't do this. She couldn't let herself be sucked into dreaming, into believing there was something more for her. All she'd wanted was a safe place to raise her son in peace. She'd found it, and she couldn't endanger that by wishing for things that were impossible, no matter how beautifully tempting they were.

She jerked away from Jakob's touch. It was too tempting, and as far beyond her reach as the stars.

"Is something wrong?" he asked, his brows drawing together in concern.

"No." She snatched the cloth and pressed it against her face. "I can hold it, that's all."

She saw his quick flash of hurt, then he leaned away, his face closing down, expressionless, they way he'd looked when she first met him. "If that's what you want."

She really didn't want to hurt him. She was trying to spare him pain; she didn't want him to think that her sharpness was his fault. "I'm just hungry, I think." She tried a limp smile. "Maybe you could begin getting out the lunch?"

"Fine." With jerky motions, he started unpacking the basket she'd stuffed with Helga's food.

But the brightness had gone out of her morning, and she sat there, her bruised temple throbbing, wondering why the one thing she'd dreamed of for years now somehow didn't seem like enough.

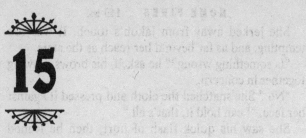

15

Amanda was expecting the rap against her door. When it came she started anyway, smoothing her hands down her skirts and taking a fast, appraising glance around the cottage.

Maybe this was a very stupid idea.

She knew Jakob had been surprised when, on the way back from the brewery this noon, she'd asked him to stop over and see her for a moment before he went back to work after dinner. Until then, she'd avoided him pretty effectively after their picnic; no use spending time mooning over something beyond her reach. But she owed him this.

He'd agreed to come by, and she'd deposited him with Helga in the luscious-smelling kitchen of the main house, hurrying back to the guest house to make one final check on her preparations.

And now he was here. The boys were still at school, and she and Jakob would be alone. Not that she had any leftover fear about being alone with him. Still, her heart skittered a bit in her chest, and there was no denying her nerves were getting the best of her.

Just get on with it, she told herself, and tugged open the door to him and the crisp, clean air.

For some reason she never remembered him with quite the impact he really had when she saw him. He stood, waiting for her, easy and contained, one hip cocked, clothed in plain old denims and a knit undershirt that pulled tightly over his shoulders and chest— too tight and totally unfashionable, but Amanda had to admit that, from her perspective, there were certain advantages to him wearing something like that.

The earth-brown waves of his hair were mussed, as if he'd run his hands through it as he worked and never bothered to comb it straight. He held a deep amber bottle of beer, and when he tipped his head back for a sip, sunlight brightened and warmed the darkness of his hair and eyes, washing them with gold.

He shouldn't have looked that good. He was messy and male; his shirt was tugged half out of his pants, and his boots were scarred and scuffed. She could have stood there all day, her hand still wrapped around the doorknob, and simply looked at him.

He lowered the bottle, holding it loosely at his side, and waited.

The breeze was cool, cutting through the pines and sneaking into the warmth of her house, and Amanda shivered. Jakob, standing there comfortably with just a trace of confusion evident, didn't seem at all affected by the chill, even though he wore only that light shirt.

"It's cool today," she said lamely, at a loss for anything clever to say.

"Is it?" Jakob looked around, as if it were the first time he'd bothered to notice the day's weather. And she knew he probably hadn't; when he was focused on work, he paid little mind to anything else. Any woman would long to find out what it felt like to have all that intensity and focus turned on her. "Yeah, I guess so. You can tell autumn's coming."

"Already?" The time had slipped by so quickly, a smooth, easy thread of one good day after another. Amazing how quickly those days went, when one didn't have to face each morning and night with the dread of what might happen. When she could simply live, just doing her job and raising her son and speaking to her friends without the dark cloud of certain disaster looming over her.

He hooked his thumb in his waistband. "Did I get it wrong?" he finally asked.

"What?"

"You did ask me to stop by, right?"

"Yes."

"Are you going to invite me in?"

"Oh, of course!" She laughed, embarrassed, and waved him in. She'd been too occupied looking at him to remember why he was there. "We don't have to do this now, if you're too busy. It can wait."

"No, now's fine." He stepped by her, out of the sunlight and into the dimmer room. He always seemed to take up too much space, too much air. Amanda breathed deeply, trying to calm her ridiculous heart that was pumping just a bit too hard. "I have plenty of time."

He always seemed to have plenty of time for her. Despite everyone's claim that he had time for nothing but work, she never felt rushed by him. Never felt that he had anything but all the time in the world for her and her son. And when she had his attention, she had it all.

She fiddled with the deep gathers of fabric at her waist. She didn't want to feel so flattered, and tried hard to read nothing into it. But even now, he stood relaxed in the center of the cottage and just looked at her, as if he had nothing at all better to do.

"You look well," he said, though he'd seen her only a few hours before.

"Thank you," she murmured.

"You've been sleeping well?"

"Sleeping?"

"I haven't seen you out at night."

"Oh, well . . ." Briefly, she considered shading the truth a bit and telling him that the nights held nothing but peaceful rest for her. Though her days now slid by, filled only with freedom and light, too many memories still lurked in the darkness for her comfort.

But she'd lied to him enough. "Not really. I guess I just don't need much sleep."

He stepped closer. She should step back, back to a safe distance, back where his comfort and nearness were no temptation.

"Then why do you stay inside?" he said, his voice as soft and intimate as it had been the night they'd sat under a willow and he'd told her of his family. "The river's beautiful in the moonlight. And winter will be here soon enough, and it will be too cold for you to wander around in the night."

"I didn't want to disturb you. These are your grounds, after all."

"You won't disturb me." He had night-dark eyes, and they were focused squarely on her. Except the night held in his eyes promised no terrors and no memories . . . only warmth. A warmth that she was all too drawn to, that she wanted far too much to believe in. "Well," he amended, his voice low, "you'll disturb me, but I don't mind."

That was exactly why she no longer wandered outside

at night. She was afraid she would seek him out, and he would disturb her as much as she disturbed him. It was something she couldn't afford.

She had so much now. She would not allow herself to be greedy for more. Contentment had been long in coming, and she would do nothing to risk it.

"No, I . . . no."

The warmth in his eyes faded, and he stepped away, tipping his head back for another swallow of beer. It exposed the column of his throat, where it broadened into sturdy shoulders, and the hollow of his neck, shadowed by his unbuttoned shirt.

Oh, no. Amanda closed her eyes. It was no longer safe to look at him, for she couldn't seem to do it without wondering how her mouth would feel pressed right there, settling into the slight depression at the base of his throat.

"What is it you want, then?" he said, clipped and businesslike. His usual tone, but one he seldom used with her. She hated it, even as she was grateful for it.

"Just wait right here," she said, and skittered into her bedroom.

She slammed the door shut behind her, not caring if he thought it was odd. She needed a moment alone.

She'd left the package in the tall, intricately painted cabinet that Helga had called a *Bauernschrank*, which served as the only storage in the small bedroom. The stiff brown paper crackled in her hands and she pulled it out, wondering why she'd bothered to wrap it up in paper and tightly tied string, like a present.

It wasn't a present. It was something she owed him, that was all. It certainly didn't matter that she was absurdly worried about whether he'd like it. Perhaps she should have chosen another color. Perhaps she'd done a poor job of it—she was more than a bit out of practice.

It was a daringly intimate thing to give to a man. Was she being forward? She hadn't meant anything by it, had only intended to replace something he'd lost because of her.

And all those excuses sounded hopelessly weak, even to herself.

Oh, Lord. Maybe she shouldn't give it to him at all.

"Amy?" He knocked lightly on the door. "Are you all right in there?"

"I'm fine." Her fingers brushed over the slick surface of the paper one more time. Enough delaying. Of course she was going to give it to him; what else would she do with it, let it gather dust in the bottom of the cabinet?

All right then, she told herself. *Just be done with it. It's not so big a thing.*

When she opened the door, Jakob was right on the other side, one hand braced against the wall, a worried frown drawing down the corners of his mouth. She liked it so much better when he smiled.

He loomed over her in the doorway, as if he'd been ready to barge into the bedroom and check on her. Startled at his closeness, she stepped back.

"I'm sorry," he said, dropping his arm and moving away.

"Here." She stuck the package in his direction.

"What?"

"This is yours." She shoved the package at him and let go; he had to scramble to catch it before it dropped to the floor. Amanda felt heat burn her cheeks. She wished she could simply disappear into the other room until he was gone.

What if he didn't like it? She wanted, too much, for his face to light up with pleasure, for him to smile at her in surprise and appreciation. Foolishness, every bit of it. Yet she didn't know how to make it stop.

He held the package awkwardly in his big hands, as if he wasn't quite sure what do with it. "What is it?"

"Why don't you open it and find out?"

"But—" He turned it over and over, inspecting it. "You have nothing of mine to return."

"I'm not returning anything."

His brows drew together in confusion.

"I don't understand."

"It's just something I wanted to give you." She didn't know what to do with her hands; her fingers fiddled with the lace that edged her sleeve until she finally shoved her fists into her pockets to get them out of the way.

"There was no reason for you to give me anything."

"Does there have to be a reason?"

"But no one's ever . . ." He cleared his throat awkwardly. "You don't owe me anything."

"Oh, would you just hurry up and open it!" she said impatiently, unable to stand it any longer.

He looked at her in surprise, a faint smile lighting his face. "Yes, ma'am."

The knotted string and paper fell apart under his strong fingers, revealing the dark brown, finely woven wool she'd chosen at Kaufenburg's store. He lifted out the suit, holding it between two fingers as if he were afraid of bruising it.

"It's to replace the one you ruined when you went into the river after us," she said.

His features gave no hint of what he was thinking. He just stared at her, his deep-colored eyes as close a match to the color of the suit as she'd hoped.

"I'm going to try it on," he said abruptly, and spun for the bedrooms.

"Oh, no, you don't need to do that," she protested, but he'd already disappeared into the room that Daniel used and clicked the door shut behind him.

This was not exactly what she'd had in mind. He was supposed to thank her nicely and then leave, putting her out of her misery. She was half-tempted to rush outside and escape before he came out of the bedroom. The waiting was killing her.

She frowned when she realized she was chewing on an already badly mangled thumbnail. Rocking back on her heels, she wished she could see through the heavy wood door and know what he was doing in there.

See through the door! Lord!

It wasn't what she had meant—she'd only wanted to see his reaction to the suit—but once her mind had come up with the idea, it didn't seem to want to let it go. She pictured him hopping out of his trousers, him tearing his shirt over the top of his head. It didn't seem to matter that she had no clue what he looked like beneath his clothes. Her imagination filled in the details rather nicely.

She knew he was built strong, his thick bones overlaid with a heavy layer of muscle. He'd be in nothing but ankle-length, four-button drawers; they'd sag low, exposing a nice bit of flat belly. He'd have just a bit of hair on his chest, she decided, dark brown and soft and curly . . .

She went to see if she could tamp down the fire in the stove. It was getting way too warm in the cottage.

There was the creak of the bedroom door opening behind her; she straightened and turned.

There. That was what she had hoped to see on his face when she'd given him the suit.

He was grinning, his eyes snapping with pleasure. In stockinged feet, he strolled into the middle of the room. Sticking out his arms to his sides, he turned around for her inspection. The clothes looked even better than she'd imagined; Jakob looked businesslike, intelligent, sober, but with all his strength and power clearly evident.

"What do you think?" he asked, but he didn't seem the least bit worried about her reaction. He knew he looked good, darn it.

"Well, the shirt's probably going to have to go. I can't say wearing just an undershirt, instead of a nice cotton one, is ever going to be in fashion."

She hadn't realized how much he could resemble Nicolaus, his eyes dancing, his smile wide, mussed-up waves of hair tumbling down around his collar. He looked young and hopeful and completely irresistible.

"Let me see," she said, and went over to him, circling slowly.

"It fits so well," he marveled, shrugging to test the jacket. "It's just so comfortable. Usually I feel all trussed up like a Christmas goose in a suit."

She tugged on the shoulder seams, checking the fit, and brushed her hand down the slope of his back. Perfect, if she did say so herself.

"That's because they weren't leaving quite enough room for your shoulders and your . . . well, it wasn't cut quite properly."

Now that she'd started, she couldn't seem to manage to stop touching him. She rounded in front of him, standing close enough to smell brewer's yeast and the outdoors, to smell warmth and new wool. To smell Jakob.

Her fingertips whispered under his lapels. She was only seeing if she'd pressed the jacket properly, she told herself, making sure the seams were crisp and square. It had nothing to do with the luscious heat creeping through the fabric and into her palms, with the solid swell of muscle underneath the fine wool.

"How did you manage it?" he asked.

"Helga helped me, of course."

"Of course." His laugh was richly intimate.

"She let me measure one of your old suits. I made a guess at how much extra to allow." She tugged at his sleeve, and it just grazed his wristbone. "I was fairly close, I think," she said proudly.

"It's perfect." His voice lowered roughly. "Perfect."

Her hands slipped down the line of the jacket, a motion that had no excuse for being anything but a caress. Oh, Lord, she thought wildly, what am I doing?

There was a slight catch in his breathing. "I thought you didn't have your sewing machine yet."

"I don't. I did it by hand."

His chest rumbled slightly beneath the light touch of her fingertips. Slowly, knowing she shouldn't, she lifted her gaze to meet his, to find his features taut and his eyes dark with heat and intensity.

"Amy," he said slowly, lifting one hand to her face. His touch was as light as hers, the barest brush of his fingertips along her jaw.

Scarcely a touch at all. Yet it was far too much. It was enough to start a low, strong ache in her belly, to make her blood run hot and thick. She dared not even *want*, and now she *needed*.

I cannot do this, she thought. It was not fair to herself; it was not fair to Jakob. She threw herself two steps back, to a safer position.

"Let me see if I got the length right," she said, though it was difficult to get the words out smoothly. Her gaze swept the length of him; across broad shoulders, snugged under rich brown wool; over the wide, white patch of undershirt revealed between the lapels; down past the hem of the well-fitting jacket.

"Oh, God." She didn't know if she said the words out loud. As much as an exclamation, they were a prayer for strength.

She'd cut the trousers wide, giving them a loose drape, and now the fabric tented out over his obvious erection. He made no move toward her, just stood there with his hands resting on his narrow hips, his weight on one leg. She should have looked away immediately and pretended she never noticed.

It was too late. She was caught, unable to do what she *should*, held as much by her own body as his. There was no air; there was no reality. She was shaking, wanting only to go to him and unbutton his trousers, to take him into her hands and her mouth and her body.

"Oh, God." This time she knew she'd spoken aloud and that he'd heard her.

She had no idea how long they stood there, doing nothing but looking into each other's eyes. The fire hissed and popped in the stove; a gust of wind rattled a loose windowpane. Need grew, shifted, took on an inevitable power of its own.

Finally, he walked over to her, his stockinged feet a soft whisper against the wood floor. *Move away,* she told herself. *Move away!*

She could no more move than she could force herself to stop breathing. Though there were only a few, bare inches of air between them, they touched nowhere. The space was small, insubstantial, but she knew once they'd bridged that distance, everything would change.

"The feel of your hands on me, Amy . . . even through the fabric, do you have any idea what it's like?" She was unable to speak, to think of anything but how much she longed for his hands on her body, too.

"Are you waiting for me to apologize?" he asked, his voice hushed. "I'm not going to."

Her breathing went slow and deep, in time with the easy, seductive rhythm of his words.

"I can't. Not for something I have no control over. Not for something so natural."

There were shadows under his eyes, under his blunt cheekbones, and she wanted to gather him in and soothe them away. Make him forget the worries, make him forget his dark memories, even as he drove away her own.

"And not for something I think . . . I think maybe you feel it, too."

He swallowed. "Am I wrong, Amy? Should I be apologizing for something?"

If he had to apologize, so should she. Her thoughts, her passions, the feelings that curled seductively through her body—they were every bit as sinful as his. They just didn't show as explicitly. And somehow, it didn't seem fair that he would be alone in this.

"No," she whispered. "No, I feel it, too."

Haltingly, so tentative she thought he'd never get there, he lowered his head, brushing his mouth against hers; once, twice, and then again and again, as if he could do nothing else. Her breath caught, and the brushes slowed, settled, became a slow, even, astonishingly wonderful pressure.

He touched her nowhere else, just the gentle meeting of their lips. So little, to cause so much. To cause a need that carved hollows deep within her, empty places that only he could fill. To cause this wild, wonderful yearning, where there was no thought or restraint. Nothing but him, and the way he could make her feel.

His hands came up to cradle her face. His thumbs stroked along her cheekbones, feather-light, a tiny, astonishing hint of what he could give her.

He could give her everything.

16

Jakob was drowning, awash in sunshine and roses and incredibly soft skin. Half-thrilled she was allowing this, half-terrified that he would do something wrong and she would pull away.

What did he know of wooing a woman? Nothing. He'd never regretted all those days and nights spent in something—anything—besides the pursuit of pleasure; that was his life, his work and what remained of his family, and he hadn't been sorry. Until now, when he wished for skill and sureness, something instead of this trembling, awkward rush of heat.

So he went slowly, concentrating on nothing but the plush softness of her lips, yielding and parted against his. But he had to touch her; he could not keep his hands still. Her face was the safest spot he could think of, and so he hesitantly cupped it, and then knew it wasn't safe at all. Touching her nowhere was safe, nowhere that he could feel the extraordinary, fine softness of her skin and wonder if the rest of her was just as smooth, knowing it must be.

He hardly dared believe she was kissing him; could not imagine there would be more. He slid one hand down; the skin under her ear was tender. The fine wisps at her hairline tickled the backs of his knuckles. There was the fragile, living pulse of her neck against his fingertips.

The delicate lace that fringed her collar caught on the calluses of his hands; it felt rough after the gossamer-smoothness of her skin. Her shoulder was round and firm under the washed cotton, heating his palm and his blood.

And then her breast was in his hand, a lush, heavy weight that filled his palm as well as his dreams. He held his breath, waiting for her to shove him away. Surely this would end now; she would realize he was inept and unsophisticated and scorn his clumsy touch.

She gave a small sob, a signal of pleasure that drew out his own groan. She threw herself tight against him, her arms linking tightly around his shoulders, her breast pushing firmly against his hand. He squeezed gently, reveling in the pliable softness. Her mouth opened, and the first slick glide of her tongue was beyond any pleasure he had known.

He no longer cared that he was shaking, for she was trembling, too, her warm cushioned body overwhelmingly arousing. He didn't even think of what could be next; *now* was more than enough, impossible and extraordinary.

"Amy," he whispered against her mouth. "Amy."

"Oh, no." She pushed hard and tore free. He let go and stumbled back. She turned her back to him and buried her face in her hands, her shoulders jerking. "I can't do this."

Numbly, he tried to rein in his careening emotions. He longed to pull her back, to bury himself in softness and sunshine. What had he done wrong? Had he frightened her, because she could tell that he wanted her so fiercely, so overwhelmingly, that he was beyond restraint?

"Amy . . ." Haltingly, he lifted his hand to stroke her back, her head, wanting to soothe and calm her, then let it drop helplessly at his side. He had no right to touch her.

"It's so wrong," she said, her voice muffled in her hands. "So wrong."

"I'm sorry." Her head was bent, and her hair slipped over her shoulder, revealing the pale, smooth side of her neck. Even now, he could hardly keep from going to her and putting his mouth there.

Guilt washed through him. "I didn't mean to do anything you didn't want. I apologize for offending you."

"No!" She whirled on him, her hazel eyes glazed with moisture, her mouth drawn with strain. "It's not you!"

How typically kind of her to try and spare him. She was attempting to take on a portion of the responsibility, when it was entirely his fault and he knew it. His, and the damn, outrageous, unmanageable, wondrous passion he'd conceived for her.

"Amy, I know I should not have touched you. It will never happen again," he said.

"It's not your fault," she insisted. "It's me."

Silence was awkward, a thin, brittle barrier that neither one knew how to break. Outside, the light had dimmed, and deep shadows swathed the corners of the small room. Ordinary day, ordinary room, when what was between them was anything but ordinary.

"Shall I go?" he asked finally.

"I should be the one to go." Her head bowed. He longed to gather her up and comfort her, but knew his presence was anything but comforting, when he was the one who'd caused her pain in the first place. "But I can't. So yes, please go."

"All right, then." A harsh wind blew in when he opened the door, and she shuddered in the cold. He left without looking back, leaving the door yawning open behind him. It blew back and forth, creaking, its faint shadow sliding across the wide-planked floor.

Amanda ran to the door and leaned against the frame. Jakob was slowly walking away, his hands pocketed, his shoulders hunched in the new jacket. He looked utterly alone, and she bit a knuckle to keep from calling after him. What good would it do?

None at all.

He'd forgotten his things. His feet must be freezing, with nothing between his soles and the cold, hard ground but thin stockings. Amanda closed the door, slicing off the cold and the world, Jakob and temptation, and went to Daniel's bedroom.

Jakob's pants were slung carelessly over the end of the bed, one leg trailing on the floor, as if he'd tossed them there in his rush to try on his new suit and paid no mind to where they landed. His brown boots, scuffed and worn, lay on their sides on the circular braided rug.

She crossed the room, sank down on the bed, and picked up his pants, imagining they still held a faint echo of his warmth.

All women are whores.

Oh, God. Of all the things that Edward had accused her of, this was the most true and he'd had the proof of it. She crushed the trousers in her fists, balling them up as if she could press them to powder, to nothingness.

Her body was prone to sordid, sinful urges she'd never managed to totally free herself from.

It was the one thing she'd never understood about herself. How her body could still respond to a man who'd hurt her so badly.

Edward had patience, a cruel and calculated, coldly gentle touch that had nothing whatsoever to do with tenderness. And he'd used it, in those long, lost nights when it had finally become easier to surrender to sensation than to think any longer.

At first, she'd thought it was his way of apologizing, of trying to make up to her what he'd done and the pain he'd caused her. She'd come to believe, however, that it was another way of proving his control over her—he could *make* her respond, even as she loathed him.

No more than she'd loathed herself. With the gray morning light, she'd sometimes have to reach for the chamber pot to relieve herself of the sick lump in the pit of her stomach. And it was those memories, even more than the fear and echoes of pain, that kept her wide-eyed and sleepless through the empty hours of the night.

Suddenly furious, she hurled Jakob's pants across the room. They hit the wall with a soft splat and fell to the wooden floor, an absurdly ineffectual release for her anger.

She allowed only one broken, harsh sob to escape. Falling back on the bed, she drew Daniel's pillow to her, the fine linen covering it as soft as his baby skin had been. Her son, the one clean, right thing in her world.

She closed her eyes and tried to forget.

Edward Sellington studied the party that swirled around him, securely satisfied that, in a room that held all of New York's richest and most powerful people, not to mention half of the country's, no one was richer and more powerful than he.

He took a sip of the deep, red wine in his glass and grimaced slightly. This was where Norbrook, whose party it was, always showed the lack of breeding in his ancestry; his decorating and food were top-notch, but he always skimped on the wine, perhaps thinking no one had the palate to even notice.

Sellingtons, however, skimped on nothing.

At least the staff was competent. He barely flicked a white-gloved finger at a passing waiter, who hurried to his side. Edward ordered a cognac to replace the mediocre wine, specifying the brand and vintage he wanted. He didn't really trust Norbrook's cellars, but there must be something decent there.

A small orchestra played a slow, European waltz; banks of hothouse flowers backed hundreds of lit candles and rimmed the hissing gas sconces. Idly, Edward watched the dancers whirl by, wondering if he would find someone deserving of the chase. Perhaps the small blond bit in ice-blue satin and diamonds. Attractive enough, but he didn't feel any real anticipation meriting the slight effort of exerting his charm.

He was horribly bored.

Nothing seemed worthy of him; women, money, power—they all fell so easily into his lap they seemed not to have any value at all. He'd been born to them, raised to them, considered them part of his due. But he couldn't deny that it might be slightly entertaining to, once in a while, have to—not work, exactly, but at least occupy himself with something for a time before it was achieved.

He'd only been at this party for less than an hour, and he was already deeply annoyed with the dullness of it all. Polite conversation, civilized music, decorative women.

He made desultory conversation with the few men

he considered equal to his notice. No one commented on his wife's absence; he really had not dragged her out into society all that much, and no one would dare question him about private matters, in any case.

No one ever dared question Edward Sellington. He almost wished someone would, just for the distraction of scorning the foolishly presumptuous fellow.

Unfortunately, when he worked his way through the room, making brief contacts with all his acquaintances, Lester Morehouse was so pathetically eager to curry his favor that Edward assumed the rumors must be true and his business was failing badly; no doubt Morehouse would be on his doorstep first thing Monday morning, trying to drum up investments.

Well, perhaps Edward would help the man out. But he certainly needn't stand here and listen to the man's determinedly bright conversation. Edward deftly excused himself and went to stand again by the edge of the dance floor.

The servant finally reappeared with his cognac, and Edward traded glasses. He tried a sip. Ah, that was better. So Norbrook was keeping the decent stuff to himself after all.

The woman in blue whirled by again, partnered by a tall fair man who gazed adoringly at his partner. She, however, slanted a glance at Edward, deep blue eyes faintly but unmistakably provocative. She was clearly available. Edward was vaguely disappointed. There was no sport to be had there, either.

He sighed. He wondered how his wife would feel if she knew that she was furnishing him with the only entertainment in his life. Tracking her down was proving to be an interesting challenge; he rather thought that after he found her, she'd provide him with a good deal more entertainment. His plans for making her pay for daring to defy him were about the only thoughts that could occupy him for longer than a moment.

"Where's your wife, Sellington?"

The deep voice from behind him startled him so that, for a moment, Edward didn't realize he was being addressed. "Excuse me?" he said, turning slowly.

He'd not laid eyes on the man for nearly ten years, but he remembered him well. "McDermott," he said, his voice a low hiss.

"Ah, you remember me?" Kieran McDermott gave a slight, mocking bow. "I'm flattered."

Edward's fingers tightened around his glass, and he nearly lifted it to his mouth and downed the entire thing before he realized what he was doing. He would not give McDermott the satisfaction of knowing he was momentarily discomfited by seeing him.

"Who let you in here?" Edward asked tightly.

McDermott smiled, and Edward wanted to slice that grin right off his face, if only for the satisfaction of watching him bleed. Irish bastard.

"I was invited."

"I believe the kitchen is that way. I'm certain servants must check in there," Sellington said dismissively, and turned toward the door, plotting his course out. He had to leave. But he must not do so quickly enough to cause any comment.

"You never answered my question," McDermott said, his voice even, slightly touched with that ill-bred Irish accent that betrayed his birth. "Where's your wife? Don't tell me you killed off this one, too."

Edward froze in mid-step. He closed his eyes, struggling for control, before he turned back to face him.

"Don't be ridiculous," he said calmly.

"I know you killed her." There was a dangerous, half-mad glitter in McDermott's eyes, enough to cause

Edward just a moment of concern, before he remembered that McDermott could never hurt him. He was a powerless man.

"Wherever would you get such an absurd idea? Cynthia merely tripped down the stairs. I was devastated; everyone knows that."

"I know you killed her." Rage softened and sharpened his voice. "I *know* it."

"How can anyone know what happened that night? No one can. And who knows? Perhaps Cynthia threw herself down that staircase. After all, you would not leave her alone. You'd taken her youthful flirtation to mean so much more, and she was distraught that she could not free herself from you."

Edward shook his head sadly, and continued. "I'd offered to help her, you know, to rid her of your bothersome attentions once and for all. I suppose I was too late. Or perhaps it was merely a tragic accident. It was a long time ago." He shrugged, attempting indifference. Hatred was only useful when it was carefully controlled, and Edward was a master at it. "I've put it behind me. So should you."

McDermott's hands jerked upward, as if he meant to throttle Edward, but when Edward merely stared at him, impassive, Kieran brought his hands back down to his sides. "I may never be able to prove it," he said, "but I can make you pay."

That was enough to make Edward laugh, the first genuine bit of amusement he'd felt the entire night, perhaps the entire month. "You poor man, just how do you intend to manage that?"

"You will not always be so well protected," McDermott said. "Someday, you will not be surrounded by servants and lackeys and privilege. Every time you look up, I will be there, and one day, when you are alone—" he lifted the champagne glass in his hand in a toast, the golden liquid reflecting the sparkling candlelight "— well then, of course, I shall kill you."

Edward nearly lost control of himself right there and smashed his glass right into the bastard's face. But he knew, very well, what was public and private behavior, and so only grew more still, his voice softer. "I should have killed you, too."

He saw the rage blaze across McDermott's features, the raw red spreading on his dark cheeks. He felt a certain satisfaction that the man was so predictable; the response was exactly what he'd expected.

Turning on his heel, he left McDermott standing alone in the middle of the room, and wound his way through the crowd, pausing to speak briefly to acquaintances, bowing low over the hands of the women, and making his excuses.

It was only when he was comfortably settled into his carriage that he realized he still held the glass of cognac, his lifeless fingers frozen around it in a rigid grip. He gulped down the contents, opened the carriage window, and tossed the expensive crystal into the street. The tinkling crash of its shattering was muffled beneath the sounds of traffic and street life.

Though he was certain he was not bothered one bit by Kieran McDermott's sudden reappearance—the man had no significance at all—it took until he was home, until he'd stripped off his evening clothes and had three more drinks, until Corinna had expertly ministered to his needs—twice—before he found himself relaxed enough to turn his thoughts from his first wife and her bastard Irish lover to his second.

Amanda had turned out to be more clever than he had expected. He'd traced her to Philadelphia quickly enough, but there she had disappeared. He'd not expected her to give up her fine clothes and luggage in disguise. And it had taken a few weeks for him to discover the simple carriage she'd hired from a local merchant to take her to Pittsburgh. She was a more worthy opponent than he'd imagined.

He had yet to find out where she'd gone from there. He would, soon enough.

And he'd learned a great deal since his first wife, also. He'd learned that the satisfaction he'd extracted from Cynthia in retribution for her infidelity was only momentarily gratifying.

With Amanda, he'd learned that it was far more amusing to keep them alive, and take his payment out over years and years.

Soon enough, he told himself, before he drifted off to sleep in his large, velvet-draped bed.

Soon enough.

17

"Daniel?" *Amanda rapped* on his bedroom door before she turned the knob and entered. "Are you ready for supper?"

Daniel spun quickly from the window, his hands tucked behind his back. His cheeks were flushed with excitement, his eyes bright, and he was the picture of a little boy who was up to something.

Amanda smiled. Daniel had spent so long being cautious, unwilling to risk the slightest misbehavior for fear of what the consequences would be, it was good to see him cautiously trying out a bit of mischief—if that was what he was hiding.

"I'm almost ready," he said. "Just a moment, Mama, and I'll be there, okay?"

Behind him, the window was open a few inches, allowing a bit of the mid-September air to sneak in, just cool enough to be uncomfortable. It smelled crisp, of ripening crops and drying leaves, layered with a touch of cooking grain from the brewery.

"That's fine. But just let me shut the window. It'll be too chilly in here for sleeping tonight."

"No, it'll get too hot," he protested. Why in the world was he insisting on having the window open? She supressed a delighted smile.

She crossed the room and tugged down the sash. A large, tan lump of sugar rested on the sill. She picked it up, balancing it in her palm. "What's this doing here?"

"It's mine." Daniel snatched it from her and tucked it safely in his fist.

"That's fine, but you can't leave it there on the sill, Daniel. It'll draw ants."

"But how else am I going to get a stork to come?"

"A stork?" She bent, bringing her face level with his. She didn't have to bend as far as she was accustomed to; he'd grown this summer. How much longer would it be until he was bending to her level? She had a feeling it would come much too soon to suit her. "I'm not sure there are storks in Minnesota, Daniel."

"There have to be!"

"Oh, yes?"

"Nicolaus said."

"He did, did he? Well, I suppose Nicolaus always knows." His face scrunched as he frowned, and she mimicked his expression. "And, even if there are storks here, I'm not sure they'll come to your window just because you have sugar there. Why would you want a stork, anyway?"

"I want a brother."

"You what?" She'd assumed he was merely trying to add to the menagerie the two boys had been collecting over the past month. Clearly, he had another plan entirely.

She sank down on the edge of his bed. "Now, why don't you tell me exactly what's going on here."

"Nicolaus said that's how you get babies. You put sugar on your windowsill for the stork, and he brings them to you."

"Oh." She wasn't entirely sure she was ready to have this conversation with him yet. "And has Nicolaus tried this?"

"Nooo," he said disdainfully, obviously appalled at her ignorance. "You have to have a mother. He doesn't. But I've got you, and if we get another baby, then I won't have to be the only one anymore."

"Daniel." His expression was earnest and hopeful, and her heart twisted. She would give him anything she could, but she could never give him this. "Is it really so bad, just the two of us?"

"No." He stuck his hands in his pockets. "But it would be nice, wouldn't it?"

"Yes, it would be nice." It was just a flash, a sweet, impossible vision of herself holding a small baby as Daniel made faces at it over her shoulder. She forced the picture away; one more thing that could never be, and it did her no good to dwell on it. "But we're doing pretty well as we are, aren't we?"

He brightened. "And now I've got Nicolaus, and he's almost as good as a brother."

"Right. And *Tante* Helga, and all your new friends at school, too."

"And Jakob," he added.

"Yes, and Jakob." Jakob, whom she'd done her best to avoid, and to whom she'd said not more than half a dozen words in two weeks. Whom she'd seen across the grounds or at the brewing house and felt as close to as when he'd held her in this cottage, and whose mouth she still felt on her own at the beginning of each night, just as sleep stole her defenses and gifted her with passionate dreams.

"I guess you're trying to tell me it's going to take more than a lump of sugar to get me a brother, huh, Mama?"

"You're so smart."

"Do I have to have a father, too, to get one? 'Cause I don't think I want a father again." His features pinched.

It was the first time he'd mentioned his father since they'd left New York. How often did he think of Edward? "Not all fathers are like Edward, Daniel. When you grow up and have children of your own, I'm certain you'll be nothing like him. But yes, we'd probably need one."

"Oh. Maybe I could be like Jakob when I grow up instead?"

"Maybe you could."

His brow puckered. "Mama, are you mad at Jakob?" he asked shrewdly.

She sighed heavily. "Not mad, Daniel." Just tired. Tired of trying to ignore the soft, gentle yearning she saw in his eyes when his gaze rested on her. Tired of cutting him off every time he tried to talk to her, and watching the hurt settle into his expression when she made it clear she had no intention of discussing anything with him.

She leaned forward and rested her forehead against his, searching for a way to explain to a child things that she, an adult, seemed to be mangling so badly.

"Daniel!" She snapped up abruptly and brought her palm up to his forehead. "You're so hot!"

"No, Mama." He hunched his shoulders and shivered. "I'm cold. Maybe you should shut the window after all."

She peered at him closely. She'd attributed his bright eyes and high color to excitement. Now she saw the unnatural paleness of the skin surrounding his red cheeks and the glaze of fever glassing his pupils. "It's into bed with you, young man." She had the quilts down and him tucked in before he had time to mumble a protest. She slammed down the window and fetched another blanket, tucking it high around his shoulders.

"Now then," she said brightly, trying not to show him the frisson of fear that was unraveling in her stomach. When she'd left New York behind, she'd also left behind the bevy of well-paid, highly trained doctors and nurses who'd tended Daniel through every sniffle. She was horribly certain she hadn't the knowledge or skill to properly care for him alone. "Do you hurt anywhere?"

He sighed, snuggling beneath the covers. "My throat hurts a little."

She smoothed his jumbled curls off his forehead, the skin dry and hot under her fingers, and swore at herself for not noticing it earlier. Some mother she was. She'd been too busy moping over her own problems to notice her son was becoming ill.

"When did it start?"

"I dunno." His lids started to droop. "This afternoon, maybe."

Not long, then. Thank God. "I'll go make you some nice broth, okay? We'll have you all better in no time."

Just before she left the room, she leaned against the doorjamb, looking back at him. The early evening light was dim, leaving the room washed in gray and shadow. Daniel was a small lump, huddled under the piles of multicolored quilts, and he suddenly looked terribly small and fragile.

Such a little bundle, to mean the entire world to her.

It's only a fever, she told herself. He'll be better by the morning. Children have fevers all the time.

That's all it was, because that's all it could be.

*   *   *

Jakob shifted from one foot to the other in front of the door to the guest house. The noon sun was warm on his back, nicely muting the crisp chill of the air that still held only a hint of autumn.

He wasn't at all sure that what he was about to do was the right thing. Certainly, Amy had done her best to avoid him the past weeks. She'd made it perfectly clear she didn't want to talk to him. She didn't want an apology, she didn't want a return to their previous friendship. She wanted it forgotten, and above all, she didn't want the thing he was almost overwhelmingly tempted to do—to try that remarkable kiss again.

Because, damn it, nothing that was that good should be ignored. He was quite positive of it.

He'd tried patience, though it came hard to him. He'd tried to give her a little space to get used to the idea, while he figured out the best way to woo a skittish widow who was bent on ignoring that powerful pull between them. And he'd been able to stand it, as long as, once in a while, he could glance up from his work and rest his eyes on her. He'd look his fill at the shiny brown spill of her hair, the deep, soft curves of her body, and think about how it could be between them, and he'd find it in him to be patient for another day or two.

But she hadn't shown up for work this morning.

He wasn't letting her get away that easily. If she thought she could just up and quit without telling him, so she wouldn't have to see him anymore, well, she was wrong. If she wanted him completely out of her life, she was going to have to tell him to his face. Because he was as sure as he'd ever been that she didn't want that. She couldn't. Not the way she'd clung to him that afternoon, the way her body had pressed so sweetly to him, the way her lips had softened and invited him in to stay. Not the way she'd sighed, and not with the deep, lonely yearning in her eyes when she'd pulled away, which seemed to echo so precisely the feelings swelling inside him.

He knocked sharply on the door, the sound ringing hollowly inside. He rocked back on his heels and waited for her to answer it, planning what he would say.

So she wasn't ready yet. He'd promise he'd stay well away—whatever she wanted—as long as she'd come back to work, where he could look at her every day, and patiently—damn, there was that *patient* stuff again—work his way underneath her defenses.

This wasn't going to be easy.

She opened the door slowly, and everything he planned to say evaporated in the cool breeze. She was pale, with fine lines etched around her worried mouth, and a faint purplish hint to the translucent skin under her eyes.

"What's the matter?"

She shoved strands of hair out of her face, and her gaze found his, her eyes wounded and worried. "It's Daniel. He's got a fever." She took a deep, shuddering breath. "It's probably nothing. Children have fevers all the time, don't they?" she said hopefully, though uncertainty broke through her thin, fragile veneer of confidence.

"I'm going for the doctor." He smiled at her weakly, trying to give her reassurance he didn't have. "You're probably right, but we'll just check it out to be sure, okay?"

Her shoulders slumped in relief. "Thank you, Jakob, I . . ." She gave a small nod. "Thank you."

* * *

In New York Amanda had grown accustomed to briskly confident middle-aged doctors in expensive suits who gave her orders in dismissive tones, never answered her questions, and whisked in intimidating private nurses who hovered over Daniel and allowed her not the slightest bit of leeway in his care.

Dr. Lobach was another sort entirely. He was old, curled over as if his shoulders were weighted with time, and he had a German accent so thick she could barely distinguish his words. He clucked in response to her automatic greeting and went straight in to Daniel.

She stood helplessly at Daniel's bedside while the doctor examined him, wringing her hands together so tightly the skin burned. Surely this ancient elf would be of no help to her son, who lay so listlessly in his bed, his skin drawn and dry with heat.

"Amy," Jakob said softly. His hand was warm and comforting on her shoulder. "Dr. Lobach will do all he can. He's taken care of us all along. He's kept Nicolaus alive through all of his adventures. There's no better doctor, I promise. If there were, I would get him for Daniel. You know that."

Gratefully, she sagged against him, accepting his warmth and strength. She no longer cared if it would lead him to believe something she could never allow. Right now, she needed his confidence, his solid, vital hold on life when her own felt so very tenuous.

The doctor's examination was slow but brief. "Well, then, young man," he said in his low, raspy voice, "we will see if we can get you well, *ja*?"

Daniel nodded, the dull blue of his eyes barely showing between his slitted lids, and Amanda's throat thickened at the effort that small motion had caused him. He looked so tired.

"You rest now," Dr. Lobach went on. "I want to

talk to your mother a moment. I will send her back right away, I promise."

He brushed his age-spotted hand gently down Daniel's face, and Amanda realized the real difference between this doctor and all those who'd attended Daniel in New York.

This one cared.

She and Jakob followed him out of the room, and Jakob quietly shut the door behind them. She was distantly surprised to find that it was late afternoon, a dim, weak, sunlight slanting through the front windows. How had the day passed so quickly? It had seemed very long.

She turned to the doctor, her throat tight with dread. Only the steady comfort of Jakob's hands on her shoulders and his solid presence behind her gave her the strength to ask, "Is he . . . is he going to be all right?"

"I wish I could answer that for certain, *Frau* Smith," the doctor said gravely. "He has the quinsy, that is for certain. And the fever is high, even for such a young boy. Is he able to swallow anything?"

"Not much." She balled her fists, and the nails dug painfully into her palms. "He says it hurts too much."

"The throat is very swollen, very red. And there are the white sacs on the back. This is not so good."

"But surely . . . surely there is medicine." There had to be something, some magic potion that would make her son well. She could pay—anything, whatever it took. But money seemed not to have the same power here as it did where she'd come from. It was part of the reason she liked it here, though right now she wished for the false comfort of believing money could buy anything.

"Unfortunately, there is not much we can do. I can

give you willow bark, for the fever. And you can
sponge him off to cool him, and try to get the liquids
down." He shook his head, *tsk*ing in the back of his
throat. "The real worry here is for the scarlet fever.
You will watch for the rash, I will come back to check
on him. But the best we can do is hope for the best, *ja*?
A little prayer would not come amiss."

After years of unanswered prayers, she'd forgotten
how. For Daniel, she would learn again.

That night and the next day went by in a blur for
Amanda, a foggy, dark passage of time that held no
meaning beyond caring for her son.

She noticed only peripherally that others were there.
The doctor came again the next day, clucking his
tongue and allowing that, if Daniel was no better, he
was no worse, either. Helga came and went; Amanda
accepted the strong beef broth she'd made for Daniel
but refused both the food Helga had brought for her—
what need had she for food?—and Helga's offer to sit
for a time with Daniel so Amanda could rest. How
could she rest? She trusted no one else to tend him.

A worried Nicolaus came to cheer up his friend, and
she shooed him away, not even having the energy to
soothe his obvious fears. She had too many of her own.
Finally, she no longer bothered to answer the knocks at
the door; they didn't matter. Only Daniel, who shivered under his covers, who drifted fitfully in and out of
sleep, mattered. Only Daniel, as she watched all the joy
and vitality that he'd so recently acquired slowly seep
out of him.

She realized night had come again only when she
had to refill the lantern that had burned out in order to
clearly see Daniel's pale, shadowed face. The second

endless, sleepless night—no, the third, she realized belatedly. When she touched him, his white skin seemed to hold the imprint of her fingers for a moment before they faded away.

She continued the remedies that Helga had suggested only because she knew no others; they seemed to do no harm, and she had to do *something*. For his fever, she mixed salt with dried hops and stuffed it into small bags, heating it on the stove and applying the warm bags to the soles of his feet and his wrists, replacing them the instant they cooled, over and over until her back ached and his skin reddened from the heat.

Daniel grimaced every time she gently shook him awake to gargle with the brewer's yeast and honey she mixed with warm water. He hated the taste, but it seemed to ease his throat enough that he could at least swallow a few spoonfuls of salty beef broth or willow bark tea. She worried over the dryness of his skin, as thin and crinkly as autumn leaves, but it hurt him too much to drink more, and she couldn't stand to force him. His breath smelled horrible, and brushing seemed to have little effect on it, so she finally gave up trying. His teeth were the least of her concerns.

Deep in the stillest part of the night, when the light of a cold silver moon streamed through the uncurtained window to blend with the fragile, flickering glow thrown from the lamp, she laid her palm against his forehead for the thousandth time, praying that this time, it would be a bit cooler. Please, God, only a little. That was all she asked for now, no longer dreaming of his sudden recovery. She would take what she could get, one slow, tortuous step at a time.

She snatched her hand back, then forced herself to place her shaking hand against his head again. She swallowed a sob. He'd grown hotter yet, as if he were burning up from the inside out.

She ran from the room and snatched a pan from the kitchen, throwing herself out of the house and down to the river. It seemed to be so far away, her feet beating a desperate rhythm as she ran across the hard ground.

The river rolled on, moonlight skimming over the surface. How could it not have changed, not be affected with what was happening to her son?

The water was cool, colder than what she kept in the barrel outside the house. She filled the pan and hurtled back to the house, water sloshing over the sides and soaking the front of her dress.

Gasping for air, she raced back into Daniel's room, terrified that something had happened to him in the minutes she'd been gone. She stripped the blankets from him, exposing his frail body in his pale nightshirt. The sodden cloth she dunked in the water plopped droplets of water on the floor and the bed, and he shivered when she wiped it across his face and arms.

"Cold, Mama," he said between clenched teeth. "Too cold."

"I know, honey," she said, rewetting the cloth and gliding it over his legs. They were decorated with the scrapes and bruises he'd proudly collected in lunchtime baseball games and rambles through the woods with Nicolaus; healthy-little-boy legs, on a boy who was no longer healthy. "I know. I'll be finished soon, and then we'll warm you."

Again and again, she drew the damp cloth over him, trying to wash away the heat that was scorching her son, her heart aching as he shuddered with chills. Again and again, she checked his fever, so terrified he would be deathly hot that she scarcely dared believe it when he seemed to have cooled a bit.

Thank God. He was still far too warm, still shaking against the cool night air, but he was no longer burning with the intense heat that had frightened her so badly earlier.

His eyelids fluttered up, his eyes stark against his pale skin, deeply shadowed like fresh bruises, catching no warm sparkle from the lamplight. "Cold, Mama," he complained again.

"I'll warm you." She climbed into his bed and pulled him to her, tucking his small, hot body close. His head fit just under her chin, the way his whole body had fit curved against her when he was a baby. She closed her eyes, willing her warmth to seep into him and stop his violent shivering, willing even more for her strength to flow into him and make him strong again.

Surely this wasn't punishment for her sins. It would be unimaginable cruelty to cause her innocent Daniel suffering to make her pay.

No, he was only an ill child, who would soon be well again. There weren't any other possibilities. Because if there were, of all the things she'd lived through, this one would be the one that would finish her.

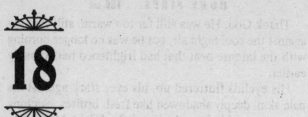

18

"*Come on. You're going* to bed." Jakob scooped Amanda into his arms.

This morning, he'd finally given up on waiting for her to answer his knocks. He'd simply walked right on into the cottage, to find her nodding, her head bent at an awkward angle, in the straight-backed chair she'd dragged beside Daniel's bed.

They were both hurting so much. He felt nearly as much for her as he did for Daniel. Well, if he could do nothing for the one, he could for the other.

"What!" she squawked, startled, and blinked in confusion.

"You need to get some rest, Amy. I figure you haven't had much in the last three days, and I'm going to make sure you get some."

She shook her head. "Daniel. I have to stay with Daniel."

"Amy," he said softly. Her hair was snarled in long tangles around her shoulders and her usually impeccable clothes were rumpled and crushed. But what made his heart turn over was the blur of fatigue in her eyes, the unnatural, dull pallor of her fine skin. She was reaching the end of her endurance. "You're not going to do him any good if you get ill, too."

"I have to stay with him," she protested, dismissing his words with a weak wave of her hand. What difference did it make if she were sick? Daniel was the only thing that was important.

"He's going to need you healthy to play with when he's all better."

She swallowed heavily, wanting to believe him. "Do you really think he'll be better?"

"Of course he'll be better. We won't let anything else happen, will we?" She was limp in his arms, her limbs loose and sagging, and he knew she had no energy left to give. If only he could give her some of his. "Have you eaten anything lately?"

"Yes . . . maybe. I don't know. Does it matter?"

"It would matter to Daniel." He tightened his hold around her, wishing he could gather both her and Daniel in and keep them safe from things like weakness and illness and all the other horrible things that haunted the world and he had too little control over. "Amy, let me watch him for a bit while you get some rest. I'll call you the instant there's any change. I promise."

"I can't leave him, Jakob."

"You're not leaving him." Her eyes were wide and uncertain, rimmed with red. "You're just getting a little food and rest so you can take care of him better when you wake up. That's all." He lowered his head, his forehead almost meeting hers. "Please, let me," he whispered. "Let me take care of him. Let me take care of *you*."

"I'm tired, Jakob." She sounded unalterably weary, as frightened as she was exhausted. A stray curl clung to her white, vulnerable neck, and he nudged it away with one finger.

"I know, Amy." He brushed his lips against her forehead. "I won't let anything happen to him. I swear to you."

Palpable fatigue seeped out of her with the soft sound of her sigh. "Maybe for just a little while." She rested her head on his shoulder.

His throat tightened. She was trusting him with her child. "I promise," he said again. He shifted her weight in his arms, making sure his hold was secure. "Come on, Amy. Let's go tuck you in."

"Amy. Amy!"

"What?" She blinked, trying to clear the groggy blur of sleep from her eyes, her brain. "What is it?" For a moment, she wasn't certain where she was. The room was quiet and warm; rosy light filled it, painting the bare white walls with blush.

"You've slept the whole afternoon, Amy. Time to wake up."

"Jakob?" she said sleepily. How nice to be awoken by that low, rumbling voice.

And then she remembered.

"Oh, God." She bolted up, whipping the quilt off. "It's Daniel, isn't it?"

"Take it easy." He hands were on her shoulders, gently holding her in place. "Daniel's okay."

"Really?" She searched his face, his eyes, hardly daring to do so, dreading what she might see. "Are you sure?"

"Yeah." He grinned, engaging and happy, and the

cold fear disappeared. Her heart was still beating fast, but now for an entirely different reason. Him bending low over her in bed played right into fantasies she scarcely realized she had. "C'mon. I've got something to show you."

He took her hand and tugged her to her feet. She scrubbed a palm over her face, trying to rub away the last stubborn vestiges of fatigue. Her hair was hopelessly snarled, and she could feel the creased imprint of her pillow on her cheek.

"I must look a mess," she mumbled, wondering why she cared.

"Yep," Jakob agreed cheerfully, dragging her out of her bed and through the main room.

When she saw he was taking her to Daniel's room, he had to tug her along behind no longer. Though her hand remained tucked in his, she dashed ahead, hitting the entrance before he did.

She stopped cold just inside the door, squeezing Jakob's hand tight. "Oh, my God."

Daniel was sitting up in bed, a crumpled pile of sheets and blankets in a sloppy heap around his skinny legs. His hair stuck out in awkward, black clumps in all directions. He looked thinner, shadows carved beneath his cheekbones, but his face was blushed with healthy color and his eyes were beautifully clear.

"Oh, there you are, Mama. I'm hungry."

She made it through the next hour like a sleepwalker, with a calm unreality that was the only thing that kept her from collapsing in a heap.

Unable to stand being away from him for an instant longer, Amanda brought some necessities into Daniel's room. She performed a quick, cursory toilet while

Jakob went back to the house and got a pot of oxtail soup from Helga. He stayed carefully out of Amanda's way as she hovered over Daniel's bed while he slurped it, her hands fluttering around him again and again as she touched his forehead, his cheeks, his neck, assuring herself that he was really cool, that the fever was truly gone. He grumpily jerked away from her fussing and grumbled about being treated like a baby when she held a cup of warm, nutmeg-dusted milk to his lips.

Her gaze never wavering from him, as if she were afraid that, if she looked away for an instant, he would disappear, she stood by his bed while he drifted back to sleep; a normal, healing sleep, a single quilt snugged around his shoulders, his breathing even and smooth.

And then her shoulders began to shake as the weeping rolled up within her, deep, welling, fierce sobs that jerked her chest and bent her over from the waist.

"Oh, Amy." Jakob had his arms around her in an instant, her head tucked against his sturdy shoulder as he led her from her son's room and into her own. "It's okay, Amy. It's okay."

He sat down on the edge of her unmade bed, sliding her into his lap, and he pulled her close. She buried her face against his chest, muffling the harsh sounds. Her hot tears soaked through the thin cotton of his shirt and wet his skin.

He slid his hands through the unbound tangle of her hair, gently freeing the knots that snarled the fine strands. He rubbed her neck, her back, her shoulders, and she burrowed closer, as if she could simply be absorbed into him, and he half wished she could.

And then, because he could think of nothing else to soothe her, and he could no longer bear to listen to her cry, he cradled her head in his hands, tipped it back, and kissed her. Little nothings, light, bare brushes of his mouth over her skin, touching away her tears. Over the smooth, silky curve of her eyebrows and along the wet, rounded slope of her cheeks.

His lips rested briefly on her temple, where her pulse beat close to the surface of delicate skin, then whispered along the edge of her damp hairline. Spiky eyelashes; faint little crinkles at the corners of her eyes that would probably turn into appealing wrinkles in a few years, if he were lucky enough to see them. He tasted the salt from her tears, underlain by the impossible sweetness of her skin.

He hadn't meant it to become any more. He'd only wanted to smooth away a bit of her pain. But she gave another sob and turned her head, her lips brushing his, and he didn't have the will to turn away.

His hands slid to her waist; he didn't need to hold her head in place. Her mouth remained, hot and wet, trembling like rose petals in the breeze. She was soft, her breasts pillowed against his chest, her rear settled neatly in his lap, and warmth was quickly sparking into heat.

"Amy," he whispered against her lips, trying to draw back, to use words to find sanity. She tilted her head, fitting her mouth better to his, and he forgot words.

She hadn't intended it, either. Hadn't meant to use him for comfort, for safety, for anything more. But there were simply too many emotions spinning through her; fear, relief, gratitude, joy, pain, and she had no other release for them. They whirled through her, twisting in her heart, and focused on him, on the butterfly-soft touch of his mouth, on the hard, solid nearness of his body. She wanted to curl around him, in him, find a way to get him close enough so that there would always be a part of him in her.

He pulled back, taking his lips from hers, drawing in a shuddering breath. She nearly cried again at his absence, at the cool rush of air that replaced the warmth of his mouth.

"Amy," he said, voice harsh and strained, "you told me you didn't want this."

She bit her lip, hard, hoping the pain would bring her to her senses. But there was only more sensation, raw and wild, and she just wanted him to calm the sting with the slide of his tongue.

His eyes were dark, deep, fiercely studying her; his nostrils flared as he drew in a ragged breath, and she knew. He was trying to be kind, trying to give her a choice, but he wanted, too. Every bit as acutely, every bit as deeply, every bit as profoundly. Even if it didn't happen now, it would happen soon. In celebration, in sadness; in anger, fear, or comfort. Did it matter which? It only mattered that it was *him*.

Air was thick in her lungs. She was grateful for the shimmering light from the lantern, so she could see his face, all blunt bones and bronzed skin. She swallowed and reached for his hand, risking what she had never risked—being the one to reach out first—and drew his palm to her breast.

He left it there, unmoving, unbelieving, as his gaze fell to her chest. That was *his* hand, big and scarred and awkward, on her, so dark against the pure, rumpled white of her tucked shirt. He could feel her heart, the heavy, slow thud in her chest; there was the faintest suggestion of her nipple, hard and pointed, under the layers of cloth. Oh, God, he thought. Was that for him? Had he caused her response?

There were no more fortunate accidents; he meant to kiss her this time, his breath escaping in a groan. She was waiting for him, her mouth open, her tongue impatient to begin the dark dance.

The golden lamplight threw twisting, shuddering

shadows on the dim wall. Jakob's voice was low, his breathing harsh; his fingers were blunt and clumsy as he struggled with buttons and ties and laces.

She was utterly quiet, her breathing only a faint whisper of sound, but her hands were quick, relentless, racing over his body, a fluttering touch, expertly flicking open his buttons.

Ah, but he was a strong man, she thought, gaining bare flesh at last. His chest felt exactly as she'd imagined, rounded with heavy swells of muscles that were hard and unyielding under her fingertips. His arms bulged and the cords of his neck grew taut as she skimmed them with her mouth.

He fumbled at the throat of her blouse and she finally had to help him. Still tucked into her waistband, it fell loose around her waist. His fingers snagged on the delicate straps of her chemise, the rough texture of his hands a wonderful abrasion against her skin. He slipped the thin ribbons off her shoulders, the fine cloth sliding down, freeing the heavy curves of her breasts.

He was unbelievably tender, his touch slow and his eyes filled with wonder. His hands closed around her waist, and he lifted her, bringing her breasts up to the level of his mouth. Her head fell back on the sudden burst of pleasure as his lips closed around her nipple, gently tugging, the slow, gliding rasp of his tongue an almost unbearable incitement.

She wrapped her arms around his head to hold him close, his hair a soft tickle on the insides of her forearms.

There was everything here, Jakob found. Darkness and sunshine, sweetness and spice. All those mysterious, female things that made him yearn, made him sweat, made him dream. Things he'd tried hard to never want, had tried to ignore. But now there was nothing else for him in the world, nothing but the pale gleam of her skin and the deep hollow between her breasts. He lowered her back down to sit sideways on his lap once more as he licked his way back up to her neck, her jaw, her mouth, that were all there waiting for him. Just for him.

Unable to help himself, he pressed up into her softness, twice, jerking at the sudden explosion of heat. She gasped; no sound, but he could feel the rush of air out of her chest. And then she scrambled up, her body twisting rapidly in his arms, and he couldn't do more than brush his fingers over her sliding skin.

She turned to face him fully, her knees tucked along his hips. The hot, hard points of her nipples seared his chest. Her fingers were busy again, this time on the buttons of his trousers. He knew that he should stop her but he couldn't find the will.

"There," she whispered as the cloth came free, "Finally."

Gently, she wrapped her fingers around his erection. No surprises, she had thought. She was not innocent, and there would be no surprises for her here. But there were, in how she wanted, so much, too much, to be filled with him. In the way she was thrilled with the feel of him, blunt and broad and hard, tipped with a drop of moisture that she had caused.

His hands were slow, moving up under her skirts, sliding up the outside of her legs, a slight whisk over the underwear that covered her. She hated the thin layer of cotton between them, wanted it gone. So she lifted up, reached under her own skirts, and tried to tug her drawers away.

It was awkward, slow; four hands, trying to hurry, and two people who didn't want to separate, couldn't stop kissing, couldn't come apart long enough to make it easy. She smiled against his mouth, astonished that she could feel so lighthearted, even when the keen, desperate edge of passion threatened to slice her in two.

They peeled her drawers off finally, managing to tear the fragile fabric only a bit. Jakob impatiently tossed them over his shoulder and brought his hands back to her, bringing her bare chest tight up to his. Closer, closer; he couldn't seem to get her close enough.

She was more impatient than he. She lifted her skirts in her hands and rose to her knees, sliding against him, searching until she found what she wanted, pushing herself right down on his hardness.

"Amy, stop," he said hoarsely, "Please, let me—" His words broke off when she lifted and settled again, a quick, wet glide along his full length, taking him completely into her body.

She couldn't stop. Not now, not ever. She had to have him deeper, closer, though she was stretched nearly to the point of pain right now. She felt the burn of tears behind her lids, and clutched his head to her chest, hugging him close. Always close.

"Amy!"

She moved her hips again, a subtle rocking, and he growled harshly. His hands went to her waist, holding her down, fully against him. And then he was shaking, shuddering in her arms, pulsing deep inside her, and she knew this was what she needed most of all. Her Jakob, giving part of himself to her.

He was finally still, his head still resting limply on her breast, his arms squeezing around her back.

"I'm sorry," he said, his mouth moving against her skin as he spoke, the wash of his breath hot, "I'm sorry. I didn't mean it to be like—"

"Don't you dare be sorry!" She closed her eyes and swallowed. "It's what I wanted. Don't be sorry."

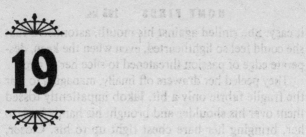

19

He smelled roses. Roses and woman and sex. The skin of Amy's breast was warm and moist against his cheek. Her fingers slid slowly through his hair. His arms were filled with her, bare skin and the bulky bunch of her clothing around her waist. He felt himself soften within her body, and felt the faint flutter of her heart against his cheek.

Half of him was stunned, delirious with joy, filled with a warm wealth of emotion he'd never known, never suspected.

The other half of him was terrified.

Scared to death he'd disappointed her. That he'd never be able to make it up to her, never be able to give her one tenth of what she'd just given him. He cursed his lack of skill, the absence of experience he'd never bothered to worry about before.

Only once. Only once, on a rare trip to St. Paul, when he'd gone to the theatre and received a note to meet the singer backstage. He'd come nearly as soon as she'd touched him then, too, but she'd only laughed softly, took his hand, and spent the rest of the night teaching him a few things.

Not much to draw on. Not nearly enough, for that distant, pleasant interlude had nothing to do with this, this deep and desperate passion that was only for Amy. Only for her.

But it would have to be enough. Somehow, it would have to be enough.

He angled his head, opened his mouth, taking her nipple inside. It responded to the slow stroke of his tongue, rucking up immediately, and her fingers stilled against his head.

They were still sitting awkwardly entangled on the edge of the bed. Fool, he called himself. He'd forgotten even that. He lifted her, suppressing a small groan when his body slipped free of hers, and turned, laying her carefully back on the rumpled sheets, setting his fingers to work, divesting her of her clothing as he should already have done.

"What . . . what are you doing?" she said faintly.

"Please." He paused and drew his fingers down her jaw, his touch as gentle as he could make it. Somehow, some way, he would find a way to make this right. If only she would give him the chance. "Let me."

Wordless, her eyes wide and bright with the pale gold reflection of the lamplight, she nodded. The strings that held her clothing were delicate and knotted, making his hands seem too big and too clumsy. She helped, lifting her hips at his urging to make it easier, until she lay naked, her deep curves shadowed and lit with the light, and his breath came out in a low hiss.

He slipped off the rest of his clothes and joined her; the bed creaked beneath their weight. She was too beautiful, her complexion pale and glowing as a pearl, and he studied her face carefully, watching for any sign that would help him learn her response.

Her skin was gossamer silk beneath his palm. Nothing in the world could be softer, he thought. Nothing. But then he reached farther down, nudging her legs wide to give him access, and he knew he'd been wrong. For this was softer, sleek and hot and heaven. He didn't know whether the slick moisture was from her or him or the two of them together, and the thought made him wild with wanting her again.

"What are you doing?" she asked, her voice high and strained.

"I think we tried that question already." Horribly uncertain, wonderfully eager, he probed lightly, seeking. "There's a place . . ."

He felt her sudden stillness. She looked at him a long moment, searching his face, her lower lip tucked uncertainly under her teeth. And then she reached down, taking his hand, guided it a bit over, and sucked in her breath abruptly.

She was the most incredibly exciting thing he had ever seen. He was determined, awkward but filled with the need to do this for her. He watched her, as her eyelids fluttered closed and her mouth opened. Her neck bowed, light shimmering down the curve, her body arching into his hand, her lush breasts quivering. When a soft cry escaped her, he thought that he would burst, too, and her shuddering, straining response was surely the one thing in his life that would remain this sharp, this clear, in his mind forever, no matter what happened to him. He knew that nothing could ever be as sexy, ever be as erotic, as watching this woman shudder at his touch.

She quieted, in long, soft seconds that were brushed with gold. Carefully, he slipped his thumb deeply inside her, causing one last, vivid tremor as she tightened inside around his finger. She opened her eyes to look at him, and she gifted him, her mouth curved up in a tentative, wondrous smile.

Thank God. His prayer was swift and thankful; he'd not made such a mess of it after all.

He lifted himself over her, taking his weight on his elbows, and her eyes opened wide when he slid swiftly inside her.

"Already?"

"Already," he said, smiling at her surprise, and the magic began again.

It was then that Amanda Sellington learned about love. About the wonder of having Jakob lodged deeply within her body, his hips completely still, as his hands and mouth worshiped every inch of her skin. Of whimpering, shattering passion molded and softened by tenderness. She no longer knew where she ended and he began, and she couldn't summon the will to care.

He linked his hands with hers, pulling them over her head. They touched everywhere then; pressed together down all the inside lengths of their arms, mouths fused, tongues meeting, their torsos tight, their bellies rubbing, legs lying fully tangled. Everywhere. Inside, outside, their skin touched, and it still wasn't enough.

For her, sex had always been about taking, feelings stolen from her against her will.

But Jakob didn't take.

He *gave*.

She slept the entire night through.

The next morning, she woke as weak early light leaked into the room, and wondered at it. She'd missed the thickest, blackest part of the night—no nightmares, no bleak memories, no stark clench of fear. Just sleep, for the first time in longer than she could remember.

And Jakob had, too.

She turned in the bed, the sheets slipping decadently down around her bare hips, to look at him. They'd slept holding hands, and hers was still securely locked in his grasp.

He looked impossibly large in her small bed, a big, bulky male out of place against her white sheets with the thin flutter of lace at the edge. His other arm was thrown up over his head, which was turned toward her. His face was relaxed, young, a rogue curl of hair sticking straight up over his ear.

There was nothing young about the rest of him. The covers pooled low on his body, just beneath where a fine line of hair bisected his belly. She reveled in the luxury of looking her fill, at the power and strength that years of hefting barrels had given him and the pure male beauty they'd wrought.

There was no doubt the man looked impossibly fine, naked in bed, with the soft wash of rose-gray light. If she'd had only one wish, she would have spent it foolishly, on wishing she could stay right there and simply look at him.

But she needed to check on Daniel. She eased her hand away from his, and he frowned a bit in his sleep, then gave a groan and flopped over.

She snatched a wrapper and threw it on as she walked quickly through the small cottage, the floorboards icy against her bare feet. Daniel woke up the instant she crossed the threshold to his room.

"Good morning, Mama. I'm hungry again."

She laughed and promised him breakfast as soon as she'd checked his forehead, finding, to her relief, that his temperature seemed normal.

He gulped down two bowls of her watery oatmeal, disguised by generous helpings of cream and sugar. She teased him that being ill seemed to have been good for his appetite, for he was eating more than she'd ever been able to urge down him otherwise.

"Maybe your cooking is getting better," he suggested, a beautiful twinkle back in his eye as he swallowed the last spoonful. "But then again, I don't think so."

"Brat," she said softly, ruffling his hair, almost overwhelmed with gratitude at this gift she'd been given, being able to tease him again.

His body still needed a lot of rest before he was completely back to normal, however, and he dropped back off to sleep almost as soon as he finished his oatmeal.

She returned to the kitchen and dumped the dirty pot and bowl into the dishpan, finding an odd, new joy in the everyday task. For it meant things were returning to normal, a routine that had been impossible when she'd been terrified for Daniel's life.

But not everything was the same. The proof of that was still in her bed.

Passing back through the sitting room, she caught sight of her reflection in the tiny mirror that hung over a sturdy side table.

So that's what an adulteress looks like, she thought.

She didn't look like a scarlet woman. There was no sign of decadence around her eyes, no slash of immorality on her mouth that she could detect.

Instead there was a high flush on her skin, a hint of softness and warmth in her eyes. Maybe a faint puffiness on her mouth that marked her. Nothing horrible. She rather thought she appeared much as she always had.

I am an adulteress, she thought again. A sinner. And I don't care.

For in one night, Jakob's touch had managed to push away so many years. Had managed to blot out so many terrible memories, to displace fears she'd been sure she would always struggle with.

For *that* was what it was supposed to be like, she was certain. Not like it had been for her, cold and dark and linked with pain. It was supposed to be about joy. Joy and affection and sharing. About waking up the next morning glad of the night before.

Was that such a horrible sin? Was she damned?

She lifted her hand to the glass, tracing her fingers down her reflection, smudging the polished surface.

What about Jakob? He'd committed adultery, too. Was his soul in danger if he didn't know what he'd done? She hadn't wanted to do that to him. Please, God, she could take his sin on her, too. It hadn't been his fault. Nothing had been his fault.

She thought he was still sleeping. But when she pushed open the door to her bedroom, she found him propped up against the pillows, his gaze focused on her, his face serious and unreadable.

"I . . ." Her voice trailed off helplessly. She had no idea what to say.

"I thought I'd better stay in here. I didn't suppose you wanted me wandering around out there while Daniel was up."

"No, I . . ." She hadn't thought about it. Well, quite honestly, she hadn't thought at all. And now she was going to have to deal with it. "Oh, Lord! What about Helga? How are you going to explain being gone all night? We—"

"We probably just made Helga a very happy woman." He grinned then, like sunlight, a much-needed morning breaking through the night. That's what he was for her, the brilliant morning she'd never thought to find. "I think we'd better make some decisions about the wedding before we go back and face her." He fluffed his pillows more comfortably. The rugged flex of his muscles doing that simple thing made her want to touch him again. Had there ever been a man as beautifully made?

"The wedding?"

"Of course."

"But we can't get married!" she burst out.

He went absolutely quiet and still. She looked down, at the bright circles of rag rugs on the floor, because she couldn't look at the shock on his face and know that she had caused it.

He moved swiftly, quietly, until he stood before her, completely naked, close enough that she could catch a hint of his warmth.

"And just why is that?" he asked, his voice very soft.

Oh, God. *Because I am already married*—it echoed in her brain, her heart, a sharp stab of words every bit as painful as a blade.

She couldn't tell him. She could not draw him into her deception, into her sin.

Somehow, she must find a way to convince him of the impossibility of their marriage. Finally, irrevocably. So he would never think there was a chance she would change her mind. It was the only thing she could do for him.

Bleakness crept in, settled firmly into her heart, dirtying all the clean, bright happiness she'd felt this morning.

Last night had been all she would ever have. And now she would lose his friendship, his companionship, as surely as she would lose what they'd shared last night. She could survive the loss of his body, his lovemaking.

She was not so certain she would survive the loss of his presence in her life.

What could she tell him? What would convince him of the futility?

Nothing that he could take as blame. He must know it was not his fault. Never, ever his fault. She could never hurt him like that, never leave him with a hint that there was some inadequacy in him that caused her to reject him.

It must be her fault. She needed to, somehow, make him believe it was her fault.

She swallowed heavily, wondering if she would find the control to keep her voice steady, as it must be. Yes, she would. She had to, and she would do it for him.

"I would guess that must be obvious," she said, surprised at the evenness of her tone. But she couldn't look at him; there was a dark knot in the oak boards of the floor, a wound in the wood, and she stared there instead. "After last night. You must have noticed I am a woman of . . . strong passions."

Her nails cut into her palms. Was she bleeding yet? Surely she was, even if it was not where it showed. "I enjoy the pleasures of the flesh. You are quite pleasurable, of course. All that strength and . . . enthusiasm. But I have always found it difficult to limit my . . . entertainments . . . to one man. I do not wish to do so now."

All women are whores. Edward's words came back to her, from that cold, dead place inside her where she'd tried to keep them walled up behind a thin shield. Somehow, they always managed to leak through and hurt her. Little had she known how useful they would be. "I intend to enjoy my freedom fully."

Silence. Dead, empty silence, the silence of her future. She was certain she could hear the beating of her own heart, an uneven, echoing ticking, like an old clock in a room no one bothered to go into anymore.

"Amy," he said steadily, no inflection marring the flat tones of his voice. "Look at me."

She couldn't. If she looked at him, she would see it in his eyes. The condemnation, the revulsion. She knew she had to send him away; she had no choice. But please, God, she did not have to look at him. For if she did, her heart would surely shatter, into a million, worthless, lusterless pieces that could never be fit back together.

His hand, his tender, rough-textured, workman's hand, cupped her chin and forced her to tilt her head back and meet his eyes. Dark, beautiful, intently serious eyes that gave nothing of his thoughts away.

Oh, God, she thought. Here it comes. She would never survive it.

His eyes squinted in what she knew was
anger. A small muscle twitched beside his mouth.

And then he broke out laughing. A deep, full laughter that bent him at the waist and rumbled through the
room.

She couldn't believe it. A big, stark-naked man,
who'd just been told that the woman he'd spent the
night with and expected to marry was a slut, was
standing in the middle of her bedroom and laughing.

She'd been so certain of his disgust. So sure of
impending pain. And he was amused.

Mentally, she ran through what she'd told him.
Where had she gone wrong? What hadn't she said?

Perhaps it was simply that he didn't believe she'd be
able to attract all those lovers that she claimed. She
knew she was hardly a raving beauty, but she'd been
quite certain that Jakob, at least, found her appealing.

"What exactly is so funny?" Miffed, she crossed her
arms over her chest.

"I'm sorry." He sobered, but humor lurked at the corners of his mouth, threatening to break out again any minute. Absurdly, it made her want to kiss him. He cupped her face, his thumbs stroking down her cheekbones. "But honestly, Amy, did you really think I would believe that? Don't you think I know by now what kind of a woman you are?"

"What kind of a woman I am?" she repeated, stunned.

"Yes. I certainly know you're not a woman to give yourself cheaply or freely. I can't believe you thought I'd fall for that."

He trusted her. How? Why?

Edward had never trusted her, not even at the beginning. And now, so easily, unconditionally, without any proof, Jakob trusted her this much.

Something inside her softened, eased. Tears prickled at the back of her eyes; she wanted to throw her arms around him and hug him tight for what he'd just given her. Another gift, freely given.

But it was one she hadn't earned. He couldn't trust her, *shouldn't* trust her. She was lying to him, and she was going to continue to lie to him.

"Now that we've gotten that out of the way," he said, still standing so near that his body brushed hers, just as his thumbs brushed her cheeks. "Are you going to tell me what the problem really is?"

"I—" She stopped, her breath lodging in her chest. Through the thin layer of her wrapper, she could feel his body hardening against her. She looked down before she thought to stop herself.

"Sorry." He dropped his hands and stepped away, and she felt a sharp, traitorous surge of disappointment. "I can't stand that close to you."

He stood there easily, unashamed, his hands on

his hips as the bright morning light glowed yellow and clear, his . . . condition . . . plainly evident. Stepping away didn't seem to have any effect. She dared not look at him, but she couldn't *not* look at him. She caught the unrepentant grin on his face and knew that was exactly what he wanted.

"Well . . . for one thing . . ." She desperately tried to come up with another reason. One he'd accept this time. "You told me your plans, Jakob. I know you're simply waiting for the time you can leave New Ulm and go on to find a life of your own someplace else. I can't do that; I don't want to do that. I'm staying here. And I refuse to take that away from you. I'd never forgive myself."

That wiped the smile from his face instantly. Now he was angry. She tried to remember if she'd ever seen him angry before. Certainly not like this. And he was every bit as magnificent as when he was smiling.

"And you think it's your place to decide this?" he asked, raising his voice.

"Shh," she said. "Daniel's sleeping."

"Sorry." He softened his voice, if not his stance. "But what do you think? That I don't know what I want?"

Me, she thought, staggered and thrilled by the thought. He wants *me.* But she wasn't free to give. "Can you honestly tell me you don't wish for that anymore? To leave this place and see the world?"

It was brief, but she caught the flash of guilt and regret in his eyes. "I will not take that away from you, Jakob. Just because you think that, after what happened last night, you must do the right thing by me. I do not want your sacrifice."

"I am a man, Amy, not a spoiled child." His anger gentled. "A man who knows well that our lives do not always run as planned. I have never wasted time on regrets. And I have no intention of spending the rest of my life regretting letting you go. So I'm not letting you go."

If only. Happiness tempted her, a precious golden dream just beyond her reach. And she couldn't even attempt to take it.

She shook her head. "The answer is still no, Jakob."

"And what if we—" he hesitated, an odd note creeping into his voice "—what if we created a child last night?"

A child. For only an instant, she saw a brief vision of a tiny, dark-haired infant with Jakob's deep brown eyes snuggled up against her breast, but she wanted it with an intensity that was almost unbearable. And it could never, ever be.

"I . . ." The words were difficult, forced around the lump in her throat. "There have been no children, all these years, after Daniel. I really doubt I can conceive."

"Maybe we got lucky."

Oh, God, she thought. Why now? Why did I meet him now? Why not when we could have had a chance?

"I can't marry you, Jakob. Don't ask me again, please."

"Is it your husband?"

Her knees nearly buckled. "My husband?"

"Yes." He ran a hand through his hair. "I know that you loved him. You have some odd idea that being with me is unfaithful to him?"

She closed her eyes in relief. "Something like that."

He moved back within arms' reach. Amanda twisted her fists in the belt of her wrapper to keep from stretching out to touch him, to keep from sliding her hands down the ridge of his abdomen one more time.

"Well then, Amy," he said, his voice a seductive rumble, "I guess I'll just have to change your mind."

* * *

He was being unusually patient, he thought. He gave her until almost the end of September.

Though the days were still sunny and unusually clear, the nights were longer and cooler. Nights in which he paced the length of his stretch of the valley and wondered how he'd become accustomed to sleeping beside her in only one night. A night in which he hadn't even slept all that much, come to think of it.

The fields up on the flats dried into harvest gold; flocks of blackbirds roosted there, growing fat on the grain. A hussy of a sumac down by the Cottonwood gained its garish fall scarlet. And Jakob thought of Amy.

So today, on his way to town, he stopped and knocked on the cottage door.

She eased it open slowly, and his breath slammed into his chest. So beautiful; he'd forgotten how beautiful she was. For the last weeks, he'd only caught glimpses of her. Sometimes she slipped out the back of the house from visiting Helga just as he got home from work; once or twice, when he walked around the grounds, he could see her, bathed in lamplight, through the lace-shielded windows of the cottage as she bent over supper with Daniel.

He'd been so sure he knew what she looked like. But now, with her hair twisted up into a chignon, all sheeny and soft-looking brown, and her pale, pure skin set off by the flutter of ice-blue ruffle at her neckline, he realized he'd completely underestimated her impact on him. And he'd counted her effect on him as pretty damn high, as it was.

"I was just on my way to town." He jerked a thumb over his shoulder in the direction of the wagon. "Have to drop off the rest of the *Wiesenbier*—the meadow beer—for the festival. I thought I'd stop and see how you are—how Daniel is," he added hastily.

She wiped her hands on the limp dishrag she was carrying, then flipped it over her shoulder. "He's fine. We're both fine."

Jakob shifted his weight. "Are you—do you have enough work? Without coming in to the office, I mean."

Damn! He hated this, this awkward, floundering conversation between them, when he'd always been so comfortable with her.

She tilted her head and a loose swath of hair fell against her neck, just under her ear, and he swallowed. He knew exactly what her skin felt like there, the way her pulse simmered close to the surface and trembled against his mouth.

"Fine. I still haven't gotten the machine, of course, but I've gotten some handwork. Mrs. Kaufenburg, and some of her friends. They've been very kind to me. I keep busy enough."

She still stood in her doorway, and he was outside in the path, several feet away, as if he were a stranger she dared not invite in. *Enough!* he thought.

"I wanted to invite you to come to the *Oktoberfest* with me."

"Oh, Jakob." She leaned against the doorway, fingering the pearly buttons that marched up the front of her bodice. "You know we can't."

"Why not?"

"You know the answer to that."

"No, damn it, I don't." His glasses were slipping down his nose, and he jabbed them back into place. "We are not even allowed to be friends, too? We have the boys in common, and this place. Do we have to give it all up just because we lost our heads for one night?"

She hesitated, and he could see she was tempted. "Do you really think we can? Go back to the friendship, I mean?"

"Of course." He felt a bit guilty, knowing he was allowing her to believe something that wasn't the precise truth. He had every intention of retaining the friendship, but he certainly planned on having a whole lot more than that.

But he knew good and well they were right together, damn it, and they needed time together for her to see it. If the only way he could get her to do that was by giving her a slightly twisted impression of his motives, well, then, that was just the way it would have to be. He just needed enough time for her to get over whatever ridiculous idea she'd gotten in her head that was keeping her from marrying him.

One of her hands was skittering up and down the wood that framed the doorway. Her hands were the only part of her that wasn't calm and controlled; he remembered, far too well, what it had felt like to have those hands playing quickly, enticingly over him.

He stepped closer, looking up into her eyes. Soft, hazel eyes that he fully intended to spend the rest of his life looking into, trying to pick out all the different colors that jumbled together there.

"I miss you, Amy."

Her fingers curled tightly around the doorjamb. "Oh, Jakob, I miss you, too."

Though Jakob told Amanda on the way to town the *Oktoberfest* was first celebrated to honor a royal wedding, it didn't take her long to decide there was really only one reason for the festival: for everyone to have as good a time as humanly possible.

The town was stuffed with people; surely all who lived in the surrounding countryside, as well as most of the nearby towns, were there. The streets were clogged with wagons and horses. All of the town's shops were doing a booming business, customers and special merchandise spilling out onto the busy streets.

The festival itself barely squeezed into both North and South German Park, separated by two blocks and Center Street. There was color, more color than she'd ever seen in her whole life. The leaves on the trees that clung to the sides of the valley were painted with red and orange, glowing like fire in the strong gold of the autumn sun. The parks were lined with brightly hued tents selling nutcrackers and elaborately painted furniture; quilts; and *Fraktur*, papers beautifully decorated with thick, curvy calligraphy and watercolors.

It started precisely at noon, when the church bells rang through the town. Jakob tapped the first barrel of the special beer he'd made and Amanda felt an unwelcome but totally undeniable swell of pride. After he downed the first stein, foam spilling over the sides and down his hands, a cheer went up. The sounds never seemed to stop for the rest of the day.

Bands played the entire afternoon, the music clashing and tangling with the constant chatter, English and German competing with the sprightly wail of the concertina. The music always seemed fast and full; no slow ballad from a single instrument here. All the bands were large, filled with brass instruments and a big, determined bass drum whose steady pounding seemed to set the pace for her thrilled heartbeat.

Amanda thought she'd never been so happy. She'd certainly never been so full, as Jakob insisted she try every bit of food that they came across. The air was rich with the smell of roast chicken and fish broiled on sticks; they tried so many different sausages that she couldn't remember which was which, and tiny, honey-sweetened pastries shaped like stars and hearts and animals.

Jakob even talked her into dipping into a stein of his *Wiesenbier.* It was much too strong for her taste, and she wondered how much of the bouyant feeling that seemed to keep her floating merrily through the day came from that beer.

Now, as she bent over the tiny carved gnomes in a tent, she chanced a glance at him out of the corner of her eye. For the festival, most of the people in New Ulm wore what Helga called their *Trachten,* their traditional dress, and Jakob was no exception. The suspenders of his leather shorts were a dark slash against his light-colored shirt, an ornamental breastband decorated his chest, and thick, woolen knee-high stockings hugged his calves.

She knew that all those elegant, fashionable people she'd known in New York would have laughed at the ridiculousness of his clothes. But all she could seem to think of was that he had really fine legs. There were certain advantages to those short pants, she mused, and decided that perhaps she had never really belonged in New York.

Maybe she'd always belonged here. Here, where the sun beat through skies that were never fogged with smoke and the people smiled at her as if she'd always known them. Where the only things that seemed to matter were family and work and fun, and no one wasted much time on envy and the convoluted games of intrigue and competition that Edward thrived on.

Where Daniel was so happy. He dashed into the tent on the heels of Nicolaus and the half-dozen little boys who'd spent the day in a pack, like puppies, tumbling through the festival, finding their way back to their parents only when they needed a few more coins to buy a cake or wager on a game.

It amazed her that she could stand to have Daniel out of her sight, here in this crowd of people. But she knew he was safe; nothing untoward could happen to him here. Because it was that very crowd of people that protected him; everyone seemed to keep a guardian's eye on the children, just as she herself had snagged a small blond girl who'd seemed bent on climbing up the back of the bandstand.

She watched as Jakob bent down to the children. He grinned as he pulled out yet a bit more money and handed it to the two boys. He was a soft touch, that one; he didn't seem to know how to say no to the two of them. Though she knew he was spoiling them, she couldn't find it in her to stop him. Not today.

"Bye, Mama!" Daniel shouted and ran back out of the tent with his friends.

Jakob straightened and looked her way, his gaze settling unerringly on her. His smile broadened, and he walked over to her, out of the sunlight and into the dusky shadows of the tent. His fingertip caught her underneath her chin, and he tipped her head back. "Well, well," he said softly. "What is this?"

"What?"

"This particular look on your face, Mrs. Smith."

His grin was entirely too self-satisfied for her peace of mind. Annoyed that he could read her feelings so easily, she swatted his hand away. "It's this—" she grabbed for the nearest figure "—it's this gnome, that's all. I think I'm in love."

The figure was tiny and wrinkled, its carved mouth cheerfully scrunched into a smile, with bulging round cheeks, eyes popped wide, and a perky red cap perched on its head.

"You like this one, do you?" he said dubiously, frowning at the appealingly ugly face.

"Yes I do."

"Why?"

"He looks sort of like you, don't you think?" she teased.

His smile vanished; the intensity that sparked in his eyes was powerful, a look she'd seen only once before, during the night she was trying very hard to forget.

"But you said that you thought you were in love," he said slowly.

Oh, no. It had tripped right out of her mouth before she'd even realized what she was saying. It couldn't be. She wouldn't allow it to be. But she couldn't seem to find the words to tell him he was wrong.

"With the gnome," she reminded him.

"Which looks like me."

"I—" She was hopeless, she thought. She couldn't even find the strength to do what she knew was the right thing.

There was too much between them, too many hopes and fears and dreams. But after a long moment, he relaxed, the smile coming back to his face, and she realized he was going to let her off the hook this time. So why wasn't she more grateful?

"We'll take it," he said to the white-haired, dirndl-clad woman who ran the booth and who was watching them with undisguised amusement.

"Please don't buy me anything else," she protested. "You've been feeding me all day long."

"They're good luck." He would hear no more about it, and quickly paid for the gnome, arranging with the woman to have it delivered to the office he kept in town so they could stop by and pick it up on their way home.

"Now then," he said, escorting her back out from under the shade of the tent. She blinked at the bright light. "What would you like to do now?"

They'd been out in the sun most of the day, and a dusky flush of color deepened the tan over his cheekbones. A tiny shadow of his beard was beginning to show, dark texture along the angle of his broad jaw, and she realized that what she would *like* to do was the thing she absolutely should not.

He looked over her shoulder and frowned. "Come on." He grabbed her hand and tugged her toward the cleared area in front the bandstand, where couples bobbed along with the music. "We're going to dance."

"I've never danced to this kind of music."

"I'll teach you," he said under his breath. "Oh, hello, Brigitte," he added loudly. He pulled Amanda along, right past a very determined-looking Brigitte Kiesling, who looked fresh and very healthy in a low-cut dirndl with tiny cap sleeves. "Can't stop to chat now. Amy insists that I have to teach her to dance."

21

She didn't want to dance with him. It would be too difficult to be held close against his body, the two of them enclosed in a circle of music and motion, to be given a hint of something she could never have again.

Instead, he taught her to *Schottische*. It wasn't even just the two of them; it apparently took four people, and the Voehringers joined in as soon as he'd demonstrated the basic steps, laughing as he danced circles around her.

It was more like skipping than dancing, she thought. They bounced around the packed earth-and-grass oval that served as a dance floor until she began to breathe a little harder with the exertion. Around her, other foursomes hopped through complicated series of turns and position changes.

One of her arms was stuck forward, grabbing onto Margarite Voehringer's. Her other hand was held safely in Jakob's; his was strong, broad, and gentle, just like he was, and she was suddenly so glad she'd had the chance to know him. Loose waves of his hair tapped against his forehead with his dance steps, and a small bead of perspiration gleamed on his temple. He glanced over at her and smiled, his grin full of appreciation and enjoyment.

It felt like the sun overhead was seeping right into her body, into her soul, filling her from the inside out with spreading warmth. It was heady and wonderful and she felt like, if she could just stop the world right now, this would be enough.

There was nothing better in life than this. Her son was safe and well, each day a bit less touched by the fear and uncertainty that Edward had beat into him. And every day, she shed a bit more of the shadows herself; the darkness had no defense against this new sunshine.

And she had Jakob. If what they would have between them couldn't be everything she might have wished, it was still so much better than anything she had ever had before. She would be happy with this; she would learn not to be greedy for more. She had no choice.

"Hey, Amy." There was a sharp tug on her skirts. Nicolaus was trying to get her attention.

"I think I'm out of money for cakes, Nicolaus," she said, and paused in her hopping, though she did not withdraw her hand from Jakob's. It felt too good right where it was. That was the essential appeal of dancing—she had a good excuse to hold his hand. "You'd better try and pry it out of your uncle instead."

He frowned, looking so much like Jakob she wanted to scoop him up and hug him. "I think maybe you'd better come."

"Where's Daniel?" she asked sharply.

"Oh, he's right over there." He pointed through the

joggling circles of dancers. "Just not feeling so good, I don't think."

"Let's go see," said Jakob. He quickly made excuses to the Voehringers, then shouldered his way through the crowds.

Daniel looked miserable, leaning against one of the posts that supported the bandstand.

"What's the matter?" Amanda flew to him, touching the back of her hand to his forehead. "Open your mouth so I can look at your throat."

"Wait a second." Jakob squatted down on his heels, the big muscles of his thighs straining the legs of his shorts. "How many sausages did you have, Daniel?"

Daniel groaned. "Six, I think."

"And maybe a little bit of beer?"

"Beer!" Amanda shrieked. "Why would anyone—"

Jakob cut her off with a jerk of his hand. "Around here, beer is like bread. No one would think twice about giving him a glassful." He turned his attention back to Daniel, his voice soft and comforting. "Now then. Maybe a little beer?"

Daniel slanted a worried glance at his mother, then gave a small nod.

"So your stomach's not feeling so good, huh?"

Daniel clutched his stomach with both hands. "Uh-uh."

"Okay." Jakob took Daniel's hand and straightened. "How about we get you home."

Karl hurried an out-of-breath Helga into Jakob's small office on the second floor of Erd's Building and slammed the door behind him.

"Now," he said in satisfaction. He pulled out a straight-backed chair and settled her into it, her back to the door, then planted himself in front of her, his big legs spraddled wide.

"What is this?" Helga said in a huff, bristling with indignation. "Why do you drag me up to Jakob's office? What are we doing here?"

"It is the only place we could be alone." Karl hooked his fingers into his suspenders, and Helga caught her breath in spite of herself. In his *Lederhosen*, Karl was certainly a handsome figure of a man. "At the house, there are always the children or Jakob or whoever else you pull around you so you do not have to talk to me. Well, I have had enough!" he roared, the wisps of white hair that rimmed his bald head flying out in abandon.

"Karl!" Her heart fluttered in her chest, and Helga pressed a hand there to try and still it. "I do not know what you mean."

"*Nein!* We will not pretend any longer. I have had enough of pretending."

"Karl, I—"

He leaned over her, so close that she could feel the tiny puffs of air from his mouth as the words exploded from him. "Do you want me to go, Helga?"

"I . . . " *Did* she want him to go? If she knew the answer to that, did not the man realize she would not be here?

He began to pace the small space left between the square oak desk and the chair Helga sat in, his feet thudding on the bare wooden floor. "We had one night, Helga." He stopped for a minute, his warm gaze resting gently on her face. "One magical night."

"Oh, Karl."

His jaw hardened, and he took up his pacing again. "But then the next morning, you are gone. I tell myself, I know she has her life back in Minnesota. She has her

Jakob and her Nicolaus that she has told me so much about. I tell myself she must feel the same way about me I do about her. She has showed me that much. She must have only been afraid to ask me to come to her, to leave my job and my home to follow her here."

He slapped his fist down on the desk, the smack echoing off the walls of the tiny room. Helga jumped at the sound. What passion this man had, she thought. As if she did not already know that.

"But then!" he went on. "I tell myself I will come to her, since she is too good to ask that of me. I come. But you will not talk to me. You will not come to me. You will not tell me what you want."

He stopped pacing in front of her chair. He crossed his arms over his big, barreled chest and glowered down at her. "So no more, Helga. I will not follow you around like a lost puppy anymore. You will tell me what you want!"

"Oh, Karl." She smoothed the apron that covered her dirndl over her legs, trying to find a way to tell him. "My Augustus—"

"Has been dead for eleven years!"

"I know, Karl." Her voice quavered. "I know."

"I am so sorry, *mein Liebling*." Gently, his fingertips stroked down her cheek. "I did not mean to make you cry."

"It is only . . . I had that once in my life already. How can I ask to have that much again? How could I be so lucky? It is not possible. I have had it once. I should be content."

"Ah, but what about me?" She tilted her head, right into his beautiful man's hand. She should not want his touch. She did. "I have not had it. I have always had the friends, my brothers, the beer . . . but I have not had this special thing that is supposed to be between a man and a woman. I thought I never would. But then I saw you, and there it was for me. Would you deny me it?"

"Oh, Karl," she said on a sigh, unable to find any other words.

"I am fifty-four years old, Helga. Do not you think that I have waited long enough?"

"What?" she squeaked. "I am si—I am fifty-eight! You are younger than me."

"So?" He put his hands on the armrests of the chair, caging her in, and bent over her, grinning. "That is good, Helga. You need a younger man to keep up with you. I remember our night, Helga. You would wear me out if I were not so young and fit a fellow."

What was a woman to do? She could not deny a man like this.

"And you?" he asked. "You remember our night well, too, do you not, Helga?"

"*Ja.*"

He leaned over her and kissed her. His mouth was warm and firm and she nearly slid out of the chair with the pleasure of it.

"So I shall stay, Helga?" he whispered against her lips.

"What about my boys? They need me."

"I am not going to take you away from your boys." Oh, where had he learned to do that with his tongue? He had learned a few tricks somewhere in all those years he had not been married. "But I need you too, Helga."

"Oh!"

"Shall I stay?"

She hovered on the edge of capitulation for a moment. It was such a big chance to take. Then she gulped a breath and jumped right in.

"*Ja.* You shall stay."

He kissed her more; how could she stop him? His hand came to rest at the base of her neck, his hands she loved so well, big, strong hands from many years of work and living. He slid his hand down, freeing her breast from the gathered, low-necked blouse she wore with her dirndl, and cupping it in his hand.

This was it, she thought, as the wonderful sensations began to spiral through her again. The touch that had almost made her cry that night in Pittsburg, when it brought forth all those old feelings she had been so certain she would never, ever feel again.

"Oh, Karl," she said again, and reached up to loop her arms around his broad neck. She fleetingly wished that Jakob kept something more comfortable than a chair in his office. She sighed deeply in surrender. The desk would have to do.

"Well, well, what do we have here?"

Helga gasped as Karl quickly pulled away and stepped behind the chair, shielding her from the view of the door. She hastily fumbled to rearrange her clothes properly, then she turned and peered around Karl.

The doorway was full. Amy, flushed pink, had her hands pressed firmly over the eyes of the two boys, who were struggling to free themselves and get a good peek. Jakob grinned from ear to ear.

"We had to stop on the way home to get Amy's gnome," he said cheerfully, rocking back on his heels. "So . . . when's the wedding?"

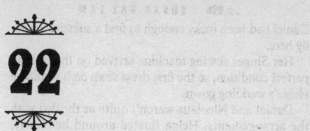

It was in three weeks.

Daniel had recovered enough by the next day to go and watch the New Ulm Brewmeisters play Mankato. Though Jakob's hitting was rusty, he pitched two scoreless innings after New Ulm's starting pitcher tired. They won 4–3, as Amanda, Daniel, and Nicolaus cheered madly.

Daniel politely declined to go back to the park and have a few more sausages in celebration.

After the *Oktoberfest*, they all turned their attention to the wedding. Since Helga was hopelessly scatter-brained, wandering around in a dazed, happy cloud, much of the arranging fell to Amanda. She didn't mind; the decision she'd made in leaving New York meant that she was never going to be there to see any of her siblings get married. This might be the last chance she'd have until Daniel was grown to be involved in a wedding. Though it made her more than a little homesick, she also was so glad that she and

Daniel had been lucky enough to find a substitute family here.

Her Singer sewing machine arrived on the train in perfect condition, so the first dress sewn on it would be Helga's wedding gown.

Daniel and Nicolaus weren't quite as thrilled with the arrangements. Helga floated around helplessly, vaguely trying to do wedding things, which meant that most of the kitchen duties fell on Amanda, too. It was not an entirely successful experiment, but they didn't seem to be suffering too badly.

In gratitude for Jakob's help in bringing him together with his love, Karl asked Jakob to be the *Hochzeitslader.* It was his honor to go door to door reciting a poem inviting all the guests to the impending wedding. The first Friday night after the *Oktoberfest,* Jakob rode out to do his duty.

Amanda dropped the dress she'd been working on into her lap and rubbed at her tired eyes. The light spilling from the lamp on her bedside table was really not bright enough for such close handwork, but her bed was warm, and she hadn't wanted to build up the fire in the stove in the middle of the night. This way, if she found herself exhausted enough, perhaps she could just slide right down and go to sleep.

She'd gotten a good two or three hours in tonight before she'd been jerked awake, her heart pounding, her eyes listening for the soft tread of all-too-familiar footsteps in the darkness. Edward's thin leather shoes had never made much noise on the thick carpets.

And she was angry, angry that she still couldn't sleep the whole night through without the nightmares pulling her awake. Damn it, they were safe. They had to be. Surely even Edward could not find her in this secluded little valley. He didn't even know it existed.

She should have been able to sleep all night long. The darkness should no longer hold such terror, such childish fears. But still she couldn't.

Only once. Only on the night that Jakob had slept next to her, the even, comforting rhythm of his breathing keeping the darkness away. Only then had she awoken the next morning truly refreshed.

It was no use thinking about it. She would learn to sleep the entire night by herself. Until then, those long, quiet hours were a useful time to get a great deal of work done.

She lifted the dress and peered closely at the gathering on the pagoda sleeve. The tucks were even and deep, requiring the sleeve to be carefully fitted by hand. It was perfect, if she did say so herself.

The dress was a fresh, apple-green that she'd suggested to Helga to complement her bright red hair. It had the simplest lines that she'd been able to talk Helga into, and would be trimmed with only a single wide band of feathery ivory lace.

It was a gown that few women of Helga's age could carry off. However, Amanda suspected that, on her wedding day, Helga was going to look quite spectacular in it. Helga's exuberance was ageless, and love added a beauty that had nothing to do with classic features or unlined skin.

The light tapping against her bedroom window startled her, bringing her up with a snap as the dress fell from her hands.

What was that?

Her heart lodged in her throat. Surely it was only a branch, blown against the panes by a light breeze.

But it came again, a short, insistent beat.

What could it be? Dare she look?

But this was her house, damn it. She would not be made to be afraid here. She eased her way out of bed and tiptoed over to the window. On second thought, she grabbed up her sharp scissors, clutching them in one hand like a dagger.

Shading her eyes from the lantern light, she pressed her nose against the cool, smooth glass and peered out into the darkness.

The moon was huge and yellow—a harvest moon, giving enough light to silhouette a masculine figure. Her heart tripped into double time. But not in fear, for she knew those shoulders.

She set down her scissors and pushed open the window. A chill crept in; she shivered and pulled her wrapper more tightly around her. Though it was warm for October, it was still October. Jakob was standing only a few feet from her window, and she leaned out to speak to him.

"Jakob! What are you doing out there?"

"Wait, wait, wait." He threw up a hand to silence her.

"Do you want to come in?" The question popped out of her mouth before she thought to stop it. Of course he could not come in. She did not trust herself that much.

"No. I have to do this here." He cleared his throat, placed one hand on his chest, and began to sing. Her elbows propped on the narrow sill, she listened, enchanted despite her best intentions.

His voice was low, slow and rich as the moonlight, and as beautiful. She didn't understand the words, for they were German, but she understood the emotions the music held as his voice twined through the night to her, wrapping her in warmth, sinking into her heart.

The cool air prickled through her nightclothes. His presence ruffled her nerve endings and stole all of the defenses she'd built so carefully.

He was still wearing his formal *Hochzeitslader* clothes: a long, dark coat that blended with the night; pure white gloves that gleamed eerily in the darkness; and a tall hat. He carried a ribboned cane, and he looked so impossibly handsome that she wished she were an artist, just so she could capture how he looked right now. But that was unnecessary, anyway.

She would remember.

When he finished, his voice fading as if it were simply absorbed in the darkness, he stood there, his eyes staring straight, unswervingly into hers. What did he see there? She wondered if he was discovering things she did not wish him to know.

He grinned, lopsided, breaking the spell, and Amanda could not decide if she was sorry or relieved. "Did you like it?"

"What are you doing?" He must be crazy, singing outside her window in the middle of an silent autumn night.

"*Fensterln*, of course."

"*Fen . . .* what is that?"

"It is tradition, that is what. Windowing. A man must sing beneath her window to woo a woman. It is how things are done."

"Oh, Jakob. You cannot woo me."

"I can't?" He frowned. "I thought I was doing a pretty good job."

"I meant you shouldn't."

"Ah, well." He waved off her feeble protests. "Who cares about shouldn't? I've been doing what I *should* my whole life. Maybe I'm tired of it."

She was weakening; she knew it. How could she not?

"Jakob—" Ignoring her, he bent down, his long coat flying behind him, and started rummaging in the bushes that trimmed the side of the cottage. The branches shook and rustled violently. "What in the world are you doing?"

"I can't get the damn—" He broke off, popping up out of the bushes, and handed her his cane. "Here. Hold this."

She took it without thinking, then looked down at the wooden cane, trailing its decorative ribbons. What was she supposed to do with this? She propped it up against the wall beside her and leaned out again, anxious to see what he would come up with now.

The bushes shuddered again, then Jakob gave a heave. There was a huge clatter as a ladder bounced against the side of the house, just to the left of her window.

"Jakob, that's a ladder!"

"Of course," he said, as if she were being ridiculous in asking. "When you *fensterlst*, you have to have a ladder."

"But I'm on the first floor!"

"Doesn't matter. It's tradition."

She was beginning to get a glimmer of an idea that crazy might not be what was the matter with him. "Jakob, are you drunk?"

He paused, his foot on the first rung of the ladder, and appeared to consider. "Yeah." He grinned engagingly. "Probably."

"Jakob!"

"It's not my fault, Amy. When the inviter does all that inviting, he gets a glass of *Schnaps* at every house. I couldn't refuse. It's—"

"I know, I know. It's tradition, right?"

"Right!" he said, delighted.

He climbed up two steps, bringing his face level with hers, and simply watched her, as if he could not get enough of just looking at her face.

He shouldn't have looked so appealing. He was obviously tipsy, there were leaves decorating the shoulders of his coat and trailing down his chest, and his high hat was askew, dipping over his left eye.

It didn't matter. This was Jakob, who made her feel safe and who'd sung for her and who meant to woo her, and she couldn't find it in her heart to send him away. It may have been wrong, it was probably foolish, but she wanted this too much to end it swiftly.

"So," she said softly, "tell me more about this windowing. Do the men really climb up the ladders?"

"Some do, if they're bold."

"How scandalous!"

"Well, we Germans are not quite so rigid about these things. We believe a couple should get to know each other well—in all ways—before they marry." He grinned wickedly. "In all ways." He flicked a finger at the rim of his hat, settling it back more securely on his head, and the pale light struck his face more fully. "There are rules, of course. You cannot put your ladder at the window of two women. That would be very bad."

"Very bad," she agreed.

"And if your ladder is seen at a certain window too many nights, a wedding is expected." The corner of his mouth quirked up, as if he were proud of the way he'd trapped her, and she wanted to kill him right then. Almost as much as she longed to kiss him. "You don't have to worry, though. No one saw me. And this is only the first night."

"I'm so relieved."

"And, of course, you cannot *fensterlst* on Tuesday or Sunday nights—"

"Why not?"

"Because it's—"

"Tradition," they finished together, and smiled at each other.

His smile slowly faded. "Amy," he whispered. He stretched out a white-gloved hand, gently stroking down the curve of her cheek, and she couldn't help but tilt her head, trying to get more of his touch. "Wait." He looped one arm around the rung of the ladder, balancing himself, and tugged off his gloves, tossing them carelessly over his shoulder. All the playfulness born of the *Schnaps* was gone. Then he touched her again, warm fingers that shook ever so slightly. "Ah, Amy," he said, his voice as gentle as his touch, every bit as mesmerizing. "Your skin . . . why is it that I think I can never forget your skin, and then when I touch you, I realize I never remembered it as fine as it really is?"

"What did the song mean, Jakob?" She should not ask. She had to know.

"It's from the thirteenth century." He did not sing this time, but spoke softly, evenly, and every word broke her heart just a little bit more.

Since creation I was thine;
Now forever thou art mine.
I have shut thee fast
In my heart at last.
I have dropped the key
In an unknown sea.
Forever must thou my prisoner be!

"Jakob." Warm wetness rimmed the edges of her eyes. How could he do this to her, touch her so much, so deeply, with only his words and the look in his eyes?

He bent his head, haltingly, as if he were unsure of

her response and wished to give her time to pull away. Surely he must know; certainly he must feel that she could not stop him, any more than she could stop the wild hammering of her heart.

If she thought his words had stirred her, his kiss was devastating. Time faded, reality dimmed; there was nothing for her, nothing but the feel of his tongue gently rimming her lips, nothing but the magical pressure of his mouth and the clear, sweet, sharp taste of him. She wondered if she, too, could become intoxicated from the *Schnaps* he had drunk, for she felt heady, overwhelmed, disconnected from the earth.

When he pulled away, she felt real pain, as if she had just lost something precious and irretrievable.

"This is the part where the woman, if her suitor has pleased her, invites him for the night." His eyes were dark, disturbing, asking for everything and more. If it was hers to give, she would. "Have I pleased you, Amy?"

She took a deep, shuddering breath. "Do you want to come in, Jakob?"

"I want to." He leaned forward, resting his forehead gently against hers. "If I come in, will anything change between us? Will the morning be any different than it was before?"

For one wild, fierce instant, she was tempted. Tempted to tell him everything, to share every secret, to throw it all in his competent hands and let him deal with it, let him try and find a way for them to be together.

But she could not do that to him. It was not fair, that he be dragged into problems that were hers alone. She could not do that to him, not after all that he'd given to her. "No," she said hoarsely.

"Then I'd better not." He drew away regretfully.

"Why?" she said, knowing it was wrong, but wanting this night more than she could bear.

"I want more, Amy." He smiled faintly, sadly, moonlight gilding half of his face in light, leaving half in shadow. "I want it all, Amy. Everything I know we can have. And when you are ready to give it to me, I'll come in that window and love you until we can no longer tell which is you and which is me. And it will not matter, because we will be one."

23

The wedding went off without a hitch. Helga was a surprisingly blushing and eager bride, Karl a beaming and slightly stunned bridegroom. Amanda enjoyed the ceremony. Except once, when she looked at Jakob before she stopped herself, and had a flash of him as a groom, as handsome and proud as any man had ever been.

He would make a wonderful groom, someday. It was only that his bride could not be her, and she'd best stop even thinking of it. It hurt too much to think of him marrying someone else.

The reception was held at the largest beer hall in New Ulm, though even that was scarcely big enough to hold the crowds who turned out to celebrate, which included the unexpected arrival of both of Helga's sons and her daughter, Anja, who was a very smug and delighted matchmaker.

The crowds efficiently devoured massive quantities of noodles, sauerkraut, potato dumplings, baked ham, and specially shaped cakes. Now they were busily disposing of a good portion of Jakob's private stock of his dark, sweet bock beer.

The room the party was held in was massive and barrel-vaulted, dark timbers ribbing the cream-colored ceiling that arched high overhead. Sounds echoed and multiplied in the cavernous room. Small, round, scarred tables made of dark oak crowded the room and clumped in a haphazard half-circle around the dance floor.

It was the first dance. The band played a slow, European waltz. Helga and Karl, flushed and lost to happiness, circled in each other's arms. Amanda stood to the side of the dance floor with the other spectators, applauding the newlyweds as they swept by.

Amanda's wide smile wobbled, just a bit. As much as anyone had ever deserved this happiness, Helga and Karl did. But thrilled as she was for Helga, her chest warming until she thought it would burst, she couldn't deny that there was a tiny, not-terribly-nice corner of her that was more than a little envious.

No man had ever looked at her the way Karl looked at Helga right now, tender concern and near-wonder in his eyes. As if she were the only thing in the world that mattered to him, a gift that he dared not believe was truly his. A miracle.

No one had, and no one ever would.

And it was a thousand times worse suspecting that someone might have, if she had been able to allow it. She sneaked a glance at Jakob, standing stiff and silent at her side. He looked unreasonably handsome, his high collar stark white against his tanned skin, one wayward brown curl falling over his temple, where any woman who saw it would want to brush it back, just for the pleasure of touching his thick hair and uncovering the smooth slope of his strong forehead.

Since the night at her window, he'd been polite, friendly, but just a shade reserved. He'd never pushed her, never indicated any impatience with her. Except once in a while, she would turn unexpectedly and surprise a look of such intense warmth on his face that she knew, she just knew, that someday Jakob might have looked at her as Karl looked at Helga. As if she were something that the world had created just for him.

She knew she had to end it, somehow. They couldn't live much longer in this half-world of yearnings and remembered pleasure, in a friendship that, she suspected, would no more be enough for her than it would be for him. There were too many fires between them; slow-burning, uncontrollable fires that blazed all the hotter for their patience.

She needed to move out of the cottage, to sever the net of relationships that bound them together and threw them so often into each other's company.

But she could not yet find it in her to turn him away completely. Part of it was Daniel, and how much he looked up to Jakob, and how good Jakob was for him. Daniel needed a strong, honorable male in his life so much, to make up for the damage his father had done.

That was only an excuse, and she knew it. She knew Jakob well enough to know that he would find a way to continue to be a presence in Daniel's life, no matter what happened between the two of them. He was genuinely fond of Daniel, and would never make a child suffer for the sins of his elders.

No, she kept living in this world between friendship and love because *she* wanted it, with a fierceness she hadn't realized she was capable of. It would hurt too much to never see him again, or to see him only in the guise of a polite acquaintance, to pretend that he wasn't someone whom she knew, in precise, crystalline clarity, what his mouth felt like when it was warm on her breast, tonguing her nipple into acute pleasure.

She returned her attention to the dance floor, where it belonged. Thinking these things about Jakob would lead her into nothing but trouble. Edward had told her often enough how stupid she was, but she was not dumb enough to realize exactly where such thoughts would take her—running headlong back into Jakob's arms.

Helga and Karl were joined by her children now, and their spouses, a waltz for the whole, celebrating family. And Amanda was proud that she had been able to play a small role in bringing them together. Thank God she'd been able to do something right. She'd made such a mess of all else, and could see no way out of it without even more pain. The last thing she'd ever wanted to do was to hurt Jakob.

As they swayed to the music, Helga raised up on her toes, speaking into Karl's ear. He tenderly smiled down at her and nodded, the lights from the many-candled chandeliers playing off his round, bare head. How sweet; they were whispering to each other. But then they stopped dancing and, arms looped around each other's waist, walked across the wide floor to where Amanda stood with Jakob.

Helga stretched out a welcoming hand to each of them. "You must join us," she said. "We want *all* our family to be with us for this dance. It is not complete without both of you."

Jakob gave no hint of whether he wanted to dance with her; his expressions were carefully contained. It didn't matter, she found. She wanted to dance with him, though it would only make it all the harder to know that it must be the last time.

He formally offered his arm. "Shall we?"

"Of course." She placed her hand lightly on his forearm as he led her out on the floor, feeling the hard flex of muscle underneath his coat. How long had it been since she touched him, even this casually? Too long, though it must only be a week or two. It would be so easy, too easy, to let her hands wander where they wished, to fill themselves with heat and skin and Jakob.

The music swept them along, into big, slow turns that made the room spin around them. Helga and Karl beamed happily on them, Karl's face scrunching in an encouraging wink. The floor was slippery with scattered sawdust to aid the sliding turns, and Jakob had to tug her closer to keep her from skidding away.

Jakob bent his head and smelled roses, and he knew he was lost. Even asking her to dance with him, politely and with proper distance, was asking too much.

He'd tried so hard these last weeks. Tried to give Amy the time and patience she seemed to need, when half the time he'd been working on the wedding preparations he'd been wishing they were his. In the church, he hadn't dared look her way, afraid that his face would show his feelings all too clearly.

The rational side of him argued that he should give up. The rational side had lost the argument long ago. He'd seen the look in her eyes when he'd gone to her window, felt her shivering response every time he'd touched her. No, there was something so strong between them; he could not imagine she didn't feel it, too. Why was she fighting it so hard?

There must be something he was missing. Maybe something more than what she'd told him was keeping her away from him. Soon, he would set himself to finding out what it was, one way or another. Patience had never been one of his strong suits, and his was long past wearing thin. But he was damned good at doing what he set his mind to, and right now his mind—and most of the rest of him—was set on her.

Now, though, he had better things to think of than her resistance. Amy was in his arms, one hand nestled softly in his, and she smelled like roses. It was almost frightening how comfortably she fit against him. Once in a while, when they made a particularly deep turn, a soft hint of her breast would touch his chest. He wondered if he were going to be able to get off the dance floor without everyone in the place knowing exactly what effect she had on him. He wasn't sure he cared if they did; surely it was perfectly obvious from the look on his face that he was completely caught.

"You look . . ." Hell, how was he supposed to describe it? Her hair was curled high on her head, and she was wearing some pinkish-grayish-purplish concoction of a dress with pleated frills spilling from her sleeves and her bodice. She looked sophisticated and polished, smooth as expensive crystal, and he was dumbfounded that he was dancing with a woman like her. "Beautiful?" he tried lamely. Damn! What an idiotic thing to say. She'd probably heard it a thousand times. He was a small-town brewer who knew nothing of thinking up clever flattery.

But she looked up at him, shy pleasure evident in her eyes, color blushing along her cheeks. Haltingly, he drew her closer and lowered his head, resting his chin against her temple. The softness of her hair teased him, tempted him, brushing against his jaw and reminding him of so many other places that could tease and tempt him. She sighed and seemed to sink into his arms.

Maybe he would learn some patience after all, he thought. If he could hold her like this, just once in a while, he could wait for the rest. If he had to.

Amanda knew she surely must be in heaven. Jakob's hand was at the small of her back, stroking, the tantalizing pressure and heat palpable even through her layers of clothing. Her chest brushed his, and she felt her nipples harden up abruptly. She wondered if he could feel them, rigid and waiting, through the barriers between them. Though she knew it was wrong, a part of her almost hoped he did.

The music grew with a slow, swelling pulse; Jakob smelled of fresh soap and heady musk. Amanda closed her eyes, allowing herself the luxury of dreaming.

There was something between them she had never sought to find, something she had never been quite sure existed. Now that it was here, did she truly have to throw it away? It seemed too precious a gift, too clearly a bestowal from the Almighty to treat so carelessly.

She felt so utterly right here. In this town, and even more right in Jakob's arms . . . and his life. Perhaps her coming to New Ulm had been more than circumstances; maybe she'd been led here, a wondrous return from the fates for all the pain that had come before.

She'd been so certain that her only choice was to go on as she had been, to live a quiet life alone but for her son. Now she wondered. Was that truly the only thing she could do?

She could tell Jakob the truth. She hoped he would not hate her; surely she knew him well enough to know that he would understand the choices forced upon a person. And then she would no longer have to carry this alone.

But that could not be fair to him. He had burdens of his own; what right had she to add to them? How could she ask him to join in hers, when she had so little to give him in return?

I am no longer Amanda Sellington, she thought. She refused to be. The woman she was now bore little resemblence to that weak, beaten woman who'd run from New York in desperation.

I am Amy Smith.

A widow. That was who she was to this town, who she was to Jakob. Who she was to *herself.*

Amy Smith could marry.

She was probably damned to hell for the very thought of it. But it might be worth being damned for all eternity, just for the chance to love Jakob Hall for the rest of her life.

An imperious tap on her shoulder jerked her back from the wonderful, powerfully tempting world she'd created in her mind. She blinked, surprised to find herself still in middle of the crowded hall.

The decidedly ungentle finger was prodding her shoulder again, and Amy twisted her neck to find Brigitte Kiesling, beautiful and clearly impatient, standing behind her.

"The dance is over," she said in a determinedly cheerful voice. "I'm sure you don't mind if I cut in."

Amy had not noticed that the waltz had ended. In proof of Brigitte's words, the band picked up its pace, jumping into a lively polka. "I—"

She broke off when, at her back, Jakob's fingers gave her a light, warning pinch. "Of course you may cut in, Brigitte," she said sweetly.

Jakob glowered at her for a moment, and she grinned in response. It was safer for her to get away from him for a while, anyway. She needed to think clearly, without the wonderful distraction of his body within touching distance.

On the side of the dance floor once more, she accepted a stein of beer, grimacing just a bit at the taste. It was strong stuff, but she supposed she must develop a taste for it if she were to live in New Ulm forever.

Forever. Lord, what a wonderful word. For so long, forever had been something she could not think of; it had been too disheartening, to think that she would spend forever living as she had been.

Her gaze followed Jakob, hopping around the dance floor with Brigitte, their rhythm awkwardly out of step. He'd been perfectly in time with Amanda, and she smiled inwardly. He was gamely smiling at Brigitte, bobbing his head at odd moments when her mouth stopped flapping for an instant.

She took another swallow of beer and felt victorious when she didn't shudder. Automatically, she scanned the room for Daniel. Last she checked, he'd been happily huddled in a corner with his friends, plotting the batting order for their next ball game.

He wasn't there now. Perhaps he'd gone to speak to his teacher, of whom he was inordinately fond. She looked farther around the room, her feet idly tapping in time with the merry music, her gaze drifting over the crowds and toward the heavy, carved, double doors that fronted the hall.

The beer stein slipped from her hand. It crashed to the floor, scattering ceramic shards, the dark beer geysering up and staining her skirts. She didn't notice.

A moment before, she'd been contemplating heaven.

Now, instead, hell had just found her.

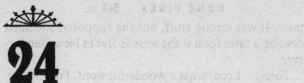

24

"Edward."

The word slid between her lips, a low exclamation like a death rattle.

He looked utterly out of place in this jovial hall. Flawlessly dressed in unrelieved black and white, he stood tall and golden near the door, a faint, contemptuous curl to his mouth as he looked around him. He'd captured Daniel, who was still and white-faced, the vivid terror in his eyes visible even from this distance, as Edward trapped him close to his elegant side.

Blackness swept in, blotting out all the light and music, all the good things she'd experienced in the past few months. All that was left was the fear, cold and numbing. She'd lived for weeks without it, and now it was back, as powerful and debilitating as if it had never left, all the stronger for her brief freedom from it.

Around her, people asked if she was all right and bent to deal with the broken stein at her feet. Numbly, she assured them she was fine, then she stepped through the mess, her heels grinding broken shards to powder, and threaded her way through the crowds to Edward as if she were in a tunnel. A long, dark, horrible tunnel, except at the end of it there was no light but only the deepest, most inescapable darkness of all.

"Edward," she said when she reached him, as if there were no other words to say. What other could there be? Nothing she could say would blunt what was to come; if there was one thing she'd learned in all those years with him, it was that nothing she could ever do or say would change it. Change him.

She bent to Daniel, running her hands over his face, his arms, as if to check if he were sound. All the bursting life and confidence that he'd gained during these past few months seemed to have vanished, leaving only the empty shell of her beautiful little boy. "Are you all right, Daniel?"

He gave a small nod. "He just twisted my arm a little," he said, his voice nearly inaudible. "He hasn't hurt me . . . yet." *Yet*. How was she to stop Edward? Perhaps there was nothing she could do to protect herself. But this time, somehow, she would make sure Daniel did not suffer, too. She could never live through that again, but dying was not an option, for it would leave Daniel alone and at his father's nonexistent mercy.

She straightened, trying to pull herself up tall and confident, though inside she could find nothing. No reserve, no strength, no pride; she'd taken her best shot, and it had failed.

Edward had found them.

"Well, my dear," he said smoothly, as casual as if greeting her upon returning from a brief outing, his cold gaze raking her from head to toe. "One would think that you are not glad to see me. Have you not missed me?"

"I'll be glad to see you when I see you in hell."

That amused him; he threw back his head and laughed. "Well, I have missed you. Though finding you provided some small entertainment all of its own. You are not quite so stupid as I'd always assumed, Amanda. I believe I shall enjoy instructing you again in the proper behavior of a wife."

How could she be standing here, so still and outwardly calm, surrounded by all this gaiety? she wondered. Surely she was curling up into a small, dead ball. She wanted to crumple at his feet and vanish, like the life she wanted just had. After a few short months of glorious living, how could she go back to the waking hell she'd endured all those years?

"Well, Amanda, I must say you look much the same," he said conversationally. "How unfortunate."

Her nails must be close to drawing blood, so deeply were they cutting into her palms. But the pain was better, far better, than the terror.

"Well? Shall we adjourn to somewhere more . . . private to talk?" His smile was as charming as always. How could it have fooled her—and so many others— for so long? How could she not have seen there was nothing behind it but empty cruelty and arrogance? "I'm certain that we have much to discuss, after all this time apart. You'll want to demonstrate how much you've missed me, of course. And I am certainly anticipating performing the same service for you."

She knew precisely what he was anticipating. It was there, in the dark, cold glitter in his eyes and the slight tensing of his long-fingered hands, which looked far too delicately made to inflict the kind of damage she knew he was capable of. She'd learned to read the signs well over the years; her survival had depended on it. The more controlled he got, the closer to the sharp edge of violence he was. And he was balanced only a razor's edge away right now.

"I'm not going anywhere with you."

He smiled again, genuinely pleased by her answer. "So you've remembered how to fight a bit, have you? That is good; it's been so many years since you've bothered with futile resistance. I've missed that, too. It is slightly more challenging this way." He released Daniel's upper arm, instead curling his fingers around the boy's small neck. "You do not have to go with me, I suppose. I could just get up on that stage and introduce myself to everyone, hmm? I'm sure they'd be most intrigued to meet your husband. Not to mention quite thrilled to have Edward Sellington in their midst."

Oh, God. She couldn't let him do that. Jakob would be so hurt, to find out so abruptly, and in front of the entire town, that she'd lied to him from the beginning. And it would be for nothing. They would all happily escort her off with her famous, powerful, and respected husband. No one would dare protect her from Edward. They couldn't.

No one ever had.

"Of course, that would cause a scene," he mused. "And you know how I detest scenes, Amanda."

And her punishment would be all the greater. She clearly understood what he didn't say.

"I'll go with you," she said, forcing the words out through lips that felt as if they had been frozen to ice, "but let Daniel stay here. It's me you want to . . . speak—" God! What a harmless word. "—to, anyway."

"Oh, no. I don't think I could do that. Our whole family must be reunited." He placed one hand theatrically on his chest and adopted a heartbroken mien, the one he'd used so effectively on her when she'd arrived at his mansion just after Cynthia's death. "I'm certain everyone would understand my wish to spend some time with the family I've been so tragically separated from."

She nodded, wordless, unable to think of anything else to do. Why couldn't she *think*, damn it? She had to think. Her brain felt as numb as the rest of her, useless and dull.

Without drawing attention to themselves—the other guests were all absorbed in dancing—they went back to his hotel room at the Dakotah. They walked through the familiar streets she'd loved so well, and now they seemed strange and sinister, tainted by Edward's presence. If someone saw them, did they look like a normal family, out for an evening stroll? She fought a rising bubble of hysteria.

The walk was far too short; she needed time. Surely there must be a way, some escape route that she hadn't yet thought of. But there was nothing there; she was too tired, too defeated.

What good would it do her to get away? He would only find them again.

The small lobby of the Dakotah was empty, the desk unmanned. He led them up the stairs and through the narrow hallway, and she wondered that she was able to keep putting one foot before the other.

He ushered them into the room with a gallant bow. "It is quite inadequate, of course. But, unfortunately there was nothing else available in this . . . place," he said with distaste.

The room was small, dark, even after Edward lit the lantern sitting on a thin table just inside the door; shadows still lurked in the corners of the room, just as they cloaked her heart. It was furnished only with a narrow, quilt-covered bed and a small chest of drawers, topped with a pitcher and basin. A single braided rug covered the otherwise bare wood floor. It was easier, Amanda found, to focus on such useless details than to think about what was happening.

"Now, then." Edward had yet to let go of Daniel, and he eased the door shut behind him with frightening gentleness. "Did you know, there's almost no one in this hotel right now? They're all out at that ridiculous wedding. Convenient, isn't it? I'm certain no one will disturb us."

"Oh, Edward." She crossed the room and slumped down on the bed, unable to force her legs to hold her any longer. "Why can't you just let us go?"

"Well, now, Amanda, I would be quite happy to let you go."

She stared up at her husband, standing just inside the door that sealed them off from the world she wanted so much to be a part of, knowing the fragile bubble of hope his words caused inside her was dangerous and probably worthless, but unable to stop it.

"You . . . you would?"

"Of course," he said mildly, "I would have to take my heir with me."

"No!"

"Do it, Mama," Daniel said urgently, his voice tiny but determined. "You can stay here. I'll . . . I'll be okay."

"Daniel, you know that I could never do that." She should have known Edward had no intention of freeing them. It was better not to have hope, for it was all the worse when it was snatched away.

"I'll go back with you, Edward," she said miserably. "I'll go back with you. I'll be exactly the wife you want. There's one condition, though."

"I wonder what that could be?" Sarcasm colored his words.

"You will never touch Daniel again." She wasn't crying, she realized, surprised. She didn't understand how that could be, when the harsh acid was burning inside her, but she was glad of it. He would have enjoyed it far too much. "Never, ever, or I shall find a way to kill you, Edward. I swear it."

He laughed aloud, thoroughly enjoying her ineffectual threats. "I would love to see you try." His voice chilled. "But as for Daniel—well, how am I to do my duty as a father and turn him into a proper Sellington if I am not to effectively punish him? I'm afraid I must decline your offer."

And suddenly his fingers tightened around Daniel's neck, twisting into his delicate flesh, bringing a startled cry of pain from the boy as he started to sink to his knees.

"No!" she shouted, anger swamping her as thoroughly as despair had. Anger was better. She flew at Edward, instinctively aiming for his eyes. She missed, but her nails raked down his face, clawing into his cheek, leaving deep red trails.

He released Daniel to hit her, backhanding her viciously across the face. Her mouth split as easily as an overripe berry. The force sent her flying back, careening into the bed.

She shook her head to clear it of the fogginess caused by the blow. The pain was minor; experience had taught her to close it into a small, tight box where it could be dealt with. She wiggled her jaw experimentally. Nothing had been broken.

"Daniel, come here!" she cried. He scrambled across the floor, instantly breaching the few feet that separated him from her arms. He threw himself at her and she enfolded him safe against her.

Safe! What an illusion. He was trembling, and she

stroked his back to soothe him. "It's okay, Daniel. It's going to be all right."

It wasn't, and they both knew it. But somehow, some way, she would find a way to keep him from harm. She was stronger now; she must not forget it. She would find a way to use it.

"Well, well," Edward said. "You have a changed a bit during your . . . adventure. You used to take the punishment you deserved so calmly." He looked down at the smears of her blood streaking the back of his hand, glistening dark and shiny in the dim light. "But I don't mind." He bent his head and licked at her blood. "In fact, I rather like it."

"I don't deserve it," she whispered, her words muffled against Daniel's head.

"Excuse me?"

"I don't deserve it!" she said forcefully. "I don't! And do you know the first time I realized that I didn't?" She glared at him, wishing that hatred were enough to strike him down in his tracks. Surely her hatred was as powerful and sharp as any had ever been. If an emotion could be deadly, hers certainly must be.

"When?" he asked, sounding vaguely intrigued.

"The first time you hit Daniel." She drew Daniel closer, as if her arms could form a protective armor around him. "He never deserved it. Never, ever. And he is your son! How could you do that to him?"

"Oh." He flicked his hand, as if dismissing an insignificant servant. "Silly girl. I'm not even certain if he is my son."

"What?" She lifted her head, disbelieving. "Cynthia would never—"

"Cynthia did." His mouth thinned. "Now, then." He began to strip off his coat. He always took off his handsome, expensive coats—they were very difficult to clean. The studs that held together his snow-white shirt were tiny chips of glittering obsidian. "I believe we have other things to discuss. You've been a very, very inadequate wife recently."

"Get under the bed, Daniel," she ordered.

"Mama, I won't leave you."

She forced herself to push him away. "Get under the bed, Daniel! And don't come out until I tell you to."

Harsh sobs shook his thin shoulders as he slipped from her grasp and squirmed under the bed. Amanda closed her eyes. It was better not to look, to anticipate. She groped for the bedpost, needing something solid and real to hold on to, otherwise her world would slip away completely into the comforting blackness. She could not afford that this time, not with Daniel in the room.

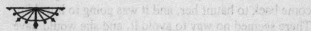

25

The crash splintered in her head, so loud and violent that at first she thought that Edward had hit her again. But there was no pain, no waves of agony rolling down from her cheek.

She swept aside the scattered hair that curtained her face.

"Jakob!"

The sound she'd heard had been the door, its lock broken, flying in and smashing off the wall. Jakob burst into the room, filling the space with his broad, familiar strength. He was what she wanted most to see, yet she would have given anything if he had not come.

"Amy, are you—" He saw her on the bed, spun in her direction and was brought up short by quietly spoken words from the man hidden in the deep shadows behind the broken door.

"Well, well, what do we have here?" Edward stepped into the weak circle of light, looking entirely comfortable. A gleaming silver pistol rested easily in his right hand, as elegant, polished, and deadly as he himself was. "My dear, perhaps you should introduce us."

She could not do it. There was no way to explain this to Jakob, no way to soften the blow. Her past had come back to haunt her, and it was going to hurt him. There seemed no way to avoid it, and she would have given everything she could not to hurt him.

"How . . . how did you find us?" she stammered. Useless, unimportant words, but she could not find the ones she needed.

Jakob's gaze was focused intently on the bore of Edward's pistol, aimed straight at his midsection. His arms swung loosely at his sides, and he rested his weight easily on the balls of his feet. He looked big, slow, harmless. Only someone who knew him as well as she did would recognize his taut, carefully leashed energy.

"I could not find you in the hall." He shifted his weight, as if relaxing even more. "When I went outside, there was a man—a stranger who saw me looking for you. He said you had gone toward the hotel. I just listened at the doors until I heard your voice."

"Stop stalling, Amanda," Edward said, his voice smooth and utterly cold.

"Amanda?" Jakob flicked a glance in her direction. From his quick, fierce frown, she knew he'd seen the blood running down her chin. There was a subtle bunching of his muscles; his jaw ticked in anger, and she knew he was preparing to attack in her defense.

She could not let him do it. Edward would shoot him; he would take great pleasure in it. She would not let it happen. This was her nightmare to deal with, to live through; Jakob had not asked to become a part of it. He had earned no portion of this pain.

"I—that's my real name." She lifted her chin, staring directly at him. It would be so much easier to lower her eyes, to hide her face as she said what she had to. But he deserved this much at least, and so she would face him when she told him of her lies. "I am really Amanda Sellington." She swallowed, the lump acutely painful. "This is my husband, Edward."

There was a flash of raw, searing anguish in his eyes. Then his expression shut down completely, becoming remote and emotionless as if he were carved from a block of solid ice.

"Where is Daniel?" he asked neutrally.

"He's—" she gulped, "—he's under the bed."

A flicker of purest rage thinned the ice before it was extinguished. Jakob turned to face Edward again, who seemed distantly amused by it all, his thumb caressing the polished metal of his gun.

"So, what brings you to New Ulm?" Jakob's question was surreal in its normalcy, something he would ask any visitor to his town.

"I've come to fetch my family, of course." Edward smiled indulgently. "Amanda enjoys playing games with me, you see. This particular one is finished now."

"I understand." Jakob leaned forward slightly, the low light making him look dark and menacing, very unlike any way that Amanda had ever seen him before. "Now, you should probably understand something," he said, biting off each world clearly. "Amanda and Daniel will not be returning with you this time."

"Oh, this grows so tiresome." Edward's hair gleamed gold. His features were perfect, patrician, like a gifted artist's image of an earthbound angel; a horrible disguise of what he really was. "You, too? And here I married Amanda because I thought her looks would prevent her from being the whore Cynthia was. I should have known the bitch would find a way to indulge her sluttish nature." He ignored Jakob, though the pistol did not waver, turning his attention to address Amanda. "Still, I must admit it escapes me. What is it you and Cynthia saw in these ill-born, rustic sorts . . . I suppose they do not bother you with conversation, is that it?"

"Edward, stop." She would rather he just beat her. She knew she could handle physical pain. She did not think she could handle these words, slicing deeply into her flesh, her soul. Not with Jakob standing there, forced to listen to them.

"Although you must admit, Jakob—that is what she called you, isn't it?—that her whorish enthusiasm is rather entertaining in bed, isn't it? She is not a cold one, at least. Or did you not discover that yet?"

She saw Jakob gather his body, ready to charge at Edward. "No, Jakob, no!" She could not let him. She could see it so clearly in her mind, the horror enough to nearly overwhelm her, Jakob falling to the floor with a red, pumping hole in his chest.

"I—" Oh, God. How could she say this? She had to. "I am going back to New York with Edward."

"See? There you go," Edward said jovially.

"I can't let you do that." Jakob brushed his thumb down his chin, as if he were feeling a trickle of blood that matched her own. "He hurt you, Amy."

"I . . . I deserved it." She nearly gagged on the words. "I want to go with him."

"Do you understand now?" Edward said. "You were simply a brief diversion. However, I will not make the same mistake I made the last time. I punished Cynthia, but I allowed her lover to live. The other way around will be much more satisfying, I believe."

He'd killed Cynthia? Impossible. Though she'd

heard the words, they did not seem to register, merely echoed over and over in the empty spaces of her mind.

Of course he had. Now she realized it.

"Yes," Edward said, lifting the pistol higher so it sighted on Jakob's head. The light caught the gun in a brilliant, intense flash. "I do believe I will like it much better this way."

"Edward, no!" she shouted, desperate to think of something, anything, to stop him. "What about the diamonds?"

Edward cocked his head, squinting down the short, bright barrel of the pistol. "The diamonds, Amanda? Ah, yes, the diamonds. I'd have thought you would have sold them by now, but you're certainly not using the money to live in style, are you?"

"I have them." It was a pitiful trade for Jakob's life, a few dozen carats of useless, flawless, outrageously expensive rock. But this was Edward, who thought the gems more valuable than almost any life but his. "If you let Jakob go, I'll tell you where they are. If you kill him, you will never get them back. I swear it, Edward. I'll never let you have them."

"An interesting proposition." Edward's teeth gleamed in his shadowed face. The lamplight flickered, distorting his features grotesquely, just as her nightmares did so many nights. "However, I do not think I will deprive myself of this particular pleasure. You will give the diamonds to me anyway."

"I will not," she said forcefully, willing him to believe her.

"You will." He nodded slightly, confident. "All I will have to do is decide to spend more time with my beloved son, won't I? And you won't be able to wait to give me my diamonds."

She would. They both knew it.

She thought she'd known despair, but it was nothing, *nothing*, compared to this, to knowing that in a moment or two, Jakob would be dead, and it would be entirely her fault.

"Any last words, Jakob?" Edward's words carried no more inflection than if he were inquiring after a distant acquaintance's family. "On second thought, I do not think that I would like to hear them. You'll have to manage without."

"No!" Amanda screamed. Searching for any delay, any diversion, she leapt for the table near the door, toppling it. The lantern smashed and shattered. Oil and flames spread over the floor.

Edward's attention wavered for an instant, the pistol swinging to cover the noise by the door. It was all Jakob needed. He dove for Edward's belly, shouldering Edward's arm so the gun jerked up toward the ceiling. They both crashed down. Edward's head made a solid *chunk* as it hit the floor. Jakob's fist connected squarely with his jaw, and Edward's eyes rolled shut and he went limp. Jakob disengaged the pistol from Edward's hand and rolled to his feet.

"Amy! You're on fire!"

The oil crept across the floor, the flames licking at the walls and the broken legs of the table, reflecting in the polished floorboards. Amy sat numbly in the middle of it, her hands resting palms-up in her lap, as the gleaming oil encircled her and ignited her wide skirts.

"My God! Amy!" He snatched up the rug and whacked at the flames, beating them out, flailing the dusty rug around her and the floor. The strong smell of kerosene and charred fabric enveloped him. When the last flame was snuffed out, he sank to his knees before her. Her eyes dark and glazed with shock, she looked up at him, raising a shaking hand to touch his cheek.

"You're not dead," she whispered. "Oh, thank God, you're not dead." Her voice broke on the last words.

"No, I'm not dead." But he'd thought she might be. Now, that seemed to be the only thing that mattered. Not all the horrifying things he'd learned tonight. "Are you all right?"

"I'm all right." She kept staring at him, as if she did not believe he was real. Then, as though she'd had all she could take, she crumpled like a puppet whose strings had been severed. "For now."

"Not just for now," he promised, pulling her close and crushing her to his chest as if he would make her part of him. She hung on to the only thing that seemed real and safe in her world. But she dared not hope that there would truly be a way out of the mess that was her life.

A groan from Edward sent Jakob scrambling back for the pistol.

"Mama? Can I come out yet?" Daniel's voice was tinny and strained, coming from deep beneath the bed.

"Yes, Daniel. It's safe enough now." As safe as it would ever be, at least. He crept out slowly, a bit at a time, as if testing to make certain it was not a horrible trick. "It's okay, Daniel."

"Mama!" He flew at her at last, launching himself into her arms. "I was so scared," he whispered.

"So was I, Daniel." She drew in a shuddering breath that was tinged with smoke and oil, and buried him close against her chest. "But we're safe. Jakob saved us."

"What do you want me to do with him?" She looked up at Jakob's blunt question. With the lamp gone, the room was lit only with wan light from the flickering sconces outside in the hall, their faint glow visible through the still-open doorway; Jakob had done too thorough a job on the door for it to shut again. Her eyes started to adjust to the dimness.

His expression colder and more remote than any she had ever seen Jakob wear before, he was standing over a moaning, curled-up Edward. The gun that fit so well in Edward's hand seemed like a toy in Jakob's, and he seemed quite comfortable pointing it at Edward's head.

"Do with him?" she repeated dully.

"Yeah." Roughly, he nudged Edward with his toe. "Get up, now."

Edward unfolded slowly. He looked small and damaged, and she wondered that he had always been able to cause such fear in her, that she had such a belief in his invincibility. But then he stared at her, his eyes cold and viciously angry, promising pain she could imagine all too well, and she remembered.

She tried to fight back the fear, but a small shudder escaped. He seemed to draw strength from that, a faint smile twisting his mouth, and he straightened, assuming once more his regal, commanding bearing. The holder of a throne of his own creation.

"Amy?" Jakob took a step toward her, but the pistol never wavered from its precise aim on Edward's torso.

"I don't know." What could she do? What could anyone do? There were no possibilities that she could come up with that her husband could not stop with his power and his wealth.

"You're going to have to think of something. We can't stand here forever," Jakob said, his words curt and expressionless.

Daniel's face was still hidden against her neck, and she brushed her hand over the familiar cap of his curls. "I can't divorce him."

The glance Jakob flicked at her was disbelieving, almost contemptuous. "No?"

"Daniel's legally his son, not mine. He was born of Edward's first wife." That surprised Jakob; his jaw dropped open for just a moment before he snapped it shut. "I'd lose Daniel. I can't do that."

"I wouldn't let him anywhere near Daniel again, in any case." Jakob's features were hard and cold. He looked nothing like the Jakob she knew. If she had seen him like this when she'd first met him, she would have run screaming in terror in the opposite direction. "I don't suppose I could count on you to just leave them alone, Sellington, could I?"

Edward laughed. "You can count on anything you want, Dutch boy."

"Maybe we can . . ." She hesitated, trying to think. Her brain felt like fog, thick and cloudy and useless. She couldn't seem to get a firm grasp on any thought. "We both heard him admit to killing Cynthia. He—he belongs in jail."

Edward's laughter was louder this time, richly amused. "Oh, Amanda. Do you really think that I could possibly be convicted of anything?"

"You killed her, Edward."

"I'll simply buy my way off, Amanda. You know it as well as I."

"Amy?" Jakob looked to her for confirmation.

"He's right, Jakob. He buys everything else. Even me," she said bitterly. She'd tried so hard, and it wasn't going to make any difference at all. She couldn't save herself, and she couldn't save Daniel.

"And while the matter is under discussion, my dear, I'm certain that my mother will be delighted to take over Daniel's care. That might be for the best permanently, come to think of it."

Her arms tightened around Daniel as he whimpered and clung to her neck. The poor child. He should not have had to be here. He should not have had to listen to this, to see so graphically what his father was.

"I will kill her myself before I ever let her get her claws into Daniel," she said, knowing she would. If only Edward would believe her.

"Why, Amanda, why ever would you do that? She is a most doting grandmother."

"Exactly what I'm afraid of," Amanda said, hatred burning in her so strongly she was faintly surprised the fire did not ignite again. "She'll try to make him into you."

"That is precisely what I intend for my loving son, of course."

"Mama," Daniel sobbed, his small body starting to shake. She rested her cheek on the top of his head. He was *her* son, damn it; she did not care what the legalities were.

"I won't let them, Daniel." Oh, God, she prayed. Please let me not be lying to him. "I won't let them hurt you again."

"Amanda." Jakob had never called her that. It sounded so strange. Awful. "I think that you should take Daniel out of here. Right now."

"Jakob?"

"Get him out of here." It was as if the words were chipped from ice, sharp and deadly and cold.

She stared at him, uncomprehending. His eyes were shards from the same brutal winter ice. Unfeeling, determined.

He meant to kill Edward.

"Jakob, you can't—"

"Now!"

Edward's smooth, inherent confidence wavered. "You can't do anything to me, Dutch boy. I'm Edward Sellington!"

"Watch me," Jakob said softly.

He was so tense and still, the planes of his face drawn taut, she thought if she touched him, he might explode. Rage could not be contained forever, and he was coldly furious. She did not know how she knew it; perhaps, because she loved him so much, she would sense anything that seethed so strongly in him.

This must be what he'd been like, she thought, when his family had been massacred. When he'd wanted to kill. Untouched by anything but the fury. And she'd brought all that pain, all that churning anger back into his life.

"If you don't get him out of here right now, I'm going to drag you out myself," he said flatly. "Daniel shouldn't see this."

He was going to kill for her.

That was what she'd brought him to. It would neatly solve her problems; Edward would be gone, to a place where he could never hurt her or Daniel again.

And it would bring Jakob more bloody nightmares to steal his sleep.

"I can't let you do this, Jakob."

He whirled on her. "I can't let him hurt anyone else."

"No, Jakob." She would not allow Edward to harm anyone else, either. She would stop him somehow; she knew now that she must find a way to do it, even if she must kill him herself. There was no other way out of this. But she could not let Jakob kill for her.

"He deserves it."

"Yes, I know—"

The gunshot exploded in the small room. Amanda hit the floor, rolling Daniel beneath her.

26

The silence was abrupt and complete, echoing eerily after the burst of sound. Perhaps her hearing had shattered, too. Then she heard Daniel's small voice.

"Mama?"

"I don't know, Daniel." What had happened? She lifted up on her elbows slightly, so she wouldn't squash him too badly, but didn't move any farther than that. He was safer where he was, with the protection of her body. Slowly, she turned her head. Her vision was blurred, banked with dark and shock. It cleared slowly, her focus shifting oddly around the edges. Jakob was lying on the floor, too, a few feet from her.

"Jakob?" She sucked in a breath. Her heart stopped beating as she waited for his answer. What if Edward had somehow gotten to the gun? Or had another one?

"I'm okay."

"Thank God."

He pushed himself to his feet, and when he moved away, she could see Edward. Sprawled limply across the floor, he appeared to have been thrown backward, one arm flung up over his head. A dark stain was spreading over the pure white of his shirt.

"Oh, my God . . ."

"Mama, what's going on?" Daniel asked, his voice quavering.

How could she explain this to him? "Just a minute, Daniel." She started to roll off him, thinking he must be horribly uncomfortable pressed flat to the floor by her weight.

"Wait," Jakob said sharply.

He went over to Edward and bent over his body, checking for a pulse in his neck. The fingers of Edward's hand curled up, clenching, then went slack against the wood planks.

Jakob straightened and his gaze found hers, his eyes very dark and unreadable. He gave a small, negative shake of his head.

Edward was dead. She waited for relief, but found only a hollow emptiness.

"Jakob, you—"

"Wait!" He snatched the quilt off the bed, leaving it bare and starkly covered in worn sheets, and tossed the quilt over Edward's sprawled body. "You can let Daniel up now."

She unrolled, her body feeling oddly disjointed, as if her motions were unconnected to her thoughts. She remained sitting on the floor, bringing Daniel into her lap, tucking his head in to try to shield him from the sight on the other side of the room, where a small, dark blotch was seeping through the quilt, nearly blending into the colorful pattern.

"I thought I asked you not to—" she started.

"I didn't!"

"I did," said an unfamiliar voice. A man—a

stranger—came through the open door, stepping around the charred remains of the table and the still-smoking rag rug. He was tall and lean and quite possibly the most handsome man she had ever seen, with a stark, tragic beauty that would burn in a woman's heart.

"Who —"

"Mama?" Daniel broke in, "is Father dead?"

"Oh, Daniel." No child should have to live through this. How could she ever make it up to him? Make sure it didn't scar him too deeply? If only for this alone, she hoped Edward was now in a well-deserved hell. "Yes, Daniel, he is," she whispered, holding him close.

"Good," he said fiercely, then flung his arms tightly around her neck. "I'm glad." But his body was shaking, his face hot and dry against her neck.

More than anything, she wanted to get him out of this room that smelled of smoke and gunpowder, lightly tinged with the coppery odor of blood. If only she could spirit him back to the wedding dance, and all this could be a horrible, distant dream. But this was real life, and there were things to be dealt with first.

"Who are you?"

"He's the man who told me where you were when I was looking for you outside the hall," Jakob said, watching the man with ill-disguised suspicion.

The stranger turned toward her, his own gun still held in his lean hand, though she felt no threat from him. Dark hair, pale skin, burning eyes, dressed in relentless black. Certainly the most handsome man she had ever seen, she amended. And also the saddest, a deep melancholy clinging to him like a tarnished, unwanted, and ill-used halo.

"I loved Cynthia," he said simply.

"You'd better explain," Jakob said.

"I've been waiting for this for a long time." He glanced down at the gun, smiled faintly, then holstered it along his thigh. "I knew he killed her. But I was never able to prove it, and who would take the word of someone like me over Edward Sellington? You know how that is, Mrs. Sellington."

His eyes glowed pale in the dim light, boring into hers, demanding her understanding.

"Yes."

"I went away. I tried to forget." His shoulders lifted and fell. "I couldn't. So I went back. I could never get close enough to him. He was always protected too well. But I waited, and I knew that someday he would make a mistake. He *had* to; he was too certain of his own omnipotence."

Smoke wavered around him, his clothes fading into the darkness, making him seem otherworldly. "I don't know how he slipped out of New York without me seeing him. But I trailed him, all the way out here, just a step behind him all the way."

"What happened tonight?" Jakob prompted.

"There was no one around at the hotel when I got here. I found his room, so I *knew* he was here. But there was all this commotion at the hall, so I went to see if he was there."

He shook his head slowly, light catching and fading off the elegant bones of his face. "He came out just as I got there. But you and the boy were with him, and I couldn't confront him then. And then he—" he hooked a thumb toward Jakob "—came out, and I told him where you went. When he came this way, I followed. I stood outside the door and waited."

"I could have used your help a little sooner," Jakob said.

"You were doing okay." The man smiled, all the

more devastating for that there was no warmth behind it. "But then you turned away to talk to her, and he bent. I thought maybe he was going for a hideout gun in his boot, so I fired."

"Edward doesn't wear boots," she whispered.

"Oh." The man shrugged. "What a shame."

Amanda sagged, feeling the last drops of energy drain out of her. It was over; her body was starting to believe it, and she wanted to curl up into a safe little ball with Jakob and Daniel and begin to forget.

"Well." Jakob cleared his throat. "Amanda, you take Daniel and go back to the party. Send the sheriff back here." He made a move toward her, then apparently thought better of it and stayed where he was. Oh, Jakob. Didn't he know how much she needed him to touch her right now? "Better get Hans Kaufenburg while you're at it. I have a feeling we're going to need the mayor before this is through, too."

"What are you going to tell them?" The man's voice was soft and lifeless.

"I don't know," Amanda admitted. She couldn't seem to think beyond this instant.

"The boy's the Sellington heir. You're just his step-mother."

"No." Still sitting on the hard floor, on the tiny square of wood that seemed to be the only safe space in the world, she held her son tighter. "Daniel's not going back to New York. I won't let them do that to him. We live here."

But they would take him from her. She knew Edward's mother, and she knew exactly where Edward had learned to play his games so well.

The faint light in the room began to shimmer and dim. Edward was dead; why was she crying now, when it was all over? "Jakob?" She whispered his name on a plea. Instinctively, she turned to him for help, though she had no right to ask. For Daniel, she'd ask anyway.

"Let me think." He stilled, as he always did when he was truly focused, when he was aiming all of his formidable energy on one problem. "Okay, let's try this."

He leaned forward intently. "You don't know who the man who was killed is, Amy. None of us do. You'd taken Daniel out for some fresh air when he accosted you. He dragged you back to the hotel, wanted to—" Jakob swallowed, as if even the thought of it was nearly too much for him. "Anyway, he'd told Daniel not to tell anyone or he would kill his mother. But Daniel was too smart for him; he ran and found me and told me what direction you were headed."

His words sharp and direct, he frowned. He reminded her very much of the unsmiling, driven man she'd met at the train station her first day in Minnesota. She had thought they had all learned to laugh together, she and Daniel and Jakob. Had they lost it now?

"I found you. Daniel was worried, and he followed me, even though I told him not to. That's why he was here. I burst in, we struggled for the gun."

"Which is when I came by," the stranger said smoothly, picking up easily on Jakob's groundwork. "I'd just arrived in town and wanted to find a room. You'd lost the struggle for the gun. He was going to shoot you in cold blood, so I fired without thinking—a reflex."

"Right." Jakob went over to Amanda finally. *Now*, she thought. Now he would enfold her in his strong arms and make it all well. But he only bent down, looking carefully into her face, making certain that she understood his words. "Here's the important part, Amy. *No one* knows who he is. A drifter, a gambler, someone who came into town bent on mischief. While you get the sheriff, we'll make sure there's nothing left in this room that could tie you to him."

She would be free. Could it be possible? "The guest register?"

The stranger shook his head. "Not a problem. He was traveling under an assumed name. I suppose he didn't want to be a target for robbery." He turned to Jakob. "What if they question the boy?"

"I'll tell them he's too upset and I don't want him to have to go through any more. It would be too difficult for him to be forced to relive the tragedy."

"And the sheriff will accept that?"

"If I say so." Jakob reached down and touched her then, his fingers barely sliding over her cheek. *Finally*. She closed her eyes, not wanting any other sense to interfere with his touch. "Is this what you want? You have to decide now, Amy. There's no going back once we start this."

So many lies. Could she never get away from lies? But these were the ones that would free them. Her past would be gone, erased as if it had never existed. And Daniel would not have to grow up as the Sellington heir, never be raised with the same forces that had shaped Edward. If he chose to reclaim his birthright as an adult, at least it would be his choice, not something he *was*.

This was the only way.

"Yes," she said, opening her eyes and looking directly into Jakob's, trying to convince him of her determination. "This is what I want."

"Okay, then." He straightened, snagging her hand and pulling her to her feet as she set Daniel on his own. She was wobbly, as if the deck of a ship had tilted beneath her without warning, and he briefly cupped her elbow to steady her. But this time his touch was impersonal, gone before she could imprint it in her mind.

"Are you ready, Daniel?"

He was so young, eyes wide in his narrow, pinched face. He squared his shoulders, her brave little man. "In a minute, Mama," he said, and marched over to face the stranger.

"What is your name, sir?"

The man crossed his arms over his chest, towering over Daniel. "Kieran McDermott."

"Are you my father?"

Kieran's cool armor cracked; Amanda could almost hear it splitting, revealing a raw, deep pain that it seemed he could hardly survive. How could a man live with that hurt? And for so many years?

"You look so much like Cynthia," he whispered. He knelt in front of Daniel. Wonderingly, with a tentative touch as if he were afraid that Daniel would disappear at the slightest jar, he reached out, tracing his hands over Daniel's features. "I wish to God the answer to that was yes."

"Are you certain, sir?"

"Your mother and I . . ." He shook his head, and faint light glimmered wetly in his eyes. "Only once, we . . . when you were conceived, I had not seen your mother for a very long time. We had decided that we could not—" He cleared his throat. "Your father was . . . "

"I know what my father was," Daniel said, and suddenly he looked very old. "I was hoping he was not really mine."

"Yes, well." Kieran swallowed heavily. "Your mother was . . . special. You are very much like her. But I am not your father." He lifted his head, looking from Jakob to Amanda and back again. "But it seems you have chosen a very good family for yourself."

"I think so too, sir."

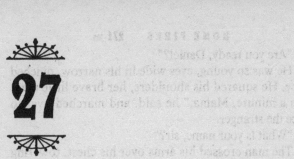

27

Jakob took care of everything.

Within a few days, the sheriff had closed his investigation; Edward had been buried in a grave that bore the name of Michael Soren, the name he'd registered under at the Dakotah; and Kieran McDermott had disappeared back into the darkness.

Amanda thought it should be easier for her. She was free! Instead, she stumbled blindly through a buffeting whirlwind of emotions, unable to capture, to feel and discard, any one of them. There was relief, yes. But also fury and sadness and lurking pain.

And loneliness. A dread, hollow loneliness that she couldn't shake, no matter how many people were around her. It wasn't the loneliness of *now* she was feeling; it was the horrible, unshakable loneliness that was to be the rest of her life.

Her life without Jakob.

She had known he would be angry with her; of course he would be. She had lied to him from the beginning, had drawn him into those awful events.

But she hadn't expected him to be so distant from her, as remote as if he felt nothing at all for her. At least in anger there was an element of emotion.

They ran into each other nearly every day, and not a flicker of emotion ever showed on his impassive face. It was as if everything there'd ever been between them was as unreal as the life she'd created for herself.

She had no idea what to do to make it right. How could she ever make this up to him? How could he ever believe anything she said again, now that he knew her whole life had been a lie?

So she clung to her son, holding him when the nightmares ripped them both awake, and tried to assure Daniel that there was nothing of his father in him.

And she thought of Jakob, turning over in her mind every conversation they'd ever had, searching for a way to repair the damage she'd caused.

What she decided to do seemed a pitiful offering to her, but it was the only thing she could think of.

She found Jakob on the bank of the Cottonwood, next to the old willow tree they'd once sat under while he told her of his nightmares and she had lied about her own.

It was a bitterly cold morning. The sun edged just above the horizon on the other side of the river, though the light was barely visible through the low streamers of fog that traced the river and the ridge of land.

She'd been up all night, as, she suspected, had Jakob. She'd been trying to think of how to approach him, the right words to use, even as she knew there were no right words.

She had no idea what had kept Jakob up all this

time, why he had not gone back to his bed when the darkness faded. The fact that she did not know frightened her; she had known him so well. What if she had caused his wakefulness, along with all the other things that were her fault? He'd always had difficulty with the night, but it was morning now. What if her nightmares had now invaded not only his nights but his morning?

Many of the leaves had fallen from the willow, damply crushed beneath her feet as she walked toward him. Those that still clung to the branches were a sad, dull brown.

Amanda brushed aside the trailing streamers of the tree. "Jakob?" she asked softly.

Oh, God, he thought. What do I do now? He'd known she was there, long before she spoke. He'd hoped that if he pretended not to notice her she would slip away and they would not have to discuss this now. He was too raw, too torn; what he felt, what he thought, what he wanted were concepts that seemed beyond him. How could he know what he wanted when he did not know her at all?

Liar! his mind shouted. He knew what he wanted, what he'd wanted from that first night at the river.

Her. He wanted her, whoever she was.

"Jakob?"

She called his name again; he had to acknowledge her. Slowly, unwillingly drawn, he turned.

This was why he'd avoided looking at her all week. Because it just hurt too damn much. Her split lip was healing, there was still the faint purple-blue shadow of a bruise across her cheek, and every time he saw it there was room for nothing inside him but rage.

He wanted to kill. It didn't matter that her . . . husband—God, he could scarcely bring himself to think the word!—was dead and buried; he wanted to bring Edward back to life, just so he could have the pleasure of ripping him limb from limb.

She glanced up at him once, then her gaze skittered away. Her shoulders hunched in her cape; the chill air brought a becoming blush to her cheeks, and he wanted to fold her in his arms to warm her.

"Jakob, I . . ." She stumbled, stammered. "I need to speak with you."

Perhaps she had come to tell him she was leaving. She had money; he knew that now. And she was free of her husband. She could go anywhere, be anything; she no longer had to hide away in this little town.

"Go ahead," he snapped.

What now? she wondered, trying to drum up a bit of courage. He sounded so abrupt, so angry. Why had she thought this might make any difference? She'd brought him nothing but pain.

He seemed oblivious to the cold wind that ruffled his hair and stung her cheeks. A yellow-brown leaf escaped the tree and spiraled down, landing on his shoulder before he impatiently brushed it away.

"I know—" Damn it, she couldn't seem to make her tongue work right, couldn't force out the words. "I know you must be upset about my being married—"

"Upset?" His eyes narrowed, glittering dangerously. "Hell, I'm not upset. I am goddamn *furious*." The words were ground out, carrying all the more impact for their low tone.

She swayed and swallowed heavily. Oh, Jakob, she thought, regret so strong in her she could taste its bitterness. Why can I never seem to get anything right?

"But I don't give a damn that you are—were— married."

"What?" she said, confused.

"I'm mad as hell that you didn't think that you could tell me." His jaw clenched, and he viciously tore a trailing branch off the willow, making the entire tree quake and shudder, raining down a dozen limp, damp, dead leaves. He wound the pliable strip around his hands, twisting and trying to break it. "Goddammit, Amy, didn't you trust me enough to tell me something that important? If you couldn't, then we had nothing—nothing!—like what I thought we did. Like I'd hoped we had."

He looked down at his hands, seeming surprised at the mangle he'd made of the branch, and dropped the destroyed mess of bark and leaves to the ground. "Ah, hell, it's not even Amy, is it? Amanda, I—"

"No," she said fiercely. "I'm not Amanda. I'm *not* her anymore."

Amanda had been gullible and weak, more concerned with surviving than living. She would never, ever be that way again. No matter what.

"What, then?" His expression softened, just a little. "Mandy, maybe? Amy never seemed to fit you quite right anyway."

"Mandy?" How did he always seem to find that place inside her she'd forgotten existed? "That's what my family used to call me." It had been such a long time ago. "Edward thought it was too unsophisticated."

"Mandy," he said, an odd, wistful note threading through the words. "Yes, that's it."

Memories bubbled up, ones she'd tried to keep buried because they hurt too much to think of, knowing she might very well never see her family again. Her mother, her father, her brothers and sisters. "Mandy, will you fix my hem?" "Oh, no, Mandy's cooking dinner!" "Mandy, are you sure the party will be properly chaperoned?"

"Oh, Jakob, I've been so confused, I hadn't even thought of it. I can contact my family now!"

She looked so beautiful to him, her eyes suddenly lit up, the deep navy of her cloak setting off her whipped-cream skin.

This was how he would remember her.

She was so excited by the thought of talking to her family again; he should be happy for her. But he couldn't seem to dredge it up.

She wasn't going to need him any longer. There was no way of getting around it; as much as he loved her, she didn't feel the same way about him. For if she had loved him as much, she would have understood that she could have told him *anything* and it would have been all right; they would have found a way through it together.

No, she'd only needed him. For safety, for companionship, for her son. He didn't begrudge her that; he'd do it all over again, the same way, if she needed him again. But now she would have her family back, and her life, and why would she need him anymore?

But if only, if only . . . he couldn't help but think what it could have been like if only she'd loved him, too.

Her smile disappeared. "Don't look at me like that," she said.

"Like what?"

"Like you . . ." She bowed her head, scuffing a toe in the brown grass. Light droplets from the fog beaded her hair, tiny silver crystals against the glossy brown strands. "Like you still want me," she said in a rush, almost inaudible.

"Whatever gave you the idea that I don't?"

She didn't expect that; her head came up with a snap.

"But then, that kind of *wanting* was never really our problem, was it?" he said.

"No, I guess not." She squared her shoulders, looking steadily at him. She dug deeply into the pocket of her cloak, pulled out a folded rectangle, and handed it to him. "Here."

"What is this?" A good-bye note? He wanted to hurl it into the river. Couldn't she just *tell* him?

"I was looking for a way to make up to you all the—the—trouble I've been. To thank you, for everything you've done for me and Daniel. I know this isn't enough—nothing would ever be enough—but this was all I could think of."

Gratitude. The last thing he wanted was gratitude. God, he'd had so much gratitude in his life that he was going to be sick if he ever heard the words "thank you" again. Damn it, he didn't want it from her!

"Mandy—" he began.

"Just open it."

"Fine." The outside paper was soft from the water-logged air and tore easily under his fingers. "A train ticket? What is this?"

"It's to Chicago. From there, you can go anywhere you want to. Anywhere at all."

"You're sending me away?" he said in disbelief.

"I've heard you, Jakob. The way you always wanted to go away, to see something besides this place. To be free." She had to make him understand. He'd given her the life she wanted; she needed to do the same for him. "It's all arranged. Karl will take care of the beer. I'll take care of the office and the paperwork. And all of us will take care of Nicolaus."

"Helga agrees to this?" He could hardly credit the thought that Helga was going to make it possible for him to go off by himself, where she couldn't keep an eye on him.

"Well, she wasn't too crazy about the idea at first, I'll admit, until I explained it all to her." She shoved her hands deeply into the slashed pockets of her cape. "Let me do this for you, Jakob."

Freedom. He'd dreamt of this for years, planned for it, wanted it with a passion he'd felt for little else. But that was before her, before he'd learned what passion really was. How could he go?

But how could he stay? It would only be worse, to stay here and not be able to touch her, to try to forget the way he felt about her. To fight the memories of her that lived in every corner of his home, every corner of his soul.

He knew he'd never get over her if he were here, to see her every day. He'd only fall all the more deeply in love with her.

But it wasn't in him to give up this easily. "Look at me, Mandy."

Her eyes were wide, misty as the fog that drifted around them. What would he see in them? he wondered. The truth? Could he trust that? Perhaps he only saw what he wanted to see.

"Forget that I told you I wanted to leave, Mandy. I have to know. What do *you* want?"

Soft, pure yearning; that was what he saw in her eyes. Longing, wanting, need.

Now, he thought jubilantly. Now she will admit that what she wants is me; now she will ask me to stay.

Moisture welled in her eyes, shimmering along the rim. "I want you to go," she said, her words cracking, "I want you to go."

"Damn it!" he shouted. Why couldn't he get her to admit it? He forced himself to lower his voice, to try and work through this rationally. "You'll fight for everyone else. You'll fight for Daniel. You'll fight for your family. You'll fight for Helga. And right now, you're fighting for me, and what you think I want, aren't you?"

She stared at him mutely, her mouth trembling, and he wanted her so much that he nearly shook with it. It couldn't end like this, not after everything they'd been through. He wouldn't let it.

"Mandy, you're going to have to learn to fight for *yourself*, for what you want."

"I'm not sure I can," she whispered.

He touched her then, gentle but unyielding hands cupping her head to hold her in place, as if he were afraid she was going to disappear. The fog shifted and thickened, sealing them in a world bound only by the spill of the willow branches and the quiet rush of the river.

"I would fight for you," he said. "For the rest of my life, happily. Hell, I would kill for you; you know that. Only problem is, how would I know what to fight *for*? I can't guess. I can't read your mind. You'd have to tell me, and I'm not sure you could."

She took a shuddering breath, trying to find the strength to do what she must.

She was so unworthy of him. A sinner, a liar. A woman with a monstrously failed marriage behind her, who was quite probably barren. Didn't she realize she was fighting as hard as she could to do the right thing for him? It was tearing her in two, making her chest hurt and her heart grow cold, but it was the only thing she knew to do for him.

If she did nothing else right in her life, she was going to love him right. And that meant giving him his freedom.

"You'd have to tell me what you want, Mandy," he said, intensity pouring from his eyes, his hands, his voice. "What do you want?"

Oh, God. She wanted him to be happy.

"I don't deserve you," she said helplessly.

"Yes, you do!" He dropped his hands and stepped away, turning his fierce gaze on the fog-blurred river. His shoulders were set, and he was suddenly as far away from her as if he'd already left on his journey. "Who deserves anybody, if it comes to that? Especially me? I work too much and I know too little, and I've got all these damned, dark corners of my soul that I'm trying to forget, and I can't, so I wake up screaming from the nightmares."

Frustrated, he kicked at a rock, sending it hurtling over the edge of the bank and tumbling down into the water. "What the hell does *deserve* have to do with it, anyway?"

The anger disappeared, leaving only a bleak, hollow regret. The anger had been better, for in the anger, at least there had been hope.

He made himself look at her, to see if he could face her when they finished this. To make certain she could look straight at him and still tell him good-bye.

"We can't make it like this, Mandy. We'd fall apart at the first bump. Until you can say you *want* me, and you *deserve* me, and believe it, we can't be together."

The cold wind blew a sheet of mist from the fog, sheening her skin with moisture. The cape whirled around her body. She grabbed the sides, yanking it close around her tightly, her knuckles turning white. How could he leave her? he wondered again.

"You're going, then?" she said.

And he knew there was no way he could stay.

28

It snowed all afternoon, big, fluffy, white crystals that spiraled thickly down from gray skies to layer deep and soft on the ground and frost the pines with generous powder.

It stopped by suppertime, the sky clearing to pure, icy black, just in time for them all to head into town for the St. Nikolaus Day celebration. Fortified by hot potato soup and a generous supply of the cookies Helga had begun baking on the first day of Advent, Karl drove them all into New Ulm. Bells jangled on the horse's tack and their breath smoked the cold air.

St. Nikolaus, regal and resplendent in his red bishop's robe and long white beard, came to Turner Hall, gifting the children with oranges and nuts and gingerbread. Nicolaus was shocked to find out that he received as many gifts as the better-behaved Daniel, but decided that St. Nikolaus must have taken pity on him because of their shared name.

Afterward, the adults lined the streets on the way

down to the river and waited for the children to parade past.

Mandy stamped her tingling feet, trying to warm them, and huddled deeper into her cloak. The cold temperatures seemed to purify the air, making it as clear and sharp as spring water. Moonlight spangled the fresh, blue-white snow, its sparkly surface a twin of the star-strewn sky.

Sleet earlier in the week had glazed the trees, and now their dark, skeletal boughs appeared to be encased in crystal, shining silver against the black sky.

It was wondrously beautiful. It was also freezing, and she marched in place again, trying to force the blood to her feet. The snow creaked beneath her boots.

"Cold?" Helga asked sympathetically.

"A little." One of Karl's arms was thrown around Helga's shoulders, and her round, red-cheeked face glowed above a fur-trimmed collar, a recent gift from her happy bridegroom.

"Here." Karl lifted his other arm, inviting her. "I would be happy to warm you, too. I have two sides."

She took him up on it immediately, snuggling against his big, sturdy frame, and was instantly warmer.

He grinned down at her. "See? I am warm on both sides now, and am holding the two prettiest ladies in New Ulm. What a lucky fellow I am."

She laughed and settled in. As they'd worked together to keep Jakob's brewery in good trim, Karl was quickly becoming nearly as beloved to her as her own father. His hearty laugh and down-to-earth sense were good antidotes to the blue moods that settled over her all too often.

She'd contacted her family more than a month ago, shortly after Jakob left New Ulm. It was wonderful to be in touch with them again, to get letters and news of her brothers' new jobs and sweethearts and her oldest sister's betrothal.

Her mother and father were well, and urged her to come home and live with them—she had not told them what happened, but word of her husband's disappearance had spread through New York like wildfire.

Perhaps someday she would. But now, she had her promise to Jakob to keep, and she did not want Daniel to be uprooted again. She did not know if returning to New York would bring up too many painful memories for him. Perhaps this summer, her family would come and visit her. Until then, she had a family here she loved deeply, too.

"Here they come!" Helga said.

She heard them first, singing, their dissonant, joyous children's voices almost unbearably sweet to her ears, tinkling and high as the bells that had rung on the horse's harness. They marched in unsteady rows as wide as the street was broad.

The children carried the lanterns they had built, fragile, inexpert and beautiful structures of wire or wood. Stars, snowflakes, sunbursts, or miniature houses, bobbing along high above their heads on long poles. The lanterns were lit, warming the streets and snowbanks with flickering, dancing ovals of light.

The children passed her, and she rose on her toes, craning her neck to find Nicolaus and Daniel. Ah, there they were, at the near end of the third row. Nicolaus skipped along, his light swinging wildly, and she thought he'd do well to reach the river with his lantern in one piece.

Daniel was intent, drinking in the sight of the lantern that Karl had helped him build, which swayed gently as he walked, the light spilling down and illuminating his upturned face.

"Daniel!" she shouted.

She was surprised he heard her over the singing, but he must have, for he turned to her and flashed her a brilliant smile, pointing up at his glowing lantern. She smiled back and nodded in approval.

He looked so happy, so much at peace. Daniel was doing a much better job of dealing with the aftermath of Edward's arrival and death than she was. He seemed relieved, less fearful, and the sadness that came upon him at unexpected moments was gone with a few tears, several hugs, and frequent reassurances that he was not, in any way, like his father. He was quieter, and a little somber, but she thought that perhaps no longer having the threat of Edward, of being dragged back to New York and that life, hanging over his head was balancing out the horror of having been there when his father was killed.

She, however, was echoing, empty, and lonely. Except when she was with her son, a deep sadness colored her days that she couldn't seem to shake. It seemed impossible; though she had exactly what she'd wanted for as long as she could remember, now it wasn't nearly enough.

The crowds closed behind the parade, following them down the streets and to the edge of the river. The children disengaged their lanterns from the poles and set them adrift on the current.

The lights were startlingly bright against the black, glassy water, as if a piece of the star-brightened sky had been captured and poured into the river. The flames spun and dipped; some caught along the bank and had to be nudged on their way again.

Nicolaus let out a wail of protest when his lantern collapsed, tipping on its side and sinking into the water until the flame was snuffed out, and he had to be consoled by Helga.

"Come on, Mama." Daniel found her, and took her

hand in his to lead her down to the water. "Help me set mine free."

She bent with him by the water, the bank rimmed with crusty, pitted ice that crunched and broke when she inadvertently stepped too close to the edge. His lantern was an elaborate star, painted white, and its glow splashed through the wood slats, lighting his face from below with warm orange tones.

Together, they pushed the lantern out into the current. It moved slowly at first, then got swept into the flow, rapidly gathering speed.

She watched Daniel's face; young, beautiful, rapt, and surprisingly peaceful. So much of Cynthia, so much of her. Why had he been able to accept when she was having so much trouble with it?

"I wish Jakob were here," he said wistfully, his gaze following his lantern as it bobbed in the middle of the river. Momentarily caught in an eddy, it spun dizzily, then popped out into the current once more.

"Me too, Daniel," she said. "Me too."

Yes, she missed him. She admitted it at last; the reason she was so lonely, so empty, was because so much of her heart had left with Jakob. And she had been the one to send him away.

She tried to tell herself it was for the best. He'd deserved this chance, and she'd owed him this much, and more.

But he hadn't wanted to go. She knew it, had known it even then. She just hadn't been able to accept it.

Ah, damn. As hard as she'd tried, as much as she hadn't wanted to believe all the things Edward had called her all those years—stupid and unworthy, sinful, whorish, fat—she'd absorbed them, like a poison administered through her skin, and she'd never been truly able to scrub them all away.

Worthless. Those were Edward's words, brutal and familiar, echoing through the nightmare-studded corners of her soul.

Jakob had been right. She'd never learned to fight for herself, because she'd thought she was undeserving, because Edward's accusations had tainted her even more than she'd realized. And so she'd pushed Jakob away.

And she knew that all that had been done to her was nothing compared to what she'd just done to herself.

Damn it, it would stop now! She would kill this, the last of Edward's holds on her, as surely as he himself had been killed.

She would learn to fight for herself. And she would be good at it, as good as she was at fighting for Jakob and Daniel and everyone else she loved.

For she *was* worthy; she had to be. Jakob could not have cared about her the way she knew that he had if she were not. It was not possible.

Yes. She nodded her head, and her hand tightened around her son's. He squeezed back, then leaned against her side, a light, warm, loved weight against her.

Sweeping swiftly downstream with the current, Daniel's light caught up with the mass of the lanterns. Turning, drifting, bumping, a cluster of tiny lights survived on the powerful river, drifting peacefully around a bend, disappearing out of sight as the river did, flowing away to the rest of the world.

All right, then. She would give Jakob some time to have his adventures and his freedom; he had certainly earned them. But he would come home someday, and by the time he did, she would have learned to fight, for herself and him and what they would have together.

Jakob shivered, turned up the shearling collar of his coat, and huddled deeper into it. Though he knew the temperature was considerably warmer than it would have been back in Minnesota, it felt colder, with a heavy dampness that seemed to go right through clothing and skin, settling deeply into his bones.

Off to his right, below the hill he stood on, he could faintly see the lights of San Francisco, wan and distant through the dense, heavy blanket of fog. In front of him seethed the ocean, black and layered with mist, visible only when a wave broke, the edge catching a pale ridge of light.

Clearer than the sight of the sea was its sound, smashing on the rocks, quieting to a low, sliding murmur, followed by another startling, thunderous crash when water met granite.

In the weeks since he'd left New Ulm, he'd seen both oceans, vast and wild as he'd always imagined. He'd seen New York, busy and dirty and vibrant. He'd seen mountains, sharp, huge, and closer to the sky than he'd known possible.

He'd also seen a great deal of the inside of trains.

He'd seen many of the things he'd dreamed of. But now, what he dreamed of most was having his family with him, of seeing Nicolaus burst into blurring motion when he first caught sight of Chicago's massive train station. Of Daniel's still, rapt absorption when they came unexpectedly across an elk traveling the same path through the valleys they were.

And, always, of Mandy, of her deep, quiet pleasure in the rare surprise of an out-of-season wildflower, her dancing hands the only clue to the fierce emotions that she kept so carefully hidden—except when he touched her.

A biting wind blew in from the sea, carrying salt-laden air that dampened his face. A foghorn blew, the loud blast momentarily drowning out the determined pounding of the waves.

There was no place he had to be, no one who looked to him for assurance. No responsibilities, no one to look after. It was exactly what he'd spent the last ten years waiting for.

And he didn't like it at all. He was good at those things, damn it, good at doing his job and taking care of his family, at being a part of his town.

Freedom, he'd discovered, could be a very lonely thing.

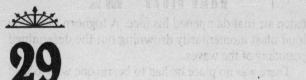

29

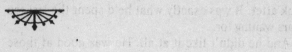

"You go in and make sure everything is ready," Helga whispered to Mandy. "I shall go feed the boys a little snack first."

She and Karl herded Daniel and Nicolaus down the hallway to the kitchen, keeping a firm hold on Nicolaus to prevent him from angling straight for the closed doors of the parlor that held the Christmas tree.

"Mama?" Daniel called over his shoulder, "you did remember my things, didn't you? You said I could sleep here with Nicolaus tonight."

"I did at that. It will be too late after we open the presents to take you back out in the cold to the cottage."

Humming the last strains of *Stille Nacht* to herself, she tugged off her gloves and unwrapped her long scarf, looping it over the carved newel post at the base of the stairs. The air had been perfect and cold on the way back from the Christmas Eve church service, and the warmth of the house was welcome.

On the polished side table that stood just inside the front door, the apple twigs they'd put in warm water the first week in December had burst into full, glorious bloom right on schedule. The petals were a white, delicate spring against the intense dark green of the pine boughs.

She breathed in deeply of the heady sweetness of the apple blossoms, the clean, sharp spice of the pine, and the rich nutmeg and cinnamon from the holiday baking. Next to the vase stood a white-painted Christmas pyramid, fashioned of stacked wheels and trimmed with tiny carved animals. With the tip of one finger, she idly spun the paddles.

That afternoon, she and Karl had decorated the tree behind the locked doors of the parlor. In order to foil Nicolaus's snooping, they'd slipped the gifts in at the last minute, when he'd already been bundled outside to the wagon. Now, she would make certain everything was ready before the tree was unveiled to the boys for the first time.

She pushed open the double doors and caught her breath. The tree was beautiful, full and shaggy and crooked, a deep, lush blue-green. The branches bowed under the weight of small, embossed silver and gold cardboard ornaments and elaborate, realistic roses fashioned from paper. Shiny wire was twisted and shaped into butterflies and stars, and marzipan fruits and vegetables were bright spots of color, nestled among the silver tinsel.

Beneath the tree, the wooden manger scene rested on a bright green bed of moss, dug from the woods in September and carefully tended in the cellar until now. The presents were tucked back, underneath the lowslung braches, leaving the nativity scene alone in its place of honor.

It was perfect. It took her a moment to register that
something was different, because she'd imagined it this
way all along.

The tiny white candles that tipped each branch were
already lit, their small, dancing flames reflecting off the
shiny surfaces of the ornaments, making the whole tree
appear as if it had been showered in stars.

"Who —"

"Hello, Mandy."

"Jakob!" He stepped from the shadows behind the
door, and she stared at him, afraid for a moment that
he was not real, that her mind and heart had simply
conjured him up because she wanted to see him so
badly.

He looked much the same. A bit leaner—there'd
been no one to badger him into eating dinner, she
thought. His hair was longer, curling against the white
collar of his shirt. No glasses, and his beard shadowed
his jaw, as if he'd been in too much of a hurry and forgotten to shave today.

His eyes were dark, and she was caught, stunned
into silence, content to drink in his presence. The
secret Christmas wish she hadn't even admitted to herself she'd made had just come true.

"Mandy, I—"

"Are you ready yet?" Nicolaus burst into the room,
a blur of color and energy, followed by a puffing Helga.

"I am sorry, I hope you have the candles lit already,
I could not catch him—" She froze just inside the door,
her hand going to her chest. "Jakob!"

The room exploded with motion and bright sound as
Jakob was surrounded. Nicolaus launched himself at his
uncle, the words spewing out of him as he tried to update
Jakob on every single thing that had happened since he'd
gone away. Karl wrung Jakob's hand in welcome, and

Helga alternated between dabbing at her eyes with her apron and hugging him tight.

"But—but what are you doing here?" Helga sputtered. "You are supposed to be off adventuring!"

"I wanted to be home for Christmas," he answered simply.

Daniel stood a bit off to one side, as if he were uncertain if he should break into the welcoming group. Mandy wanted to urge him to go, to take the chance, as she was trying to learn to take the risk herself. Jakob glanced his way, then disengaged himself from Nicolaus with a quick hug and walked over to Daniel.

He squatted down and opened his arms wide, making a place for Daniel, who smiled and walked straight into them. The man she loved, the boy she loved above all else—it was the way it should have been all along.

"I missed you, Daniel," Jakob said.

Daniel turned his head, resting it on Jakob's shoulder, and hung on. "Are you going away again?"

Mandy held her breath, waiting for his answer.

Jakob lifted his gaze, straight to Mandy, his eyes darkly intent, searching, and her heart skittered. He raised one eyebrow and inclined his head, as if he were waiting for her to answer her son.

It was up to her, she realized.

Pray God she got it right.

Rat-tap-tap.

Jakob blinked reluctantly awake from a very pleasurable dream—a dream he'd had often the last few months, but one that seemed all the more vivid for having the object of it only the short length of the garden path away.

Rat-tap-tap.

What the hell was that?

Bang-bang-bang.

Whatever it was, it was getting a lot more impatient, and was going to bust his window pane if it crashed on it like that one more time.

He threw aside the quilt and bounded out of bed. His toes curled up against the cold boards of the floor and he ran quickly over to the window. Scrubbing at the icy pane, he cleared a spot in frost. He leaned close to the window and peered out into the night.

A white face stared right back at him, and he jumped, startled.

"What the—" He jammed up the windowsill, revealing a pale, shivering Mandy wrapped in navy blue wool.

"Oh, thank the Lord. I'd thought you'd never get here." She stuck her head in, tipping over the edge of the sill. "Remind me to do this in the middle of summer next time, okay?"

Cold air streamed in about her, and Jakob hopped from foot to foot, goosebumps chasing up and down his naked back. A single pair of long drawers wasn't much armor against a Minnesota December.

"Damn, I'm caught on something." Mandy was struggling in the window, her rump pointed straight up. "Well? Are you going to help me in?"

"Sorry." He reached his arms around her and grabbed, lifting her over the sill and into the room. There was the unmistakable sound of fabric tearing as she came free of the window.

"Heavens." On her feet, she shook down the cloak that was twisted around her. "No wonder only men do this windowing thing. Skirts are a distinct disadvantage on a ladder."

"Mandy—"

"Wait just a moment." She turned back to the window and, with a huge heave, pushed the ladder away from the house. It stood straight up for a moment, teetering as if trying to decide which way to go, then toppled over. Snow flew up as the ladder dropped into the deep drift and disappeared, leaving a cold blue outline where it had sunk into the white.

"There." Mandy dusted off her hands, as if satisfied with a job well done, then tugged the window back down, shutting out the night and—thankfully—the icy air. "You're stuck with me now."

Jakob didn't think this was a particularly good time to mention that there was always the door. Besides, being closeted alone in his bedroom with her was just about the best Christmas present he could think of, so he wasn't about to remind her that there was a way out.

He couldn't believe that she was here. His Mandy, bringing with her the scent of snow and the roses he remembered so well. Exactly as he'd imagined.

And yet she was different tonight, fair to bursting with fierce excitement and determination. It hummed around her, as tangible as her quiet strength had always been.

"Now then—"

"Wait just a moment." He groped through the darkness to the nightstand and found some matches, fumbling as he tried to light the lantern. "I want to see you." He swore at his fingers, made clumsy by confusion and a burgeoning, breathless anticipation, but finally got the wick to catch, and the soft, flickering light spread through the room. "Okay."

He turned to find her still standing by the window, at the edge of where the light blurred into shadow. She'd stripped off her cloak and thrown it over a rocking chair, and was dressed in a loose white blouse and simple gathered skirt. She fidgeted with her waistband, her fingers gliding back and forth.

"Why don't you sit down?" she suggested.

"Okay." She was in his room, in the middle of the night; hell, he'd do anything she asked. He plopped down on the edge of his bed.

"All right." Her shoulders squared, and she stepped forward, into the golden, shifting wash of lamplight. "I thought about what you said, before you left. Actually, I haven't thought of much else."

He was so stupid. He'd wished a thousand times he'd never said those words to her, though he knew they were true. But he should have been patient, should have given her time, should have shown her the truth instead of demanding she acknowledge it.

That was why he'd come home, to try to give her what she needed; how could he make it work from a thousand miles away? That, and because he could no longer stand to stay away.

"Mandy, I'm so sorry, I—"

"No." She cut him off with a quick slash of her hand. "Let me finish." She took a deep breath and lifted her chin, her gaze holding his. "I want you, Jakob. I deserve you. Damn it, I want us, and I know it's worth fighting for. And so I will."

Her hands went to the throat of her blouse. She slipped the first button free of its hole, and that small gesture made the blood start to roar in his ears, for it promised so much.

"And I'll fight with every weapon I have," she whispered, working her way down the row of pearly buttons. Her blouse gaped, deep shadows between the white slashes of cloth. What did she wear beneath? She shifted, tugging the shirt from her waistband, and it fell open, revealing a pale flash of skin.

Nothing. Oh, God, she had nothing beneath. He may not survive this. And he didn't really think he cared.

He came off the bed, intending to go to her, to take her in his arms and help her get those clothes off as fast as possible.

"No," she said, shrugging the shirt from her shoulders. "Let me."

And then he understood. She needed to do this, to prove to herself and to him that she could be the one to fight, to take the risk, to go after what she wanted. And he needed to allow her to do it, even though it might very well drive him insane in the process. With a groan, he bounced back down on the bed.

The shirt slid down her back and off her fingers, disappearing into the shadows behind her. Her breasts were full, all shadowed hollows and deep, gold curves tipped with large, round nipples that hardened abruptly in the cool air. Slowly, with a seductiveness he hadn't suspected she was capable of, she brushed a hand over her breast, lightly circling the nipple, and desire slammed into him with as much force as if he'd touched her himself.

"That's—" He swallowed, hoping he was reading her right, trying to give her the confidence she needed, "—I'm not sure that weapon is even fair, Mandy."

Her answering smile was full of feminine power and promises. Thank God; he'd gotten this right, at least.

A swift fumble at her waist, and her skirt sagged low against her hipbone as she kicked off her boots. The shadow of her navel drew his attention to the full, round curve of her belly. She bent; her skirts slipped to the floor.

No drawers beneath, she was naked but for the high black lisle stockings that tugged at her lush thighs, all abundant flesh and pale, flawless skin. It was a good thing he was sitting down already; he was certain his legs would not hold him.

"And yes," she said, a wonderful, freeing glint of mischief sparkling in her eyes, "it was very cold out there with nothing up my skirts."

"Oh, my God." He jumped to his feet and went to work at the buttons of his drawers.

"You don't have to do that."

"We're a bit unequal here, don't you think?"

He jerked them down, hopping on one foot to get them off, his only thought to get as naked as she and do it now. And then he stood beside his bed, wondering if he should go to her or if he should wait for her to come to him. It felt overwhelmingly important to do it right, and he was far beyond rational thought.

He watched as her gaze swept down his body, settling at his groin, and he felt himself swell bigger under her approving regard. Her smile widened with pleased anticipation. Pure passion misted her eyes, her breath going shallow.

She walked over to him slowly, her heavy breasts swaying with her motion, and his heart beat harder with each step she took. When she was close, so close the tips of her breasts scored his chest, she lifted her hand and streaked it down his side, her fingertips playing over his ribs, her thumb flicking along the angle of his hipbone.

She slanted a glance up at him through her eyelashes, inquiring, daring. Then she dropped to her knees in front of him.

It was too much, the soft brush of her hair against his thighs, the wet heat of her tongue on him, the sight of her closing her mouth around his erection. Gently, he tugged her to her feet.

"You didn't like it?" she asked, though she didn't seem too concerned for his answer. Why should she? Surely she could read exactly that thundering reaction she caused in him.

"I didn't like it," he said hoarsely. "No. I loved it. But I think we're going to have to work our way up to that one."

She was in his arms at last, and he tumbled back onto the bed with her, the cold rumpled sheets at his back a marked contrast with her warm smooth skin along the entire length of his front.

His hands were filled with her, with the yielding swells of her rear and the plush warmth of her thighs, the ribbed, textured cotton of her stockings giving way to silky skin. Too precious, too joyous to be real.

All the time he was gone, in cold, stale hotel rooms and dirty train cars, she'd filled his dreams. Now he was filled with her, his heart and his mind, his soul and his life.

She writhed on top of him, her legs tangled with his, her hands twitching and stroking and greedy. He slid his hands up the inside of her thighs, beyond the tight band of her stockings, warmer and softer each inch he traveled, and a low purr sounded back in her throat.

Wanting to slow the headlong race to pleasure, needing to remember this, he tried to concentrate on her, on her shivers when his thumb circled her nipple, on the way her lips parted when his finger slipped deeply inside her body.

Kissing should have slowed this, he thought; surely it could not have the effect on him that her hands on his body did.

But nothing eased his drive, his need; her mouth was eager and hot, her taste so compelling, that he was only drawn deeper and deeper into her passion, pushed farther along the wild, uncontrollable river of his own.

She rose above him, holding his hardness steady with her hand so she could glide right down on him.

"No," he said. Catching her hips in his hands, fingers pressing into her soft flesh, he tried to lift her off.

She ignored him, settled on to his body, pushing back the tangled streamers of her hair so she could look at his face. "Why not?"

"I . . ." It should have been different this time, he thought. He should have been able to find some control. Instead, he felt blindsided by her, by her heat and his passion, by that love that only sharpened his need. How could he tell her that he would burst any moment?

Just to touch her, he reached up, gliding his hand over her collarbone, then cupping the soft weight of her breast in his hand.

She'd opened herself to him tonight. Had taken the first step and told him what she wanted. He couldn't be any less honest with her.

"I want you too much . . . it's been awhile."

She went suddenly still, intently focused on him. "You didn't—" She swallowed. "There was no one while you were gone?" she asked carefully.

"No." He smiled, lopsided, a little embarrassed. "Just me and my hand and my memories of you," he admitted.

She grinned. "Really?"

"Really." He shrugged. "I missed you."

"Well, in that case." She leaned down to kiss him and her hair slid over her shoulder, curling against his neck. "I missed you, too."

"You mean you—"

"Mmm-hmm."

He'd thought it was not possible to get him more aroused, but her shy admission did so. The picture was so clear in his mind: her touching herself, at first slowly and then faster, imagining that it was his hands on her flesh, pleasuring her, because she wanted him so badly.

She rocked on him and he groaned. "Really, Mandy, if you move one more time I'm going to—"

"I don't mind," she said.

"I do." He slid his hand down between their bodies, the back of his knuckles caressing her, watching as her breath caught and her eyes fluttered shut, the incredible softness of her hot against the back of his hand. "Mandy, if you only knew what this felt like . . ." His words trailed off on a hiss as a ripple of muscle deep inside her stroked him.

With his free hand, he captured one of hers and brought it down to join his. "Feel," he said roughly.

Her eyes flew open, stared into his, the soft hazel glazed with passion and gold from the lamplight. So beautiful, so strong. "Oh, Jakob," she said. "There's soft and there's hard, and there's you and there's me—Jakob!"

She shuddered, cried out, and he was lost, his seed spilling deep in her body, his pleasure magnified and blending with hers until he no longer knew if it was hers or his or something new that they made between them.

He was hers, she was his, and they were one.

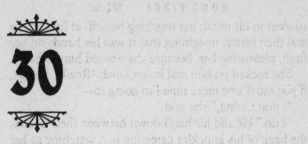

30

"If I lose you, Mandy, I feel like, all the rest of my life, I'll be lonely." He spoke against her hair, the soft current of his words stirring stray strands along the edge of her forehead.

He held her close against his side, one arm secure around her back as if to make sure she was going nowhere. Her leg was drawn up over his thighs, and she idly fingered odd designs on his chest.

She was warm and safe and secure in a way she'd never, ever been, even before Edward.

"I think I already was," she said.

He brushed a knuckle under her chin and tipped her head, so she would look into his face. "What now, Mandy?" he asked. "Are you going to marry me this time?"

She knew this was coming, had planned what to say. Yet it was so hard to say it, because everything she wanted was so close, and she had to take the risk of letting it slip away.

"I do love you, Jakob," she began.

"That's good," he said warily. "You do know that I love you, too?"

"Yes." She did. His love had never been what she questioned; he'd shown her in so many ways. "Jakob, I was married to Edward for eight years. There were no children. I know it was not him, for he had Daniel."

She swallowed hard, her heart lodged in her throat. "It must be me. I think that maybe I am barren, Jakob."

"And?" he said gently.

He would make her say it? "And you deserve the chance to have children of your own. I will not hold you to this. I want you, I can say that now. But if this is all we can have, I will understand and take that, too."

"Mandy." His fingers whispered over her brow, smoothing away a wisp of hair as his gaze traced equally gently over her features, as if he would memorize each one. "How many couples who marry know if they can have children?" His smile was so full of love that tears stung the backs of her eyes and she blinked them away. "If God chooses to gift us with children, we will be so happy." He shook his head slightly.

"If not, we already have Nicolaus and Daniel." He gathered her even closer, drawing her up against his heart. "And I will have you. That is more, much more, incredibly more than I had ever thought to have."

"Jakob?" she asked, listening to his strong heartbeat thunder beneath her ear, "Will you marry me?"

"Will you tell me what else you want?"

She did, in precise and very sexy detail.

Mandy tiptoed into the parlor, wincing at the creaking as the door swung wide. It sounded loud in the dead silence of the big house, and though dawn was more than an hour away, she did not want to take the chance of waking the children.

The room was dark, and she waited until her eyes adjusted enough to make out the dark bulk of the furniture and the towering Christmas tree. She found the matches on a side table and scratched one against its box. It flared to life, a tiny, shuddering spark of light.

One by one, she lit the half-burned, white candles on the tree. Each flame caught, sputtered, then strengthened, the small, individual flames warming her hands and face. Some of the candles were twisted and lumpy with melted wax from earlier that night, but they burned just the same, strong steady lights that gleamed bright and added their glow to the others until the tree was shimmering with those pure little flames.

"There you are." Jakob slipped into the room on bare feet and came up behind her, sliding his arms around her. She leaned back into his warm embrace. "I wondered where you'd gotten to. Couldn't sleep?"

"No."

"You should have woken me. Nightmares?" He nuzzled behind her ear and she tilted her head to give him access, his warm breath flowing over her skin.

"No. Too happy, I think. I didn't want to waste a moment of this night." She breathed in, the air rich with pine and Christmas and Jakob. "I won't have any more nightmares, I don't think."

"Mama? Are you in there?" Daniel's small, bare feet padded on the wood floor in the hallway. "I thought I heard you."

"I'm in here, Daniel," she called. Jakob loosened his hold, ready to step away, but she stopped him. "No, stay. He may as well get used to it."

"I thought you were sleeping back at the cottage."

Rubbing at his sleepy eyes, Daniel wandered into the room. "Jakob, you're awake, too?"

"I decided it was too late and too cold to go back to the cottage," she said.

"So you slept over, too?"

Against her back, she felt Jakob's chest shake with repressed laughter. "Something like that," she said.

"Come here, Daniel." Jakob held out one arm, and Daniel eased into it, next to them both, settling light and warm against her so that the three of them stood in one embrace. They stared at the sparkling tree until the soft, pure light of a Christmas dawn crept in, painting the room with warmth.

"It's a nice tree," Daniel said. "I liked my baseball glove, Jakob. I'm sorry I didn't have a present for you."

"I know something you could give me. If you want to."

"What?" Eagerly, Daniel looked up at him, his eyes as bright and shiny as the candlelight.

"You could give me your blessing to marry your mother."

"Mama? So you'd be—" He paused, and Mandy could see his struggle, hope and fear and tentative joy mixed together. "Does this mean that you wouldn't go away again?"

"Well, maybe I would. But if I did, we'd all go together. As a family."

"And you'd be—you'd be my father?"

"Yes," Jakob said gently, "if that's okay with you."

"I'd—I'd like that."

"So would I, Daniel," Jakob said, his voice catching. "So you'll give us your blessing?"

"Yes," Daniel said. He looked at the shimmering tree and up at their beaming faces, and smiled. "But I think maybe Someone already did."

Author's Note

    St. Nikolaus' Day is Dec. 6; the German communities that have lantern processions generally hold them on Dec. 12 or 13. I have combined the two festivities here.

In 1873, there were actually three breweries in New Ulm. The one in the story is very loosely modeled on Schell's Brewery, which still exists in the valley where the Cottonwood River meets the Minnesota. (My husband recommends the bock.) It is surrounded by gardens, a deer park, and a lovely home built in 1885.

However, the facts surrounding the tragedy now known as the Dakota Conflict are portrayed as accurately as I could.

I welcome letters from readers. You may write to me at: Box 828, Hopkins, MN 55343.